6/20

Shine

Shine

JESSICA JUNG

SIMON & SCHUSTER BFYR

NEW YORK   LONDON   TORONTO   SYDNEY   NEW DELHI

SIMON & SCHUSTER BFYR

An imprint of Simon & Schuster Children's Publishing Division
1230 Avenue of the Americas, New York, New York 10020
Text copyright © 2020 by Jessica Jung and Glasstown Entertainment
Jacket design and art by Sarah Creech copyright © 2020 by Simon & Schuster, Inc.
All rights reserved, including the right of reproduction in whole or in part in any form.
SIMON & SCHUSTER BFYR is a trademark of Simon & Schuster, Inc.
For information about special discounts for bulk purchases, please contact
Simon & Schuster Special Sales at 1-866-506-1949 or business@simonandschuster.com.
The Simon & Schuster Speakers Bureau can bring authors to your live event.
For more information or to book an event contact the Simon & Schuster Speakers Bureau
at 1-866-248-3049 or visit our website at www.simonspeakers.com.
Interior designed by Mike Rosamilia
The text of this book was set in Adobe Caslon Pro.
Manufactured in the United States of America
First Edition
2 4 6 8 10 9 7 5 3 1
This book has been cataloged with the Library of Congress.
ISBN 978-1-5344-6251-9 (hc)
ISBN 978-1-5344-6253-3 (eBook)

To all my Golden Stars

One

Head up, legs crossed. Tummy tucked, shoulders back. Smile like the whole world is your best friend. I repeat the mantra in my head as the camera pans across my face. The corners of my lips turn up in a perfectly sweet "don't you want to tell me all your secrets" pink-glossed smile.

But you probably shouldn't. You know how they say three can keep a secret if two of them are dead? Well, that couldn't be truer for my world, where everyone is always watching and your secrets can actually kill you. Or, at least, they can kill your chance to shine.

"You girls must be thrilled!" The interviewer is a middle-aged man with oily, slicked-back hair and fair skin. He might have been handsome if his garish hot-pink satin tie and red shirt combo weren't so distracting. He leans forward eagerly, his eyes gleaming at the nine girls seated before him, a sea of perfectly tousled beach waves and unblemished faces glowing from years of skin-brightening face masks, choreographed down to the angle of our sleekly crossed legs and the descending order of our pastel rainbow-hued stilettos. "Hitting number one at all the music shows, and with your debut music video no less! You're one chart away from an All-Kill! How do you feel?"

"We couldn't be more excited." Mina jumps in eagerly, flashing her perfect teeth in a beaming smile. My face muscles ache as I stretch to match her.

"It's a dream come true," Eunji agrees before loudly popping her gum and blowing a huge strawberry-scented bubble.

"We're so grateful for the opportunity to do this together," Lizzie chimes in, her eyes practically glowing under layers of silvery eye shadow.

The interviewer's eyes light up, and he leans in conspiratorially. "So you all get along? I mean, nine incredibly beautiful girls in one group. That can't always be easy."

Sumin gives a soft, effortless laugh, pursing her flawlessly lined bright-red lips. "Nothing is ever 'always easy,'" she says. "But we're family. And family comes first." She links arms with Lizzie sitting next to her. "We belong together."

The interviewer flutters a hand over his heart. "Just precious. And what do you love about working together?" His eyes travel slowly over the group, finally landing on me. "Rachel?"

My eyes immediately shift to the huge camera sitting behind the interviewer. I can feel the lens zooming in on me. *Head up, legs crossed. Tummy tucked, shoulders back.* I've been preparing for this moment for years. I smile wide, turning the interviewer into my best friend. And my mind goes completely blank.

Say something, Rachel. Say anything. This is the moment you've been waiting for. My hands have gone clammy, and I can sense the other girls start to shift uncomfortably in their seats as my silence fills the room. The camera feels like a spotlight—hot and prickly on my skin—as my mouth dries up, making it almost impossible to speak.

Finally, the interviewer sighs and takes pity on me. "You've all been through so much together—training for six years before making it big! Has the experience been everything you hoped it would be?" He smiles, lobbing me an easy question.

"Yes," I manage to croak out, a smile still plastered on my face.

He continues. "And tell me a little more about what life was like as a trainee before your big girl-group debut. What was your favorite part of living in the trainee house?"

My mind spins around for an answer as I discreetly wipe the sweat off my hands and onto the leather seat beneath me. An idea pops into my head. "What else?" I say, lifting a hand, awkwardly wiggling my perfectly manicured fingers, all white and lavender stripes, toward the camera. "Eight girls to do your nails for you. It's like living in a 24/7 nail salon!"

Omg. What is wrong with me? Did I really just say my favorite part of training was having eight girls to give me free manicures?

Luckily, the interviewer's laughter booms loudly throughout the room, and I feel relief coursing through my body. *Okay,*

I can do this. I giggle along with him, and the other girls quickly join in. He flashes his greasy smile at me. *Uh-oh.* "Rachel, you've received high praise for your talent as the lead vocalist. Do you find your talent inspires the other girls to do better, work harder?"

At this, I blush, putting my hands on my face to cover up the color rising in my cheeks. My head starts buzzing again. I've practiced answering these questions a million times, but every time I get in front of that camera, I freeze. The lights, the interviewers, the knowledge that millions of people *out there* are watching me. It's like my brain disconnects from my body, and no amount of practice or preparation can make the two come together again. My throat fills with a lump the size of a golf ball, and I notice the interviewer's smile growing more and more frozen on his face. *Crap. How long has he been waiting for me to answer?* Quickly, I blurt out, "I mean—I *am* talented." Out of the side of my eye I notice Lizzie and Sumin glance at each other, eyebrows lifted. *Shit.* "Wait, but not *the most* talented. I mean, well, the group—all the girls. We all—"

"I think what Rachel means to say is we all love what we do, and we inspire each other every day," Mina cuts in smoothly. "Speaking as lead dancer of the group, I know I learned a lot from my father about a strong work ethic—"

She's cut off by the sharp ringing of the class bell over the speaker system. The cameras click off and the interviewer's smile wilts off his face. He takes his time, slowly peeling off his suit jacket to reveal huge sweat stains darkening the satin under his arms as the nine of us—some of the top K-pop train-ees at DB Entertainment—wait for our mock-interview media assessment. "I'd like to see a little bit more energy for next week—remember, the only difference between a trainee and a DB K-pop star is how much you want it! Eunji . . ." She looks at him, eyes wide and scared. "How many times do I have to tell you, no bubble gum during mock interviews! One more violation and I'm sending you straight back to newbie classes." Eunji's face turns pale, and she bows her head low. "Sumin! Lizzie!" Their heads snap up. "More personality from both of you! No one's paying two hundred thousand won for a K-pop concert full of stars who use makeup to hide the fact that they have nothing interesting to say." Lizzie looks like she's about to cry, and Sumin's bright-red lips match the blush blooming on her cheeks. Finally, he turns to me and in almost a bored voice says, "Rachel, we've been over this before. Your sing-ing and dancing is some of the best we've ever seen, but that's only part of the job. If you can't even sell yourself to me dur-ing a training interview, how do you expect to perform in front of huge crowds every night? Or do real interviews with live audiences? We expect more from you." He gives us a curt nod before walking out of the training room, shaking a cigarette from his front pocket.

I practically melt off the tiny stool I've been sitting on for the past hour, my smile fading away as I massage out the stiletto-induced cramp in my right leg. I've heard it all before. *Do better, Rachel. Get comfortable in front of the camera, Rachel.*

K-pop stars must be lovable, eloquent, and perfect at all times, Rachel. I let out a grunt of pain as I twist around to pull on my Converses. Mina glares at me from her seat.

"What now?" I sigh.

She lifts a hand, showing off her perfect French manicure. *"Eight girls to do your nails for you?* Seriously? We're not your servants, Rachel." She rolls her eyes. *You would know,* I think to myself. Of everyone at DB, Mina's the most likely to have servants. She's the eldest daughter of one of Korea's oldest and most powerful chaebol families, the Choos, also known as the C-MART family. There are thousands of orange-and-white C-MART stores all over the country, selling everything from kimchi and Yakult and freshly made japchae to neon-yellow sweatshirts with knockoff Sanrio characters spouting ridiculous Konglish phrases like "Your mom is my hamster"— meaning Mina is richer than rich and a huge pain in my ass. "You know you're the reason we have so many of these media training classes, right?" My insides heat up. It's true. I know it's true. But that doesn't mean I want to hear it from Mina. "Can you at least try answering like a K-pop star and not some starstruck little girl at a slumber party? Or is that too much to ask from our poor little Korean American princess?"

I stiffen. It's no secret I was born and raised in the States (New York City, to be exact), but between my dance trainer screaming at me for being three minutes late to class this morning and my failed interview performance, I'm in no mood to deal with Mina and her attitude today. "I don't remember the interviewer asking you *any* personal questions, Mina. Maybe you're just not as interesting as you think you are."

"Or maybe I don't need the practice," Mina says.

I sigh. I skipped breakfast this morning, and the effort to keep up this verbal sparring with Mina requires at least one meal, if not two. I turn away, scooping my heels into my old white leather tote bag.

"What, you think you're too good to talk to me now? Didn't your umma teach you any manners?" Mina says.

"What do you expect from her?" Lizzie says, checking her mascara in her monogrammed compact mirror. She snaps it shut and narrows her eyes at me. "Sweet little Princess Rachel, whose mom won't let her step foot in the trainee house. Maybe that's why she thinks we all have nothing better to do with our time than each other's nails."

"It must be nice to be Mr. Noh's favorite," Eunji says with a loud sigh. "You know, some of us actually have to work hard to get where we are. You don't see *us* getting any favors from the head of DB."

"I hope you don't think you're *some of us*," Sumin says, whipping around to face Eunji. "I can't remember the last time I saw you break a sweat over anything."

"Speaking of sweat, you might want to freshen up a bit, sweetie," Eunji says, drawing a circle in the air around her own face. "You're looking a little . . . shiny."

"Well, your nose is looking a little plastic," Sumin bites back.

"The two of you are giving me a headache!" Lizzie whines to Mina. "Sunbae, make them be quiet!"

Mina smiles. "Of course, Lizzie, sweetie. Why don't we just turn the camera back on? That will shut them right up! Oh wait . . . that only works on Rachel!"

The room dissolves into giggles as my face flares in anger and embarrassment. I should bite back, but I don't. I never do. I like to pretend it's because I'm taking my mom's advice to heart—you know, be the bigger person, always take the high road, never let them see you sweat, the mantras of strong, American-minded feminists everywhere—but the huge lump that's returned to my throat knows that's a lie. I finish lacing my shoes and stand. "If you'll excuse me," I say, winding my way out of the room.

"Oh, you're excused," Mina says innocently. Out of the corner of my eye, I see her motion to the other girls, whispering wildly as sly smiles start to spread across all their faces.

DB Entertainment's training campus is exactly like the K-pop stars it churns out: flawless, sparkling, and pretty much impossible to look away from. It's prime real estate in the heart of Cheongdam-dong, the capital of K-pop. In the summer, trainees gather for yoga and Pilates on the rooftop garden, fighting over the coveted umbrella-covered spots to avoid even the hint of a sun blemish. Inside, giant fountains with spring water flown in directly from Seoraksan grace the teakwood and marble-clad lobbies. The DB execs claim the fountains are there to help us channel our inner peace in order to achieve our highest potential—but we all know what a joke that is. There's no inner peace to be had here.

Especially not with the yearbook staring you in the face every day.

The yearbook (so named because most of the trainees here never get the chance to have an actual high school yearbook) is what we call the walls surrounding the fountain in the central wing lobby, decorated with framed photos of every single K-pop star who's debuted out of DB's training program. Their picture-perfect smiles and glossy hair remind us mere trainee mortals of what we aspire to be every day as we scurry from class to class. And smack in the middle of the wall—the one place we all hope to see ourselves someday—is a gold plaque with the names of every DB solo star or group who's had a song debut at #1 on the Seoul music charts.

As I walk past, I stop and stare, my eyes blurring as I go over the names I memorized years ago. Pyo Yeri, Kwon YoonWoo, Lee Jiyoung . . . and the most recent, NEXT BOYZ. I feel a familiar squeeze around my heart, that patented K-pop trainee combination of stress, panic, and dehydration, as I flash back to my disastrous interview performance. Wincing at the memory, I quicken my steps, hurrying toward the independent practice rooms that line the west side of the building.

The hallway is full of random toys and props used by the best of the best stars in worldwide concerts. Half of the paraphernalia has the insignias of Electric Flower and Kang Jina (a gold-plaque legend and the leader of the biggest and best girl group in K-pop for the last few years). They debuted at the top spot and never left it. When I joined DB, I worshipped those girls—Jina especially. I admire them even more now, knowing what they had to go through to get to where they are. But part of me wonders about the girls they left behind. The ones that didn't make it in the group.

Will I be the one on top or the one left in the shadows?

Bass reverberates into the hallway as I peek inside one room and see a second-year trainee practicing Blue Pearl's iconic "Don't Give Up on Love" dance. She flubs the side-to-side arm movements and wilts, dragging herself over to the speaker panel to start the song from the beginning. My whole body aches just watching her. From the sweat dripping off her forehead to her bright-red cheeks, I can tell she's been in there for hours—a typical day for a young trainee. At the end of the hall, I run my finger over the electronic sign-up screen that dictates practice room availability. It's still pretty early on a Saturday, so I'm hoping for some afternoon times to work on my dance moves, but . . . Ugh. Unbelievable. Every single slot is filled.

My hands clench as I feel my body temperature skyrocket. Lizzie wasn't wrong—I'm not like the other trainees who are here 24/7, singing and dancing in practice rooms until 4:00 a.m., sleeping at the nearby trainee house, and waking up and doing it all over again, every single day. Back when I first got recruited to DB, my mom almost didn't let me come. It meant uprooting our family from New York City to Seoul, my sister giving up her school and her friends, both of my parents giving up their jobs. But more than that, she couldn't understand why K-pop meant so much to me, and she *definitely* didn't understand the trainee lifestyle—the intense pressure, the years of training, the plastic surgery scandals. Then, about three weeks into begging my mom to change her mind, my halmoni died. I remember how sad I felt, how I cried with my mom and Leah for hours, how when she was alive, Halmoni would sit me down every morning during our visits and braid my hair, whispering old folktales into my ear, telling me in her soothing voice how I would grow up to be beautiful, wise, and very wealthy. My mom wouldn't let us miss school for the funeral, and when she got back from Korea, I had practically decided to let go of the whole trainee thing, but to my surprise, Umma made me a deal: We would move to Seoul and I would go to school during the week, get an education, keep my prospects for college open, and every weekend (starting Friday night), I would train. (Once, a few years ago, I asked her why she changed her mind after Halmoni died, but all I got was a blank stare followed by a quick smack on the back of my head).

The DB execs didn't really go for Umma's arrangement at first, but for some reason, Mr. Noh decided to bend the rules for me. Umma thinks it was because of her "American female empowerment" (as she calls it), but I know I'm just one of the lucky few Mr. Noh favors—one of the lucky few he has decided to pluck from trainee obscurity and pay extra attention to. (Although in the trainee program, extra attention really just means extra pressure.) Still, the situation was pretty unheard of, and it wasn't long before I was known as "Princess Rachel," the most pampered trainee at DB; the full-blooded Korean whose American passport (and American attitude and American dislike of Spam . . .) put more distance between me and the other trainees than the entire Pacific Ocean had. Now, six years later, even though I've been here longer than almost all the other trainees, the nickname still lives on.

You'd think they'd judge me based on how hard I train. How I work my body to the bone at DB headquarters on the weekends. How I sleep four hours a night during the week because of the hours of practice I put in after finishing my homework. How I begged my school to give me an independent study in music so I can have fifty minutes alone every day in the music room, practicing scales to keep me sharp. But instead, they judge my clean clothes, my neatly brushed hair, and the fact that I get to sleep in my own bed at night.

And the worst part is? They're right. Every single one of them puts in twenty-four hours a day, seven days a week. Most of them live at the trainee house and go home once a month (if that). They eat, sleep, and breathe K-pop. No matter how you look at it, I can't compete with that. But that's exactly what I have to do.

Digging the heels of my palms into my forehead, I try to take calm, even breaths. As I got closer and closer to debut age,

I begged my mom to let me train full-time, but all I ever got back was a resounding refusal. How can I tell my mom that it's almost unheard of to debut in a girl group if you're out of your teen years? How can I explain that I'm three years away from being past my prime? It's been almost seven years since DB debuted Electric Flower, right before the last big DB Family Tour. They haven't debuted another girl group since. Rumors that DB is looking to debut a new girl group—and *soon*—have been swirling for months, and I can't afford to wait another seven years. I can't afford to wait seven months. By then it might be too late for me. Debuting is everything I've been working toward, and there's no way I'm going to let myself be passed over. No matter what Umma says.

"Rachel!"

I jerk my hands away from my face and plaster on a pleasantly neutral expression, bracing myself for another confrontation with Mina. I exhale and smile, however, when I see Akari bounding down the hall, her thick black ponytail streaming behind her.

Akari Masuda moved to Seoul with her parents when she was ten years old, after her father, a Japanese tech genius, was recruited to work at the Osan Air Force Base. She had been on the short list to start training at L-star Records, a huge J-pop label in Tokyo, but her parents didn't want her living on her own at such a young age. Instead, her dad pulled some strings to get her into the DB program. Maybe it's because we both understand what it's like to be an outsider in Seoul, but we've gotten along since the day we met. It's not easy making friends when everything here feels like a competition, but Akari is one of the few people at DB I can really trust.

"Where have you been?" she asks, linking her arm smoothly through mine. She has the natural grace of a dancer, having been in ballet since she was four years old.

"Media training," I respond lightly. Akari takes in the dark circles under my eyes and my red, splotchy face and gently starts to ease me away from the practice rooms.

"Well, I've been looking everywhere for you. I was worried you might miss the newbie bowing ceremony!"

I groan, stopping in my tracks. "Um, no. Please don't make me go to that. You know I hate it."

"Hate it or not, 'the bowing ceremony represents family—and at DB, family comes first.'" Akari giggles, her face contorting into a disturbingly accurate replica of Mr. Noh, DB Entertainment's CEO—or, as he would say, the head of the tight-knit DB family. Ha. She wiggles her eyebrows. "Plus, I heard there's catering."

My stomach rumbles at the thought of food, and I remember I haven't eaten anything all day. "You should have led with that," I say, letting her drag me down the hall. "You know I never say no to free food."

"Who does?" Akari shouts as we step out into the main lobby. It's teeming with people—trainees rushing to classes and staff rushing to their offices, prepping for the big Electric Flower concert in Busan next weekend. We pass the cafeteria—famous for being the only Michelin-starred corporate cafeteria in all of Asia. Even international superstars like Joe Jonas and Sophie Turner have come here just to eat the food. Too bad it's wasted on most of the trainees and idols who are actually repped by DB, as we're meticulously weighed each week. Can't afford to pop out of our costumes onstage (sarcasm intended).

The auditorium is one of my favorite places on campus, all gleaming blond wood and faux-industrial iron chandeliers dangling from the ceiling. The stage rises dramatically in the center of the room (to more accurately reflect the experience of a stadium tour, of course) with plush, velvet-covered seating surrounding it.

Mr. Noh is already standing onstage with the new trainees lined up behind him as we slide into the first row of seats. I look at the kids onstage; they are fidgeting and smiling with the excited, nervous energy that other kids might feel on their first day of school. Mr. Noh, tacky as ever in head-to-toe Prada, looks the way he always does: narrowed, critical eyes hidden behind mirror-tinted glasses, able to spot an underperforming trainee from a mile away, but with hands resting gently on the newbies' shoulders in a failed attempt to seem fatherly.

As he drones on about the challenges that await this fresh batch of future K-pop stars, my eyes wander over to the food set up on tables at the side of the auditorium. It's a lavish Western-style spread of prosciutto and fig sandwiches, rosewater doughnuts, and fruit platters bursting with fresh mango and lychee. A small group of DB execs and senior trainers have already set up camp around the banquet tables, stuffing their faces. I see a familiar flash of neon-pink hair among them and wave at Chung Yujin, DB's head trainer. Yujin was the one who first scouted me while I was singing "Style" inside a noraebang in Myeong-dong. I was eleven years old, and Leah and I were visiting our halmoni in Seoul for the summer. I'm seventeen now and Yujin's still the person at DB I look up to most—she's my mentor, my unni. No one but Akari knows about our history, though, and how close we really are. Yujin always says my life as a K-pop trainee is already hard enough (what with Mr. Noh's interest in me and my special schedule), that she doesn't want to pile on by telling everyone I'm her favorite. She waves back discreetly, pretending to look interested as a wrinkled old exec grabs her by the arm and starts gabbing in her ear. She catches my eye from across the auditorium and mouths, *Help*.

I giggle to myself, my eye sliding to a big orange-and-white sign displayed on the table: ON BEHALF OF CHOO MINA AND HER FATHER, WE ARE PROUD TO BE PART OF THE DB FAMILY. BON APPÉTIT! My grin vanishes. Maybe I can say no to free food after all.

"I think I just lost my appetite," I say flatly.

Akari follows my eyes to the sign. "Oh," she says. She laughs, trying to lighten my mood. "Come on, Mina's not that bad."

"Remember what happened at my bowing ceremony?"

Akari smiles, eyes crinkling. "Ooh, yeah, I love this story."

On my first day as a DB newbie, I had no idea I was supposed to bow to the senior trainees at this ceremony. I was fresh off the plane from New York City—and even though both my parents are Korean, bowing isn't really something you do all that much in the States. When I was a kid, it was just something we did when we visited my parents' friends from church during the new year, and that was the full formal Korean bow (and it was worth it too, for the crisp twenty-dollar bill they always handed to us afterward). I thought the ceremony was just a welcoming event, a chance to meet the other trainees. Yujin-unni, knowing I wouldn't know what to do, whispered in my ear that I should bow to the elder trainees. So I did—to the older teens standing in a row. But when I got to Mina, a girl my own age, I just stuck out my hand to shake hers, thinking it was the right (and polite!) thing to do. I might as well have kicked her in the stomach and spit in her hair for the tantrum she had.

By now Akari has taken over the story, mimicking Mina's world-class meltdown. "'Who does this bitch think she is?'" She crows with laughter. "'She thinks she's some kind of hotshot because she's from America? Learn some manners, newbie.'" I roll my eyes, recalling how she immediately tattled on me to Mr. Noh, demanding I be punished for my lack of respect to a sunbae (literally *anyone* with more experience than you, even if that person is your same age or younger). Thankfully, Yujin put a stop to that. But since then, Mina has basically made it her goal in life to destroy me.

"God. The temper she has."

"But you still didn't bow, did you?" Akari says.

"It'll take more than some rich daddy's girl with a god complex to make me bow to Mina," I say.

"That's my girl." Akari pats me on the back. "Young Rachel would be so proud of you." I flash her a quick smile, but inside, my heart starts to sink. If I could go back in time, knowing the proper etiquette, would I really do it the same way? I want to say yes, that obviously I would put Mina in her place, but even I don't know if I'm being honest with myself. I think back to the way I ran out of the training room this morning, the way I avoid confrontation with all the other trainees—Yujin's always telling me to rise above, to focus on training, and I play those words over in my head constantly. But . . . would eleven-year-old Rachel be proud of me? Or would she call me a coward?

Akari and I join the ceremony onstage, waiting our turn in line with the other senior trainees to receive bows from the newbies.

"Excuse me," Lizzie snaps at us. "Princess and her pawn to the back of the line." The girls around us gasp in shock.

Beside me, Akari whirls around to face her. "Excuse *you*," she snaps back, her face inches from Lizzie's, her eyes narrowed in anger. "We're more senior than you. We're not going anywhere."

Lizzie's eyes nervously dart over to Mina, who's looking at us with a smug smile on her face. But there's nothing she can say—they both know Akari is right. "Whatever," she huffs, clearly defeated. "You're still foreigners." All around us, trainees are staring and giggling. I've had enough.

"Come on, Akari," I mutter, my cheeks bright pink. "It's not worth it."

I can tell Akari is seething by the way she walks, back tall and stiff, but she follows my lead. It's not worth it, I tell myself. It's unprofessional to throw down at the newbie ceremony. I'm no Mina.

Instead, we make our way over to the banquet table. Yujin grabs my hand, squeezing it hard. "Everything okay up there? It looked . . . tense."

I give her a tight smile. "It's fine. Nothing to worry about," I say as I ignore her arched brow and grab a plate. Distractedly, I reach for a sandwich, intent on eating away this shame spiral that's started to grow in my stomach, when Akari pulls my hand back, shaking her head.

"Cucumber," she says, pointing to the sign.

"Gross." I shudder, plopping a white pizza bacon grilled cheese on my plate instead. "Thanks. You saved my life."

"What are friends for?" She smiles. "Plus, I'm never reliving the horrific cucumber catastrophe of 2017. I still get nightmares thinking about you vomiting all over the cafeteria after one tiny bite of cucumber salad."

"Don't blame me! Cucumbers are like the jogging exercises of the vegetable world! People pretend to like them because they're supposed to be healthy for you, but really, they're the worst. And they leave a horrible taste in your mouth. And they should be illegal."

"Sorry, but I believe cucumbers are technically a fruit?" Akari laughs, and I throw a crumpled napkin at her face.

Walk into any K-pop trainee lesson and you'll find some of the most talented teens in the world—expert dancers, accomplished singers, and of course, world-class gossipmongers. "I heard he dyed his hair orange," Eunji says.

"Not just any orange, but the *exact* same custom shade that Romeo from BigM$ney has," a first-year trainee in silver pants chimes in, his voice barely past puberty.

Looks like class is in session.

All the gossip, of course, is focused on one thing: Jason Lee, DB's newest K-pop star and the latest addition to the coveted plaque on the yearbook, after his group, NEXT BOYZ, debuted at #1 with their single "True Love." You couldn't take a step onto campus—or anywhere in Seoul, really—without hearing Jason's brooding tenor singing about finding his one true love. Mr. Noh had never looked happier. But now, apparently, sweet, humble, loyal Jason and the execs are in a big fight and no one knows why. I sip a can of Milkis, happy to forget all about my day and listen to the theories swirl around me.

"I heard he stole from Mr. Noh's vinyl record collection," a third voice whispers, hiding behind thick reddish-brown bangs.

"Angel Boy? Stealing? He would never!"

"Would Mr. Noh even notice? He has, like, a thousand records."

"Are you serious? He's obsessed with those records."

"Who cares if he's a thief? He's too cute to be fired!" Half a dozen trainees all start nodding in agreement.

I shake my head slightly in disbelief. Stolen records and dyed hair? That's the worst the vicious DB rumor mill can come up with? A few months ago, when a female trainee, Suzy Choi, was suddenly let go in the middle of a training cycle, rumors had run rampant that she had a drug problem and she owed thousands of dollars to her dealers, who sold her to one of those North Korean–themed restaurants in Cambodia. (Akari, on the other hand, claimed she had seen Suzy on the street holding hands with some cute boy, but I don't believe it. There's no way Suzy would have ever broken DB's strict "no dating" rule—in this industry, illicit drugs are more believable than an illicit boyfriend.) Another time last year, my mom and dad were both working on a Sunday and asked me to bring Leah to training with me—the rumors that she was my illegitimate child and that I took care of her during the week and *that* was the reason I didn't train during the week have only just died down. Of course, the fact that I'm only five years older than her didn't seem to matter to anyone.

"What we should really be focusing on is training harder, not gossiping," Mina says primly, stretching as she stands up and glances in Mr. Noh's direction. I resist the urge to roll my eyes. Could she get any more obvious?

Zeroing in on me, she saunters over, smiling brightly at the plate in my hands. "Rachel. So sorry you couldn't participate in the bowing ceremony. It's probably better left to those of us who know what we're doing, don't you think? But I do hope you're enjoying the food."

That's it. I've had enough of Mina for today. "Yes," I say brightly back, plucking a piece of bacon off my plate and crunching down on it. "I'm lucky to be so naturally thin that I don't have to watch what I eat." I let my eyes linger on her plateful of peeled celery and dotori-muk while a group of younger trainees swivel toward us, eyes agog and giggling.

Mina's eyes narrow in shock and anger—she's not used to me biting back. I'm sure she'll make me pay. Raising her voice several decibels, she says, "If you and Akari are free tonight, why don't you join us for vocals practice at the trainee house? We do it every Saturday night, and I wouldn't want you to fall behind."

The trainee house. Yeah, right. Umma would never let me go and Mina knows it.

Before I can respond, Mr. Noh strides over. Mina's loud voice has obviously paid off. At least she's getting something out of all those extra singing lessons; the girl knows how to project.

"What's this I hear about a late-night practice?" His eyes move across the group, landing on me. "Rachel, was this your idea?" he asks, smiling. "Our most hardworking trainee!" His eyes focus in on me as all around us trainees have gone silent, everyone sitting up as straight as they possibly can, alert and ready to be called on and impress at a moment's notice.

Beside me, Mina looks furious that Mr. Noh has singled me out yet again. I force a smile onto my face and open my mouth to respond, but Mina cuts me off at the last moment. "I'll be there, sir!" she practically shouts, a few pieces of celery flying off her plate.

Mr. Noh's eyes widen in shock, but he quickly recovers. "Wonderful attitude. And good for you, Miss . . . uh . . ."

"Choo. Choo Mina. My father is Choo Minhee. . . ." Mina's face falls. "You two are old friends. . . ."

"Right, right, of course, Minhee's daughter!" Mr. Noh chuckles, a look of relief in his eyes. "Thank you for reminding me."

A smile bursts across Mina's face. "Thank *you*, Mr. Noh," Mina says, simpering. "Will the two of you be getting together anytime soon? Father's always saying how much he enjoys your company at the annual Choo Corporation's Christmas party. . . ."

"Yes, yes, I'll have to give him a ring." He chuckles before turning his attention back to me. "And what wonderful taste in friends you have, Rachel! You and Mina are fine examples for the other senior trainees. You should all be making this late-night session a top priority." Mr. Noh's eyes lock with mine, and I can see myself in the reflection of his glasses. "Especially those of you who wish to debut soon."

My insides are on fire, but I don't waver. I can feel Mina's smug expression burning a hole in the side of my head, but I take another sip of Milkis and smile.

"Count me in," I say. Mr. Noh nods in approval, and I raise my can to him as if making a toast. *To family and to being utterly screwed.* "I can't wait."

Two

Sweat pours down my forehead as I take another swing at the sagging punching bag in front of me. *Thud.* Mina's smug smile. *Thwack.* Umma's strict rules. *Bam.* Me, walking away from all those girls in media training instead of standing up for myself. *Ugh.* I beat them all to a pulp, everything that annoys me, everyone who stands in my way—even me.

Appa, who's holding the punching bag steady, grunts as I throw blow after blow. "You must look up to me a lot," he says.

"Why do you say that?" I ask, my breath ragged from exertion.

"You're obviously trying to follow in my steps." He chuckles. Appa is a former pro boxer. "Why else would my sixteen-year-old daughter be torturing this punching bag?"

"Seventeen, Appa. In Korea, I'm seventeen." In Korea they consider you to be age one when you're born, which means you're a year older than you are in the US. *A year closer to passing my prime. A year closer to being too old to debut.* I punch the bag again.

"Sorry, Daughter," Appa says with a sigh.

I deliver one last punch and take a few steps back, breathing hard. My ponytail is sticking to the sweat on the back of my neck. If this were DB, I would be embarrassed—trainers hate it when the trainees sweat, even after hours of practice, saying it makes us look unprofessional and sloppy. Plus, most of the girls practice in makeup, and runny mascara is never a good look. But at the boxing gym I revel in the sweat. It makes me feel like I've just kicked someone's ass, even if it is imaginary.

Appa gives me a thoughtful look. "Is everything okay?"

He nods to the other side of the gym, where Akari and my friends from school, the Cho twins, are sparring, decked out in helmets and gloves. They come with me now and then when I visit Appa at our family's boxing gym; Appa tells us stories about his glory days and we get our cardio fix.

"Fine," I say. As cool as Appa is, I know that whatever I tell him about training life will eventually make its way back to Umma. Not that Appa can't keep a secret. In fact, I know he's keeping a pretty big one of his own from Umma. "How are those classes going, by the way?"

He glances around as if Umma might be hiding behind a punching bag. But aside from me and my friends, the gym is empty. As usual. "They're fine." He clears his throat. "You still haven't told your mother or Leah, have you?"

I shake my head. The only reason I know that Appa's been taking secret law-school night classes in the first place is because I spotted a law textbook in his office during one of my gym visits. When I asked him about it, he got flustered and tried to pass it off as light reading. Eventually he broke down and told me the truth, but he made me promise not to tell Umma or Leah. "No. But it's been, what, two years? Don't you think it's time to mention it to them? I mean, you're about to graduate!"

"I don't want to get their hopes up," he says now, the same as he did the day I found out. "We all know the gym isn't doing well. It's not like before . . ." He pauses, and I think about what life was like back in New York. Appa was semi-famous from his pro-boxing days, and the gym he ran in our neighborhood in the West Village was always brimming with people. Umma was close to getting tenure as an English Literature professor at NYU. Everyone was busy, but somehow the four of us were always together. After school, Leah and I would sit in the back row of Umma's classes, coloring and doing our homework. On the weekends, we used to run around handing out cups of water and towels to all the boxers at Appa's gym, and Umma would be helping out in the office, arranging class schedules and taking deliveries. Afterward, we would always get ice cream and take Leah to see the guy who made gigantic bubbles in Washington Square Park.

But everything is different now. Umma's working twice as hard to get back on the tenure track at her job, which could be years away. Leah spends hours alone after school each day while our parents are working and I'm doing homework or trying to keep up with my training. And Appa's gym . . . well, he bought this gym about a year after we moved to Seoul, but it's never really taken off. Some weeks, me and my friends are the only ones who come in at all.

For the third time today, I feel a lump in my throat. I know Appa is happy for me and my life as a K-pop trainee, but I can't help feeling guilty for the dreams he gave up in order to let me pursue mine. Appa shakes his head and gives me a small smile. "I love this gym, but I love you and Leah and Umma even more. You three are what's important now, and becoming a lawyer will give us some financial stability. But I just . . . don't want to disappoint them. Especially Leah. She's only twel—thirteen!— and you know how excited she gets about the smallest things. Let's just wait a little longer to see if I even have a chance at suc-ceeding."

I nod my head in understanding. The thought of disap-pointing my family—the ones who gave up so much so I could train at DB, so that I could be a star—haunts me. But that's why for me it's not a matter of if, but when. For me there's no other choice but to succeed.

"Enough old-man talk," Appa says, trying to keep his tone light. "Go have fun with your friends."

Now Akari is holding the punching bag for the twins as they take turns jabbing and crossing. Cho Hyeri and Cho Juhyun are my best friends from Seoul International School, since the first day of fourth grade, when the principal assigned them as my official welcoming committee. I was so nervous of what every-one would think of my K-pop training—would they think I was weird? Or spoiled? Or maybe they would want me to bow to them like Mina?—but Hyeri and Juhyun waved it off like it was nothing, grabbing my hand before I could move or say a word and racing me around the school. They were more interested in the glittery patches I had sewn on to my Converses and what growing up within walking distance of the boutiques in SoHo and the tents at Bryant Park during fashion week was like—not that I had much to say on either subject. They're both willowy and tall, with high cheekbones and silky brown hair that falls in natural (or so they claim) waves over their shoulders. They could be models if they wanted to be and, as heiresses to the Molly Folly makeup corporation, they'd have the connections to get there too. But the only thing Hyeri is interested in doing for the family beauty company is revolutionizing their entire engineering and design department. She's always going on about chemical reactions needed for glow-in-the-dark liquid liner or obsessing over experiments for 100 percent organic, compost-friendly packaging for a new range of eye shadow palettes. As for Juhyun, she's practically famous due to her YouTube beauty channel. Even while sweating it out in the gym, her makeup is impeccable, from her matte red lipstick to her perfectly curled eyelashes.

"Water break?" I suggest, tugging off my boxing gloves.

"God, yes please," Hyeri says, getting in a final jab. "I think I heard talk about ice cream and hotteok after this?"

"*You* were the one who mentioned ice cream," Juhyun says.

"So?" Hyeri grins, giving her sister a soft punch on the

shoulder. "You were the one who said, 'Who can eat ice cream without hotteok on the side?'"

Juhyun lets out a snort. "Well, I'm not wrong."

Akari lets go of the punching bag, and it creaks back and forth. We all grab our water bottles and take long swigs, Akari squirting some all over her face.

"You okay, Rachel?" Juhyun asks, wiping her mouth with the back of her hand. "We saw you going extra hard today."

"Are you still thinking about what happened with Mina?" Akari asks worriedly.

"Ay, shib-al! What did the bitch do now?" Hyeri groans.

I fill in the twins about Mina's invitation to the late-night practice in front of Mr. Noh. They nod understandingly. It's not my first time venting to them about DB and Mina.

"She totally set me up!" My face flushes as I remember what I said to Mina. I let out a heavy sigh. I never should have made that comment about being able to eat whatever I like. "My mom never lets me go to the trainee house, and when I don't show up tonight, you know she'll make sure Mr. Noh hears about it. And then I can kiss my future goodbye." The thought of it makes my skin prickle with panic.

"So go," Akari says. "Go and show her and all those other trainees that you deserve this just as much as they do."

"What about you? She invited you, too, you know."

Akari shrugs her shoulders. "It's 'family night' on the base and attendance is mandatory. I would if I could—not that it really matters, though. I've been at DB for five years and I don't think Mr. Noh even knows who I am. If it wasn't for Yujin-unni, I'm sure they would have cut me by now."

I wince. Even though she lives on the base with her family, she's at DB every single day, training alongside Mina and the girls. And Akari's dancing skills are unbelievable—Yujin even says she puts Frankie from Red Hot, objectively the best female K-pop dancer in the industry, to shame. But everyone knows that when it comes to being a trainee, talent will take you only so far. That's why we're all desperate to do whatever we can to get noticed by Mr. Noh and the rest of the DB executives. Because every thirty days, like clockwork, trainees gather in the auditorium with DB's executive board, waiting to be evaluated and judged, deemed worthy of staying in the program or getting kicked out. After six years the constant judgment was almost starting to seem routine, but a few months ago Akari was called into Mr. Noh's office after appraisal day—a sure sign she was being asked to leave. That she hadn't done enough to stand out. I don't know what Yujin said, or did, but Akari was back the next day, a little quiet and sad-looking, but still there. She hasn't brought it up since. I glance at the twins, who shrug their shoulders, at a loss for words.

"It's fine. I'm not trying to have a pity party!" She smiles, quickly changing the subject. "It's just one night. This is your career we're talking about."

"I gotta agree with Akari on this," Hyeri says, capping her water bottle. "You want this more than anything, don't you? If a late-night practice at the trainee house is going to set you up for success, you have to take it."

I sneak a glance at Appa. He's all the way across the gym, practically demolishing a bag, sweat flying everywhere. He's in the zone. "I don't know," I say. "My mom would freak."

Juhyun tilts her head to the side. "Is it worth it?"

I wipe the sweat from my face. Is it worth it? That's a question I ask myself every day. All the training, the lost weekends, the family sacrifices. The constant feeling of never quite belonging somewhere you desperately want to be. All to fulfill my dream of becoming a K-pop star. I think of eleven-year-old Rachel. The little girl who used to be chronically late because she couldn't stop watching K-pop music videos in the bathroom between classes. In some ways, not a lot has changed. In other ways, everything has.

"It's everything to me."

"There you go," Akari says.

Juhyun's eyes glint underneath the gym's fluorescent lighting. "Mina underestimates you, *Princess Rachel*." She pulls off her boxing gloves and unravels her hand wraps, revealing intricately manicured pale-pink and navy-blue floral nails underneath. "Now go show that bitch who's boss."

I punch the elevator button for the eighteenth floor, antsy to get home and shower after Appa goaded me and Akari into going thirty minutes in the ring with him.

The first thing I hear when I enter our apartment is the

sound of K-pop music, followed by Leah laughter and a group of giggling girls. I slide into my slippers and walk toward the living room, where Leah is sprawled on the floor with four other girls from her class, watching the newest Electric Flower music video on their phones. I recognize it immediately—the legendary Kang Jina along with the rest of the group, all dancing in glowing orange jumpsuits against a pure black soundstage. It's the quickest viral video in DB history, getting over thirty-six million hits in only twenty-four hours. Leah stands, holding a hairbrush to her mouth like a microphone, and belts out the lyrics, matching Jina's powerful soprano note by note. I can't help but smile. The girl's got talent.

Seeing me, one of her friends, a girl with a heart-shaped face and diamond-encrusted Hello Kitty earrings, nudges Leah in the toe. "Your unni's home," she says, nodding in my direction.

Leah spins around and holds the hairbrush out to me. "Take it away, Unni!"

I make a half-hearted motion to grab the brush, but the song is already fading to an end, leaving the room in an uncomfortable silence.

"Too bad," Heart Face says. "We could have had a performance from a real K-pop trainee."

Another girl in a striped shirt arches an eyebrow at me, taking in my matted, greasy hair and drooping sweatpants. "Um, are you sure *she's* the K-pop trainee? Maybe Leah was talking about another sister."

Leah laughs awkwardly, plopping back onto the floor and setting down her hairbrush. "Nope . . . that's her. I only have one unni."

"The one and only," I say.

Stripes looks stunned. "Are you serious?"

Damn, Mina and the others are no match for these vicious preteens.

Leah chokes out another laugh, her cheeks turning pink. "Come on, guys. Trust me. Remember those ninth-grade girls from school who followed her on the bus all the way to DB headquarters just to see if she was really a trainee? Don't be like them."

"If you're a real trainee, what can you tell us about DB?" one of the other girls asks. She leans forward, her eyes wide. "Do you ever see Jason Lee?"

"I heard he has a secret girlfriend that he only sees during the full moon," the fourth girl says. "Is that true?"

"That's so romantic." Heart Face sighs. "Is it true that he picks a superfan off social media to surprise and spend the day with? He's just the best!"

I laugh to myself. Even outside of DB, gossip can't touch Jason "Angel Boy" Lee's pristine reputation. "Um. Right . . . well, the thing is, I don't really see him around." It's the truth, but I can tell that's not the answer they were hoping for.

"Well, what about Electric Flower? Do they all get along? I bet Mr. Noh favors Kang Jina. She's obviously the prettiest."

"I don't . . . know?" My body is really feeling that thirty-minute spar, and I can barely keep up with their questions.

Stripes lets out an exasperated sigh, blowing her bangs out of her face. "How . . . interesting." She tiptoes around my sweat-soaked sweatshirt that I threw on the floor. "I guess being a trainee isn't as fun or . . . *glamorous* . . . as we thought it would be. Our bad . . . come on, girls. Let's go shopping at Coex." She nods at the other three but doesn't make eye contact with Leah. They all get up and quickly walk single file past me, putting on their shoes.

"Um, but . . . wait! I love shopping!" Leah stumbles to her feet, watching as the girls leave. Her shoulders slump as Heart Face slams the door behind them. Ouch.

"I'm sorry, Le—" Before I can finish, she whirls around to me, her face flushed with anger. "Unni! Would it kill you to at least *pretend* to be a cool trainee?"

Stung, I draw back. "What? Don't try to make this about me! Every week you have some new group of girls over here— why don't you try making some friends that like you for *you* for once, instead of for the gossip they think you can deliver?"

"Well . . . maybe they would have liked me eventually! You know, if you hadn't scared them away with your ahjussi sweatpants and gross hair," she claps back. "I know there's a women's locker room at Appa's gym. Stop being so lazy."

I sigh. I know those girls aren't real friends, but I also know that Leah is upset. Just like Appa, she never asked to leave New York and the life our family had there and move across the world so I could pursue my dream, and yet she's supported me every step of the way. She was too young before, but I think there's a part of her that wishes she could audition for the DB training program now. But after everything I've gone through, though, Umma would never allow it and Leah knows it. So I probably could have put on a little show for her friends. What would have been the harm in it?

But it's too late now.

I think of a way to cheer her up instead.

"Well, maybe the real reason I didn't want to tell your friends about what's happening at DB is because I wanted you to hear it first." I plop down on the couch, patting the seat next to me. "Sisters get the inside scoop before anyone else."

Tentatively, Leah sits down next to me. She makes a big show of not sitting too close. She isn't ready to *not* be mad at me yet, but she's too curious to resist. I ham it up, telling her all about my showdown with Mina in media training, Mina's loaded invitation to the trainee house, and Mr. Noh's proclamation about how my future at DB depends on showing up tonight. She leans in closer and closer as I talk, her eyes widening with every word until she's practically sitting in my lap.

"Unni," she screams, shaking my shoulders. "A night at the trainee house! That sounds like a dream come true."

I laugh, letting her jiggle me around like a bobblehead. "Don't get too excited, little sis. You know there's no way Umma will let me go."

"Oh, you're right," Leah says, putting her face in her hands.

I think back to my conversation with Juhyun. "Of course," I say determinedly, "I could always sneak out . . . ?"

Leah squeals. "I'll help you with an escape plan! I already have one in mind!"

I narrow my eyes. "I hope it doesn't involve climbing out the window of our eighteenth-floor apartment." My younger sister is well-known in our family for her obsession with The Rock.

"Okay, so I'll come up with a plan B." Her eyes gleam. "As long as you get me Jason Lee's autograph. You know he's my ultimate bias!"

"Who should I get him to make it out to? Leah Kim, My Darling Future Wife?"

She screams again, falling back on the couch and kicking her legs up in the air in delight. "I'd die! No, first I'd frame it. *Then* I'd die." She sits up, grabbing my hands. "Promise you'll bury it with me."

I laugh.

We hear the front door open and Umma's voice calling out for us. Leah and I exchange glances. We lock pinkies, each of us leaning forward to kiss our fists and bump our cheeks together, our special Kim sister pinkie promise we created years ago.

Umma enters the living room, carrying a bag full of take-out from Two Two Fried Chicken. Dinner. Umma is a linguistics professor at Ewha Women's University, and with her tenure review coming up, she's usually too tired to come home and cook. Not that we complain. Umma's idea of a home-cooked meal is cracking an egg over a pot of Shin Ramyun and topping it off with a slice of American cheese—delicious but not easy on the stomach. Plus, I feel like she feeds me noodles on purpose to make me bloated when I go into training the next day. Like some kind of subconscious, calorie-based sabotage.

"Hungry?" she asks, holding up the bag.

We dig in, pulling out boxes of steaming fried chicken and an array of banchan, including daikon kimchi and crisp salad smothered in what tastes like Big Mac sauce. It's chilly for April, so the heated floor underneath our kitchen table is on, making it nice and toasty as I sit down and reach for a piece of yangnyeom chicken, the sweet and spicy sauce already sticking to my fingers, while Umma sets aside a few pieces of the green-onion chicken, Appa's favorite. He's at the gym late tonight, giving the punching bags their weekly scrub down (which is really code for his class in Intellectual Property Law), so it's just the three of us for dinner.

"So how was your day, Leah?" Umma asks.

Leah chatters away about Kang Jina in Electric Flower ("She's *so* pretty"), Jason Lee ("I heard he's starting a charity to bring music therapy to young kids in Korea. Isn't he just the sweetest?!"), and the latest K-drama on Netflix ("If Park Dohee on *Oh My Dreams* doesn't get her memory back soon, I swear I'm going to stop watching"). Umma nods along, smiling distractedly as she picks at her salad. I carefully peel the skin off my chicken and wait for her to ask me how my day was. It's Saturday, so she knows I've been at DB.

Finally, Leah's chatter slows down and I mentally prepare, dreaming that, this time, Umma will ask me how my day at DB was and be sympathetic and understanding as I tell her about Mina and Mr. Noh and give me her blessing to go to the trainee house tonight. But when she finally turns to me, she says, "Did you finish your homework, Rachel? And the chores I asked you to do?" She shoots a pointed look at the sink full of unwashed dishes.

Poof. Dream gone.

My jaw tightens as I clench my teeth. "My day was great. Thanks so much for asking. I was training all day, and then I went to see Appa at the gym." I pause. "Sorry about the chores," I add, choking the words out like a chicken bone stuck in my throat. Not that I'm sorry for focusing on training, but her eyes are narrowing at me in that "I will make you regret the day you were born" way that she used to get whenever Leah or I were misbehaving on the subway during rush hour in New York.

She sighs, reaching into her tote bag on the table. "Always training. Why don't you try something different? It's not healthy being so obsessed with one thing." She pulls out a huge stack of papers and hands them to me. I glance down and see UNIVERSAL COLLEGE APPLICATION stamped across the top. I feel dizzy with panic as my mom claps her hands, a huge smile on her face. "Rachel! I brought these home for you— tomorrow at Ewha there's an educational seminar! It's meant to prepare high school students for the college-application process. Why don't you go? They can help you start to fill these out, and maybe I can even show you around the campus after."

My chest fills with heat as I raise my hand to push away the stack of applications. But then I see Umma's face—lips smiling, eyes hopeful—and a wave of guilt washes over me. We've been here for six years and I've still never seen the campus where she works—a far cry from the hours I used to spend reading books under her desk while she held office sessions. I pull the applications toward me with a sigh. "Umma," I say carefully, "you know I would love to see Ewha, but I just . . . can't. Tomorrow is *Sunday*."

"We're talking about the rest of your life, Rach, not just one day," Umma says lightly.

"Sure. But . . . training *is* the rest of my life. Isn't it? I mean, isn't that why we came here?"

Leah puts down her chicken, her eyes moving between us worriedly. She's used to me and Umma tiptoeing into these arguments.

Umma looks down at her plate and sighs. "There are . . . a lot of reasons why we came to Korea." She opens her mouth like she's about to say something more, but then she shakes her head slightly. She turns to me, and when she does, I can almost see tears in her eyes, but her voice is even and clear. "You know I used to be a volleyball player." I resist the urge to roll my eyes—is Umma really going to compare her high school volleyball days to my K-pop training? "But where would I be now—where would our family be—if I had given up everything for that dream?"

"But that's exactly what you're asking me to do—to give up everything I've been working for just for some college seminar." I shove a piece of chicken in my mouth, skin and all. To hell with the extra calories.

Umma shrugs, looking sad but determined. "I'm just suggesting that maybe you should keep your options open." She picks at a piece of seasoned watercress on her plate. "You never know what the future might hold, Rachel. And if things don't work out with your training . . . I just don't want you to feel surprised."

My eyes fill with tears, and I blink hard, unwilling to let them spill onto my face. Even after six years, my mom's attitude toward my training still gets to me. Sometimes I wonder if she regrets moving to Seoul—if she wishes she had just sold Halmoni's apartment and washed her hands of the whole thing. Or if she even believes in my talent. I bite my lip, about to excuse myself from dinner, when Leah jumps in, pushing herself onto her knees as she turns to face Umma.

"Actually, funny you should mention that seminar, Umma," she says. "The Cho twins are having a weekend-long study session to prep for college. They're even hiring a private tutor and studying late into the night. A study slumber party, I think they called it. Right, Unni?" She smiles innocently up at our mom.

I straighten up. *It's now or never, Rachel.* "Right," I say slowly.

"How did you know about that?" Umma asks Leah, raising her eyebrows.

"I overheard Rachel talking to Hyeri on the phone," Leah lies easily.

I focus on chewing my chicken, trying to keep my face neutral. My sister, ladies and gentlemen, the future Oscar winner.

Umma's gaze turns to me. "Why didn't you mention this, Rachel? This is just what you need to get you on the right track."

I nod, swallowing down a fresh surge of frustration along with my chicken. "I just . . . didn't want to spend the night away when I haven't even gotten to my chores yet." I glance toward the full sink. "Sorry," I add again for good measure.

"Oh," Umma says. "Well, those dishes won't take too long. Why don't you finish up and head over to the Cho house? Knowing their parents, they'll have hired the best tutor in Seoul. I'll pack some leftover chicken for you to take."

"Really?" I feel guilty for lying, but it's quickly replaced by a buzzing energy that spreads across my body. My first night at the trainee house! One step closer to my dream. "Thanks, Umma."

She smiles and begins to clear her plate away, packing a few pieces of chicken into a small bright-green Tupperware container. When her back is turned, Leah gives me a big thumbs-up. I wink at her and mouth, *Thank you.*

As soon as I'm done with the dishes, I hurl myself into the shower and quickly twist my wet hair into tight Dutch braids.

I slip into a pair of black leggings and a creamy, cozy oversize off-the-shoulder sweater top that is the perfect amount of slouch. I throw on my comfiest pair of pajamas—the cartoon Snoopy ones I bought at Dongdaemun last spring—over the whole ensemble so Umma won't get suspicious seeing me all dressed up. With one last glance in the mirror, I grab my bag, quickly scooping up Umma's Tupperware, and head out for my first night at the trainee house.

⭐ *Three* ⭐

Umma's words are ringing in my ears as I walk to the bus stop. *If things don't work out . . . I just don't want you to feel surprised.* Of course I've always known that being a K-pop star is not a guarantee, but I've wanted this dream for so long, I'm not sure I even know what the alternative looks like.

It all started when I was six years old. There was one other Asian girl in my class, Eugenia Li. Even though she was Chinese, everyone was always asking us if we were cousins or twin sisters. I didn't think much of it until one day when I got stung by a bee during recess. I was sitting in the nurse's office, waiting for Umma to come and take me home, when Mrs. Li walked through the door. The nurse didn't realize she had done anything wrong and instead was all smiles as she told me that my mom was there to get me. For the first time, I realized the world didn't see me the way I saw me, or the way my family saw me. All they saw was my face; the shape of my eyes and my nose; my thick, straight black hair—and it made me interchangeable with girls like Eugenia, even though we looked nothing alike. When my mom finally picked me up at school, I couldn't stop crying. The bee sting was still burning on my skin, but when Umma asked me what was wrong, all I could think about was Mrs. Li. "I wish I wasn't Korean," I remember sobbing into her shirt. So she scooped me up and carried me home, and when we got there, she tucked me into bed and grabbed her laptop. That was the first time I saw a K-pop music video. We watched them for hours, and I marveled at the singers—all so unique and beautiful and talented.

I was hooked. I watched K-pop music videos constantly, memorizing the lyrics to my favorite ones and putting on little shows for Leah on the weekends. The music made me feel proud to be Korean.

I wish I could say that time with Mrs. Li and the school nurse was the only time I ever felt rejected by the world, but it wasn't. There were the kids who made fun of the kimchi Umma packed me for lunch; the woman who once came up to me in our corner bodega, screaming at me that I should "go home" (even though I lived around the block, I got the feeling that wasn't what she meant); there was the time I dressed like Hermione Granger for Halloween and everyone insisted that I was Cho Chang. Through it all, there was K-pop. It made me feel understood, like there was a place in the world where I belonged, where people would see me for me.

I'm thinking about all this as I walk to the bus stop.

The spring Seoul air is breezy and crisp, sidewalks littered with so many fallen cherry blossoms that they stick to the bottom of your shoes, turning the whole city into a haze of pearly pink petals. I walk to the corner, popping into the GS25 for a Pocari Sweat, and then hop on the bus to the trainee house, a few blocks down from DB headquarters. The seats are filled with young couples in matching sweatshirts sharing earbuds, businessmen and -women watching old episodes of *Running Man* on their phones as they head home from work, and halmonis clutching canvas granny carts stuffed to the brim with groceries and empty bottles. I plop down on a seat and tip the last of my drink into my mouth as the breeze from the open window whips back my braids. The old lady next to me pokes me in the side, gesturing to my empty can. *"Dah mashussuh?"*

"Neh, Halmoni," I say, handing it over.

"Komawoh," she replies, pinching my cheek. *"Ahh ipuda!"*

I bow my head. *"Kamsahamnida."*

The bus careens down the street, barely skidding to a stop when people want to get on or off. In New York, I was never allowed on public transportation by myself, so getting used to it when we moved was a big learning curve. Luckily, just like the rest of Seoul, the buses and subway system are fast, super clean, and easy to use. But the best part of life in this city? There is free Wi-Fi literally everywhere you go.

I pull out my phone and send a quick text to Hyeri: If my mom asks, I was at your house tonight.

She immediately texts back: Sure. Juhyun says "Don't have too much fun without us tonight!"

I laugh but shove my phone back in my pocket without replying. The less they know, the less likely it is that they'll slip up if interrogated. I'm so buzzed from the adrenaline of lying to Umma and going to the trainee house that I get off one stop early and walk the rest of the way. I need to get some of this energy out before I face Mina and the others.

I'm about half a block away when I realize I still need to change out of my pajamas.

I duck behind a particularly large bush lining the sidewalk and unbutton my pajama top, stuffing it into my tote. I'm watching the street, making sure that no one is approaching as I wiggle out of my pajama pants. They catch on my ankles and my fingers fumble, but I can't stop myself in time. I trip over the pajama's pretzel twist around my legs, spinning and falling face-first in the dirt.

I groan, sitting up slowly and brushing the dirt off my sweater. Thank god no one saw that.

"Wow . . . that looked like it hurt."

Everything in my body freezes. I turn my head and see two brand-new white-and-black Nike sneakers standing on the sidewalk. My gaze drifts upward, taking in a pair of perfectly tailored Ader Error track pants and a Burberry sweater that I'm sure cost more than my entire wardrobe, all worn by a boy with silvery highlights in his hair, sparkling brown eyes, and cheekbones that could probably cut glass.

Not just a boy. *The* boy. Jason Lee.

Holy shit.

"You okay?" he asks, a concerned smile on his face. "Here, let me help you." He holds out his hand.

"You're . . . Jason . . . Lee," I stammer as I struggle to my feet. Even before shooting to stardom with DB, Jason was famous for his YouTube K-pop covers. After one of his videos went viral, Mr. Noh himself flew to Toronto and convinced Jason to move to Seoul, where he quickly became Korea's most beloved pop star. Being half-white, half-Korean actually works for him here, with everyone from preteens to stalker fans to ahjummas praising him for his big, double-lidded eyes and olive complexion, as if he handpicked his genes himself. Somehow his foreigner status gets him voted "Korea's Sexiest K-pop Star," while mine gets me mandatory Korean culture lessons.

"Oh, so you've heard of me?" He arches an eyebrow, his smile widening. He's definitely got the smile-like-the-world-is-your-friend thing down—for him, the world probably is. "What kind of things have you heard?"

"Well, my sister Leah told me about your musical therapy chari—"

"Voice of an angel? Smile of the devil? Body of a god?"

"Uh . . . what?"

"You know, most girls faint when they see me. But I guess you did fall, so that's something," he says, almost to himself. "So, tell me, what are they saying these days?" He beams down at me, his mouth open in a ridiculously cute smile.

"Mainly that you steal vinyl records from Mr. Noh's office," I say, slightly rattled by his obvious arrogance. So much for the sweet, humble star boy who starts charities and loves his fans. "And that you have a secret werewolf lover that you only see during the full moon."

"Whaaaat? That's wild! Who said that? How dare they!" He looks wounded, flashing me his signature puppy-dog eyes before a sly grin spreads across his face. "I'd never steal from Mr. Noh."

I roll my eyes. *This* is the K-pop star the world is so in love with? "Of course not. God forbid you do anything to mess up your perfect reputation. But rumors about your magical, shape-shifting girlfriend you're fine with?"

"A gentleman never kisses and tells," he replies smoothly. "Besides, you know what they say: the more people are talking about you, the more you're worth talking about."

"Maybe that's how it works in your world," I retort. Of course the infallible Jason Lee wouldn't need to take the no-dating rule at DB seriously.

Jason pauses, looking down at me. "I feel like you're mad at me."

"Nope. Not mad—just trying to get to the trainee house before practice is over," I say, pulling at the ends of my sweater and hoping I didn't just give Jason a glimpse of my underwear.

Jason's eyes light up. "The trainee house! Why didn't you say so? I'm on my way there too. I'll walk you."

"No, thanks," I reply, but he ignores me.

"So why don't I know your name?" he asks, cocking his head to the side. "Any DB trainee brave enough to wear Snoopy pants in public is worth talking about."

My cheeks redden with embarrassment again, but I force my voice to stay composed. "I'll have you know these are my favorite pajamas. Sorry we can't all be beautiful werewolves," I say, rolling my eyes.

"I disagree," Jason says.

"What are you talki—"

"You're obviously beautiful," he continues.

My body freezes. *Uh . . . what?*

"And I'm pretty sure you could bite my head off if you wanted to. Plus, it *is* a full moon tonight if you hadn't noticed."

Ohmygod. I need to get out of here. I reach down and start unwinding my tangled pajama pants, shooting a death glare at Jason.

"I don't need an audience," I snap.

He has the decency to blush but makes a big show of turning slowly around so his back is to me. "Better?"

Seething, I go to yank off my pants in one final move, but I'm so flustered that the waistband gets caught around my ankle again. I trip forward, falling face-first into Jason's back. Instinctively, I wrap my hands around his waist to steady myself, my cheek buried between his shoulder blades. Without realizing what I'm doing, I inhale deeply. He smells like maple and mint.

"Rather forward of you," Jason says. I can't see his face, but

I can hear the smirk in his voice. He turns his head, looking at me over his shoulder. "Or should I say backward? Enjoying the view?"

Kill. Me. Now. I step back, my face burning as I finally free myself from these traitorous pajama pants and shove them deep in my bag. I'm torching these things as soon as I get home.

"Thanks," I say, tossing a stiff nod in his direction and running toward the house, leaving him laughing on the sidewalk.

"You're welcome, Werewolf Girl!" he calls after me. Great. Another nickname. Just what I need.

I'm cursing myself, Jason, and the entire Charlie Brown gang as I fling open the front door of the trainee house.

Holy crap.

The place is packed with DB trainees and stars, every square inch covered in empty soju bottles and soda cans, with music practically pounding off the walls and a brand-new Samsung Frame playing all the latest K-pop music videos.

And then it hits me. Jason was headed here too—to the trainee house. This isn't a training session.

It's a party.

A group of guys turn toward me and wave, yelling out their greetings. I recognize them, but I'm in too much shock to think clearly. I wave back slowly.

"Yo, Jason!" one of them calls over my shoulder.

I immediately drop my hand as Jason enters behind me. His friend walks over, and they do that bro hug thing where they clasp opposite hands and clap each other on the back. I really need to get out of here.

"Who's your pretty date?" Jason's friend asks, looking me up and down. Then I realize. This isn't just Jason's friend. This is Minjun—lead dancer of NEXT BOYZ and global K-pop superstar.

"This is . . ." Jason pauses, glancing at me.

"Rachel," I say. At least my voice is still working normally. I haven't completely shut down from shock. "I'm a senior trainee at DB."

"American," he observes, his eyes twinkling. I almost step back, bracing myself for an oncoming insult. "Welcome, Rachel. I'm Minjun," he says, like my sister doesn't keep a poster of his face taped up above her bed and kiss it every night. "Grab a drink."

I blink in confusion, looking over my shoulder at the front door. Every instinct in my body is telling me to leave. This isn't what I was prepared for tonight.

Jason puts his hand on the back of my elbow, his eyes twinkling. "Yeah, Rachel, come join us." He raises a mischievous eyebrow. "Unless, of course, you have a pajama party to get to."

I scowl. Then I straighten up, tossing my braids behind my shoulder. I made it all the way here. I have to at least show my face. If anything, I can't leave without getting Leah her autograph. "I'd love a drink."

The party is already well underway, and I trip over more than a few empty beer cans as I march toward what looks like the bar area, which borders a spacious sunken living room where people are dropping shots of grapefruit soju into beer glasses and downing the whole drink. Someone offers me one and I take it, sipping lightly around the edges of the glass. I'm not exactly a fan of anything that causes people to lose control and embarrass themselves. I'm good enough at that already, apparently.

"Rachel!" a voice calls from across the room. I tense up. I'd recognize that sickly sweet voice anywhere. Mina appears, looking flawless and party-ready with blown-out hair and sky-high glittery stack heels. She adjusts her miniskirt and crop top while Eunji and Lizzie stand behind her, both decked out in perfectly fitting skinny jeans and tiaras. "*So* happy you could make it to our training session." She glances at the other two girls, who quickly cover their mouths with their hands to hide their laughter.

"Me too," I chirp back, refusing to back down. "Thanks *so* much for inviting me."

"Cute outfit, Rachel," Eunji says, folding a piece of gum into her mouth as her eyes flick over my clothes. "Did you borrow it from your little sister?"

"I love the hair," Lizzie adds. She reaches over and flicks one of my braids off my shoulder. "What a throwback to elementary school."

"You look uncomfortable, Rachel," Mina says, her face pinching in mock concern. "You don't feel out of place without Mr. Noh here to take care of you, do you? Surely even *Princess Rachel* must know how to have fun at a party?"

Mina takes a sip from her cup and eyes me coolly. I want to snap back, calling her out for being a dirty liar and telling her exactly where she can put her "late-night training session," but my momentary bravery has run out. Instead, I take another sip from my soju beer mix, wincing at the sour taste, my fist tight around the glass.

All of a sudden Jason pops up behind me, glancing from me to Mina to the other girls with a small smirk on his lips.

"Jason!" Mina coos. "I didn't know you were here! Have you come to find me?" she asks, sipping casually on her drink.

"Actually, I was looking for Rachel," Jason answers.

"Wh-wh-aat?" Mina sputters. "But . . . how do you know Rachel?" I swear to god, if he brings up the pajamas right now, I will kill him with my bare hands.

Jason smiles at me. "Oh, we go way back. Me and Rachel and Woodstock." Mina opens her mouth to respond, but right then Jason puts his hands on my shoulders, turning me abruptly and guiding us deeper into the party.

"I'll have you know, it was Snoopy on my pants, not Woodstock. Woodstock is the dopey little bird. Snoopy is the loyal dog–slash–airplane pilot," I say, laughing as we plop down on a couch in the corner of the room.

Jason nods in mock seriousness, draping his arm over my shoulder and pulling me close. "You're right. Clearly Snoopy is the superior choice in sleepwear. Forgive me? I was just trying to make a quick exit."

I shoot him a look. "What do you mean?"

"Well, we were surrounded by three girls who were all staring at you like they wanted to rip your face off," he says, his breath warm against my skin. "Relocation seemed like a good idea."

The soju is warming its way through my body, and I smile. "Well, you know what they say."

"What do they say, Werewolf Girl?"

"The more people stare at you, the more you must be worth staring at." I giggle, and a tiny burp escapes my mouth. My eyes go wide, and I clap a hand over my mouth as Jason looks on, utterly delighted. He pulls me closer to him on the couch, so that my legs are practically on top of his. My mind is whirring—*Is this really happening? I definitely should not be flirting with Jason right now. That's basically asking to end up like Suzy Choi. Not that she had a boyfriend. Not that Jason is my boyfriend. Oh my god, what am I thinking? There's no way I'm asking him for an autograph for Leah now.* . . . I close my eyes, trying to press pause on the soju-induced monologue running through my head.

Minjun flops down dramatically on the couch next to me, his copper-colored hair sweeping over his eyes. "I'm bored." He pouts. "And hungry."

Jason rolls his eyes at his friend, shifting so that his arms are no longer around me. A shiver courses through my body involuntarily, and I hike the sleeves of my sweater top up over my shoulders to stay warm. "Why don't you go see what the chefs left in the kitchen for dinner?" he says diplomatically.

"The only thing to eat in that kitchen is kale and spinach smoothies. You remember how they starved us in our trainee days!" Minjun sniffed the air. "Do you guys smell chicken?"

I gulp, remembering the Tupperware Umma packed before I left the house. I reach gingerly into my bag. "Um, do you mean this chicken?" I say, embarrassed.

"Ah-ssa!" Minjun shouts, ripping the box out of my hands and opening it. "Two Two Fried Chicken! My favorite! Jason, this girl is really okay."

Jason laughs and Minjun starts inhaling my leftovers, two pieces at a time.

Across the room, I can feel as Mina watches the three of us, her narrowed eyes flashing. Her phone beeps, and she pulls it out of her bag, scowling at something on the screen. She shows it to Lizzie and Eunji, and they both grimace, frowning down at her. Then she stuffs the phone back into her bag and jumps up, rearranging her face into a perfect smile. She claps her hands lightly, bouncing up and down. "Attention, party people! The time has come for girl bonding, trainees only!" she exclaims. "You know what that means. . . . All you non-trainees, out! That goes double for the boys! Even you, Jason—if you can manage to tear yourself away from *Princess Rachel*." She smirks at us.

Minjun wipes his greasy chicken fingers on his jeans before grabbing Jason's hands, pulling him up. "Come on, Jay-Star, let's go hit that new club in Itaewon."

Jason bends down and murmurs "Good luck" into my ear, sending shivers along my spine again. He jumps over the back of the couch and joins his friends, singing the chorus from "Fake Crush" as they disappear into the street.

Oh shit. Leah's autograph. I jump up, intent on running after him, but between the soju and unexpectedly spending my night flirting with Jason, my head is spinning and I flop back down on the couch at the same moment that Mina sits next to me, holding two glasses filled with champagne. Around us, all the other girls are pouring themselves glasses too, squealing as the champagne fizzes over the rim and drips onto their hands.

"A toast," Mina says, handing me a glass. When I don't take it right away, she sighs, rolling her eyes. "Come on, Rachel. Loosen up, will you? We're all just trying to have a little fun together."

Fun. I have to admit, even though this night is nothing like what I thought it would be, I am having fun. I purse my lips and set down my beer to take the champagne glass.

Mina grins and raises her drink, turning to the other girls. "To our family! And to becoming the next biggest, brightest stars in Korea!"

The girls cheer, linking arms and clinking glasses before downing their champagne in one gulp. I drink a little slower, the liquid burning my throat way more than I expected. I nearly cough it up, but I don't want to give Mina the satisfaction of seeing me choke. I tip the glass up, forcing myself to drink the whole thing.

I sink into the couch as the girls around me chatter away, pouring themselves more and more champagne. I look around the house, wishing Akari were here with me so I would have someone to talk to. I grab my phone to text her, but my fingers feel thick and uncoordinated and I fumble with the straps on my bag until I give up. I'll talk to her tomorrow. My hand is cold from the champagne glass, and I press it into my face, relishing the chill. I drank too much. No, I drank too fast. Everything is spinning. Eunji's loud voice is ringing in my ears, and the music is starting to sound like it's playing in slow motion. I look at Mina, who's still sitting next to me . . . and there are two of her. I'm seeing double. I try to blink away the nightmare.

I fall deeper into the couch, my head growing fuzzier with each second. I see Mina's blurry faces leaning in close to mine. "It worked! She'll never be chosen now." Chosen? What is she talking about? "Earth to Rachel! You look like you could use some fresh air, Princess." Her voice swirls slowly around me, but I can't find the energy to respond.

Eunji and Lizzie circle around me, laughing and sipping from their glasses. "Pretty little Princess Rachel—even Mr. Noh can't save you now," Lizzie gloats.

I hear it all like I'm at the bottom of a swimming pool. Somebody says something, and I start laughing, too—uncontrollably—though I have no idea why.

"Come on, Princess. Let's dance!" Eunji is pulling me to standing, and I'm still laughing—or she is—or both. I'm not sure. Through my lashes, which suddenly seem heavy, I see Mina hovering not too far away, but not dancing. Her phone is pointed in my direction, and she's wearing an evil smirk. Eunji spins me around, and the room spins with us, into a sea of sparkling lights and laughing faces.

⭐ Four ⭐

The first thing I notice when I wake up is how badly my head is throbbing. The second is the all-consuming smell of dried cucumbers.

I gag, my hands flying up to my face. It's covered in a cucumber face mask. Horrified, I rip the thin cucumber slices off my face and throw them on the floor, trying not to breathe through my nose. Nausea rises in me, and it takes all my effort not to throw up all over myself.

What the hell happened last night?

I sit up and my head spins. Squeezing my eyes shut, I take three deep breaths, then open my eyes again and look around. I'm on a couch in a living room littered with empty cups and overturned bottles. It slowly comes back to me. I'm in the trainee house. The late-night training session turned out to be a party. Jason saw me in my pajamas. I grimace at the memory. We walked into the house together. And then . . . what happened? And where is everyone now?

Head still pounding, I fumble in my bag for my cell phone to check the time. My eyes widen. *Shit. Shit, shit, shit.* It's already 11:00 a.m. It's 11:00 a.m. on a *Sunday.* I leap to my feet and stumble down the hallway, flinging open doors and trying to find the bathroom. I can't believe I overslept on a training day. This can't be happening.

I'm woefully lost in the unfamiliar house. A part of me wants to blame this on Umma. If she had ever let me come to the trainee house, I'd know my way around better. But I know that this isn't her fault; it's all mine. In one night I've proven Umma right and everyone who's ever believed in me wrong. *Oh god, Rachel, why do you have to be so freaking gullible?*

I push open doors and find only bedrooms and one disheveled linen closet with what looks (and smells) like dried vomit in it. I push back my own gag reflex as I slam the door shut.

Why is it that when you most need a bathroom, you can never find one? Frustrated after the fifth door leads me to a broom closet, I run back to the kitchen and wash my face in the sink. I dry myself with fistfuls of paper towels and, using my phone camera as a mirror, try to make myself as presentable as possible. I do a hasty job with my eyeliner, but it'll have to do for now.

My clothes are a mess. There are champagne stains on my leggings and remnants of the cucumber face mask smeared all over my sweater. I try not to gag again. Instead, I grit my teeth and grab the only other clothes I have. Looks like Jason isn't going to be the only person who has to see my Snoopy pajamas.

I yank my hair out of its flyaway braids as I run out of the house. I may smell like a cucumber compost bin, but maybe my hair can be salvaged. I take a quick glance at my phone camera, hoping to see beach waves. Instead I see half my hair flattened against my head while the other half is frizzing up like an electrocuted Albert Einstein.

I'm a fucking disaster.

But I don't have time to fix anything now. I'm already way too late. I race down the street to DB headquarters, throwing my hair into a bumpy ponytail, my nausea rising in my chest with every step.

By the time I yank open the door to the auditorium, I'm out of breath and sweating through Snoopy. Mr. Noh is already onstage, introducing the DB execs, all of whom are sitting in the first row of seats.

The execs. The execs are here. My stomach fills with dread. Appraisal day.

All the head trainers are onstage. Yujin. The lead dancing trainer. The lead vocal trainer. The head nutritionist. Mr. Bae, the head of marketing and publicity. Everyone is gathered to watch the progress of the trainees, to decide if we get to stay in the program, if we're really worth their time or money. It's the one day that I can't be late. The one day I can't show up looking like I got run over by a cucumber-filled garbage truck. My heart is permanently lodged in my throat, and I can feel tears burn at the back of my eyes, but I push them away. *Don't show weakness. If you're going to survive this, you have to be strong.*

"We're looking forward to seeing how far each of you have progressed in the last month," Mr. Noh says, the reflection off his shiny bright-blue Prada suit making my eyes water. "The executives and I know you've all been training very hard, so—"

He breaks off when his eagle eyes catch mine. For a second he looks stunned, taking in my unkempt hair and ridiculous pajamas. Everyone else in the auditorium turns toward me. Whispers rise, harsh sounds that fill my ears and make my head feel like it might split open right on the auditorium floor.

"So, ah, remember to do your best today," Mr. Noh continues, regaining his composure. He raises his eyebrows at me. "Your very best."

There's nothing to do now but pretend like I'm not so embarrassed I want to melt out of my own skin. I hold my head up high and make my way toward Akari, who's staring at me with her jaw dropped open. A wave of envy sweeps through me as I take in her perfect makeup, bouncy ponytail, and a cropped, floral sweatshirt we bought at A-Land together a few months ago. She looks polished. Prepared. Well rested. Like I *should* look. Like everyone expects me to.

"What happened to you?" she whispers as I take a seat next to her.

"It's a long story." I sigh. "But I'm not too sure what exactly . . ."

I trail off as I notice Mr. Noh staring at me from the stage, his face frozen in a dangerous smile. "As I was saying, today is not just about your monthly appraisals. . . ."

Out of the corner of my eye, I see Mina and the other girls silently laughing behind their hands. Mina catches my eye and wiggles her fingers. She mimes holding up an invisible champagne glass for a toast and mouths, *Cheers*. Last night comes rushing back at me in a vicious wave. The champagne. Mina's face and seeing double. Her gleeful voice crowing, "*It worked!*"

". . . an exciting new opportunity—the chance every young trainee in Korea would kill for. Today, one of you . . ."

A wave of nausea hits, and I almost double over.

I didn't drink too much or lose control. And this isn't just some terrible and unlucky coincidence. This whole thing is Mina. *She* did this. She's the one who handed me the glass of champagne, who goaded me into drinking it as her friends watched.

She put something in my drink.

She *drugged* me.

The reality of it hits like a ton of bricks. I'm completely frozen and powerless. Violated. Furious. I grit my teeth so hard I feel like they're going to crack. I'm going to explode. In my head I keep replaying the image of Mina standing over me, cackling, "*She'll never get chosen now!*"

". . . chosen to be featured in a brand-new single with DB superstar Jason Lee!"

My stomach cramps as a collective gasp rises throughout the auditorium. Akari turns to me, her mouth open in shock. "Can you believe this?" she asks excitedly.

I shake my head, focused on last night and Mina. "I really can't," I respond.

"Rachel!" Akari nudges me hard in the ribs. "Pay attention! Did you even hear what Mr. Noh just said?"

I stare at her blankly, my stomach and my head a swirling mess of champagne and anger and dried cucumbers.

"Rachel. Focus. The execs, Mr. Noh . . . they're choosing a female trainee to sing a duet with Jason. A real song—not some training exercise. The appraisal today is an audition. This is it. You could be chosen!"

That last word sticks in my mind as I process what she's saying. I could be chosen. This isn't just a typical monthly assessment. This is a chance to sing with Jason. For a *trainee*—for *me*—to sing with DB's biggest star. I could be chosen.

She'll never be chosen now.

I gasp and sit up straight. Mina knew all along. She knew what today was. She set me up.

Akari pokes me again. Hard. "What?!" I say, startling before I notice that Mr. Noh has called up the first group for dance auditions, and the other trainees are making their way to the stage.

In a way I'm grateful. If something didn't force me to act normal, to move through the motions by rote, I might never recover. But I have to. I have to keep taking one step forward. And so I do—trying to hide the fact that I'm shaking.

We line up along the back of the stage. The execs are sitting in the front row with iPads (a few years ago DB went fully digital when it comes to tracking trainee progress) and stern expressions, calling us up one by one to perform. Mina slides into the spot next to me, looking me up and down with her forehead creased in mock pity.

"Rough night, Rachel?" she says. "You look terrible. Cute pajamas, though."

An image of myself tackling her to the ground and yanking out her fake eyelashes flashes through my head. But Mr. Noh calls my name and I step forward onto center stage.

The spotlight falls on me. I can just imagine how my splotchy, half-made-up face looks in the glare. But I shove the insecurity aside and plaster a smile on my face, just like I've been trained to do. I bow to the execs, then straighten up. Head up. Legs turned in, ever so slightly. Tummy tucked, shoulders back. I smile wide—*like the whole world is my best friend.*

A few of them smile back, but most are blinking in confusion at my wardrobe choice and my rumpled hair.

Make them forget how you look and care only about how you move, I tell myself. Easier said than done, though. At least there are no cameras on me today, I think ruefully, remembering yesterday's media class.

The music starts, one of Leah's favorite Electric Flower songs, and my body immediately responds. It's muscle memory. I've practiced this routine a thousand times. But my head is still pounding and I'm sloppy. I keep missing the beat, stepping left when I should be stepping right.

The frustration is building in my chest, weighing me down even more. I'm getting too much in my own head, but the more I try to let go, the worse it gets. I can't get my movements to pop as much or my legs to kick as high. By the time I land the last offbeat step, I'm out of breath and a light sheen of sweat dots my forehead. I fight the urge to wipe it away. *Don't bring more attention to your flaws.* K-pop dancing is all about luring listeners into the song—but by the expressions on the execs' faces, ranging from awkwardly smiling to looking like they want to run out of the auditorium screaming, I know I've done the exact opposite.

"Ouch," Mina whispers to me as I retake my spot in line. "That wasn't pretty." She leans in to take an exaggerated whiff of my breath and gasps. "Omo, are you hungover? You really shouldn't party so much the night before an important day like this. Or at least brush your teeth."

I don't look at her, but I'm absolutely seething. I will not stoop to her level.

Still. The image of ripping into her hair is the only thing keeping me from screaming onstage. I wouldn't take it all, just a big patch at the front so she's half-bald for a few weeks.

One by one, the girls go up to dance. Akari is graceful as always and, as much as I hate to admit it, Mina is the best of the bunch, her powerful moves hurtling her across the stage in perfect time to the music. Some of the girls make little mistakes, but none as badly as me. It's quickly becoming apparent that I'm the worst.

I'm *never* the worst.

I can't afford to be the worst.

I don't come alive in front of the camera, shiny and ador-able like Mina and so many of the other trainees. When I first got recruited to DB, I was so excited—a whole program full of kids who felt the same way about K-pop and Korea as I did—or so I thought. It wasn't long before the constant "Princess Rachel" insults and subtle comments about my American background made me feel just as rejected as I used to feel back home in the States. Their words were like this constant buzzing in my brain. While Mina and her minions strutted around in front of the cameras with this innate sense of belonging, when the camera was on me, that buzzing was all I could hear. Even after years of training, I still feel like the camera is my enemy—reminding me of all the people out there who look at my face and think, *She doesn't belong here.* So, instead, I focused on my skills, making them as close to flawless as possible—not one step offbeat, not one note out of key. And so far it's worked. I may not be perfect, but I'm talented enough that month after month, year after year, I've earned my spot.

And now it could all come crashing down. Will this be the end for me? Will I get kicked out of the trainee program? I try to tell myself to calm down, that they have to take my past performances into account, but I'm lying to myself. One year they cut a girl because she wouldn't agree to get double eyelid surgery. Another year they cut an entire trainee group for posting a single picture on Instagram. They can do whatever they want, whenever they want. And they are ruthless.

A lump wells up in my throat, and I struggle to swallow it down. Crying onstage—showing any emotion of any kind—will only further anger the execs.

I take another deep breath as they call me up again to sing. This is my time to redeem myself. I have to be the best I've ever been, right now, or it's over.

Someone hands me a microphone as the instrumental starts. It's a slow song, a K-pop classic from the early 2000s. I take a deep breath and start to sing and my voice cracks on the first note, the trapped emotion coming out and bumping me off-key. The execs' faces are unreadable, but one of them is clearly trying not to wince. *No. I can't let this happen. I won't.*

I close my eyes and keep going. I think of that day in bed when I was a kid, watching K-pop videos with my mom. How growing up, Leah and I would go to the whispering gallery at Grand Central every chance we got, whispering the songs to each other, back and forth, for hours. And then, when I was a newbie trainee, how Yujin would pick me up after school and take me to her favorite noraebang, the two of us singing cheesy K-pop love ballads from the early '90s all afternoon. Since I was a kid, music has been my happy place. K-pop has always been there for me, showing me my place in the world, giving me a reason to be proud of who I was even when the world told me I shouldn't be. Through everything, it has always felt right. Felt like a part of me.

I'm finding my stride now, my voice riding the melody like a surfer on the waves. And that's when I finally find it. The joy. The reason I'm doing all this. Despite my pounding head, I hold on to that spark, my face breaking into a smile as I continue to sing.

Just as I hit the chorus, I hear a brilliant harmony float alongside my own voice. Everyone in the audience gasps. *What's happening? Am I having a hangover hallucination?* But it's not my voice. It's a deep male tenor, and when I turn my head, I see Jason emerge from backstage, singing along with me.

I'm stunned, but it doesn't break my flow. In fact, his voice is like another strong wave, carrying me further into the song, lifting me higher. He takes a look at my pajamas and raises his eyebrows at me like he's remembering an inside joke. We don't break eye contact as our voices intertwine and blend together. He takes a step toward me from the other side of stage. Even without a microphone, his voice soars, complementing mine perfectly. I take a step forward to match him. The space between us feels charged somehow, our voices crashing together, lighting up the stage like lightning in the night sky. The entire auditorium is holding their breath, watching us.

A surprising thought flashes through my mind. *We are meant to sing together.*

We walk toward each other until the space between us is no more than a finger. He's almost as close as when I fell into his back yesterday. Or when he pulled my body into his on the couch.

He leans forward, and I can see the deep golden brown of his irises. They're locked on to me as he lets the microphone I'm holding pick up his voice. We're truly singing together now. Perfectly harmonized, perfectly joined.

He wraps his arm around my waist as the music slowly fades away, and together we sing the last line of the chorus. We smile at each other, breathing hard. His arms feel warm and strong around me, and for one moment silence hangs in the air.

Then the crowd erupts into applause and cheers. The other trainees and the junior trainers are cheering and clapping. Only Mina and her minions are silent and sullen.

I don't know what that was, but it was some kind of magic. I smile, my heart beating in my chest, and Jason smiles back. Unlike his cocky grin from yesterday, this one is warm and makes my breath catch. It's almost enough to make me forget how horrible I feel.

And then, without warning, my stomach lurches. It rolls and twists, and I barely have a second to think, *Oh shit*, before I throw up all over Jason's white shoes.

Jason blinks and stares down at his previously pristine Nikes. The silence is static. Someone lets out a burst of laughter. I don't need to look to guess who it is.

My cheeks burn with embarrassment, and my body convulses with another wave of nausea. I have to get out of here.

I race off the stage, stumbling out of the auditorium and tearing down the hallway to the nearest bathroom. I burst into a stall as I feel the acid and bile rise from my stomach. At least this time it's into a toilet and not onto an international K-pop star's shoes. Ugh.

I puke until I feel like there's nothing left in me. I puke out the entire contents of my stomach and my pride.

Groaning, I curl up on the floor and drop my head into my knees, feeling absolutely miserable. I have no idea how clean these tiles are, but I don't really care right now. I'm pretty sure that was the worst thing to happen onstage in all of DB history. I'm never going to be able to show my face here again. Goodbye, Jason. Goodbye, K-pop stardom.

The bathroom door opens, and I tense up inside my stall, curling into myself. I hear Eunji's and Lizzie's voices as they clatter around the sink, the sound of lip gloss tubes popping open.

"So, what's your bet?" Lizzie asks.

"I can't believe they didn't cut her."

They didn't cut me. My body nearly crumples in relief.

"Mr. Noh said they didn't cut anyone today because it was all about that duet with Jason."

I hear a snap of gum and I can imagine Eunji pursing her lips.

"Did anyone catch it on camera? We should get someone to leak it on social media."

Shit. Did someone film that disaster? I crane my ear to hear what Eunji says next.

"No, but trust me, the memory of it is vivid enough. It's all anyone is going to talk about for months."

Lizzie giggles and sighs. "You're right. We should make T-shirts or something. 'I survived the Princess Rachel Vomit Extravaganza of 2020.'"

Ugh. I really hope they don't do that.

"I just wish I could have seen her face when the board picked Mina to do the duet with Jason," Eunji says.

Of course. They chose Mina.

"She'll find out soon enough, and her face will be priceless."

"Let's try to get a pic of it—we can put it on the T-shirt!"

Lizzie smacks her lips together. "Okay, enough Princess Rachel talk. Mr. Noh was looking right at me when he announced the autumn DB Family Tour. . . ."

Her voice fades into the background as my head snaps up—too quickly—and I cover my mouth as my body recoils from the sudden movement. I let out a soft groan. A new family tour. The first one in seven years.

DB is debuting a new girl group.

Suddenly all the pieces start to fall into place: Mina didn't just want this duet. She wanted me out of the way. She must have known about the tour. And she knew whoever got to sing with Jason would have the best chance to debut before the tour started in the fall.

I hear the bathroom doors open. Laughter and shouts from the hallway fill the room before the doors shut. How can I go back out there? Lizzie's right—this is all anyone is going to be talking about.

The more people are talking about you, the more you're worth talking about. Jason's words from last night ring in my head.

I stand up slowly, making my way to the mirror along the back wall. Someone pale and sweaty—and oh my god is that vomit on my shoulder?!—but determined stares back at me. Mina might think she got exactly what she wanted, but she didn't get everything. I'm still here. And I'm going to make sure I'm worth talking about.

★ Five ★

"Look alive, Rachel!"

I duck, covering my face with my tennis racket as a fluorescent yellow ball whizzes over my head. *Whew. That was close.* I peek over my racket to see our newest tennis coach crossing her arms. Our school doesn't really believe in gym teachers. Instead, we have a rotation of professional-athlete instructors—Adam Rippon for ice-skating, Katie Ledecky for swimming, Simone Biles for gymnastics. Right now I'm being scowled at by the sixteen-year-old Canadian wunderkind who just beat Serena Williams in the Australian Open and is on the most recent cover of *Sports Illustrated* and *Vogue*.

"The idea is to use your racket to hit the ball," she says, rolling her eyes. "Not use it like some kind of Captain America cosplay shield."

"Sorry, Coach Sloat." I straighten up, adjusting my white tennis skirt and matching white visor.

Most days when I'm at school, I'm counting down the

minutes to the weekend, to getting back to DB and to training. I even have a countdown app on my phone set to 3:30 p.m.
every Friday afternoon. But right now the app is on silent and
school is an absolutely necessary distraction to keep me from
constantly reliving the moment I threw up all over Jason, on a
stage in front of every single trainee, trainer, and exec in DB.

It's been three days, and the burn of embarrassment has
faded from a raging fire threatening to engulf me from the
inside out to a full-body sunburn. Still stinging and in need of
some major damage control, but I'll survive. Probably. As long
as I don't get taken out by a rogue tennis ball in gym class.

I jog over to the Cho twins, who are serving tennis balls
into cones arranged around the court.

"Rachel, you've got terrible panda eyes," Juhyun says,
lowering her racket and leaning in to inspect my face. "I
have Depuffing Raspberry Eye Gel in my locker. You can
borrow it."

"Are they really that bad?" I ask, touching my face self-
consciously.

"Let's just say I wouldn't be surprised if you said you had
gotten into a fistfight with Mina and lost," Hyeri jokes, serving a tennis ball perfectly into a cone. She pumps her fist in the
air. "Ah-ssa! It's all about the angles, baby."

I sigh, stifling a yawn. "I wish a black eye was all Mina did
to me. I haven't been able to sleep since the Incident."

"You have to stop replaying it in your mind," Juhyun says.
"Don't think about how you totally flubbed your audition and

threw up all over the most famous and adored K-pop star in the world."

"Just his shoes," I say defensively.

"Right, exactly. That's not even that bad. Pristine white Nikes, was it?"

Hyeri sighs mournfully, raising her eyes to the sky. "RIP Jason Lee's shoes. Your time came far too soon."

The twins giggle behind their tennis rackets. I'm about to jab back, but I interrupt myself with a humongous yawn.

"Damn, you really have been staying up all night thinking about it, haven't you?" Hyeri says.

"Not just thinking about it," I say. Our coach walks by, and I pretend to swing my racket back and forth. She nods in approval and continues on. I slip my phone out of my tennis skirt and pop up a photo of Jason and Mina singing together on Instagram, holding it out to the twins. "*Looking* at it too. DB announced Jason and Mina's duet." I grimace. As their voices burst out of my phone, the only thing I can find to take solace in is the fact that Mina's face has that squashed-in look I'm familiar with from six years of voice lessons with her— meaning she can't quite hit the high notes in the chorus she's singing with Jason. But clearly DB hasn't noticed. Like all K-pop labels, DB has a zero-tolerance policy for social media (to go along with their zero-tolerance dating policy)—as in, trainees do not post and are not posted about, ever. On pain of being cut from the program and, if the rumors are true, shipped off to military school. If they shared this about Mina, that means they have some seriously big plans for this duet. And for her.

Hyeri scrolls through the comments, reading them out loud. "'Daebak, I've been waiting my whole life for a Jason Lee solo. And this girl is sooo pretty!'"

"'If she's singing with Jason, she must be the best trainee at DB,'" Juhyun reads over her sister's shoulder. "'They look so good together. Imagine the babies they would make.'"

I groan, grabbing the phone back and shoving it in my pocket. "Please. I was up all night reading the comments. I don't need to hear them out loud."

From across the court, Coach Sloat blows on her whistle. "Game time, girls! Tennis doubles. Line up for your turn."

"Hey, Juhyun! Loved your video on wing-tip liquid liner last night." Wan Somi smiles sweetly at the twins and squeezes into line between me and Hyeri, her tennis racket smacking me in the knees as she boxes me out.

I'm used to it. Seoul International School is one of the most exclusive private schools in Korea, educating the one percent of the country's one percent: children of K-drama stars, government officials, and girls like Somi, whose parents and grandparents have run the Sitisung corporation for the last fifty years. She's constantly sucking up to Juhyun and Hyeri, but with my lack of a trust fund and no heiress status to speak of, I've never been important enough for her to notice. Even my K-pop trainee status doesn't get me on her radar. I take a swig from my water bottle when suddenly Somi whips around to face me.

"Hey, Rachel, I heard about the duet."

I choke on my water. *Wan Somi is talking to me?* I glance over at the twins, who look as mystified as I do.

She purses her lips in mock pity. "Choo Mina's the daughter of the C-MART president, right? We spent a summer with them in Provence once, when we were kids." *Of course you did.* "Rich and talented." She clucks her tongue at me. "That's two for two, and you're still at zero. And here I thought DB had standards for their K-pop trainees."

Juhyun takes a step forward, looking ready to swing her tennis racket into Somi's face, but gets pushed back by Goo Kyungmi, another classmate, as she hurls herself between me and Somi.

"Don't listen to her, Rachel!" Kyungmi shouts. I stare at her in shock. Kyungmi is Juhyun's biggest fan and is always offering to carry Juhyun's books and her lunch tray and leaves little presents taped to her locker. Once she even brought a puppy to school for Juhyun to play with between classes, but the principal made her take it home when it peed all over the putting greens in the south lawn. But this is the first time she's ever spoken to me.

Kyungmi throws her arms around my shoulders, nearly whipping me in the face with her high ponytail. "You must have so many mixed feelings about the duet. Are you okay? You know I'm here for you if you need to talk, right? You can tell me *anything* about your trainee life."

"Thanks . . . Kyungmi . . . ," I say, extracting myself from her surprisingly viselike grip. "But I'm fine."

"Really? Are you sure? Hey, we should take a selfie together in our tennis clothes!" She pulls out her phone.

"No phones on the courts!" Coach Sloat says, stomping over to us. She points to Somi and Kyungmi. "You two, get out there. You're next on doubles."

Somi grumbles and drags her feet onto the court. Kyungmi shoots me a regretful look as she follows after Somi. Sloat whirls on me next, her eyes narrowing.

"Sorry, Coach," I say hastily, bouncing into some jumping jacks. "Warming up for my game now!"

"Wait," she says. She glances over her shoulder at the rest of the students and then leans in and whispers, "Is it true that Mina and Jason are dating?"

I gape at her. *Seriously?* Even famous tennis champions and magazine cover stars?

She notices my expression and chuckles, scratching the back of her head. "I'm just kidding. Obviously." Clearing her throat awkwardly, she turns her attention back to class. "Good serve, Kyungmi!"

Seoul International School was built on the edge of Hannam-dong, across the Han River from Gangnam, one of Seoul's trendiest neighborhoods. It's surrounded by three of the city's most exclusive residential areas, all highly prized by Seoul's elite not only for the suitable selection of designer boutiques and hotspot restaurants, but by the fact that Hannam-dong, unlike the rest of Seoul, has the luxury of space. Which might explain why our school sits on five and a half acres of pristine, uninterrupted land in one of the world's most crowded cities. Aside from our regulation clay tennis courts, Olympic-size indoor swimming pool, a full track, and soccer field, the school has outdoor and indoor amphitheaters, a movie screening room, and ice-skating rink. The horticulture club plants bright-fuchsia orchids that line the main driveway all the way up to the central school building, and every Wednesday the pyrotechnics society and the AV club put on a fireworks display worthy of any Fourth of July celebration.

As the twins and I head for the locker room after class, I see a huge poster advertising next month's career day. HAVE YOU THOUGHT ABOUT YOUR FUTURE? MARK ZUCKERBERG AND MEGAN ELLISON ARE HERE TO HELP YOU! I wince. I know my mom would want me to go to that. It's part of the reason she and my dad sacrificed so much to send me and Leah to this school. Halmoni left Umma some money when she died, and I know that most of it has gone to paying our tuition—instead of helping Appa get more business for his boxing gym. "Think of the opportunities," she said, shushing me, when I told her I was fine going to the public school down the street from our apartment.

What is my future? I think to myself, warm water rushing down on me from the waterfall showerhead in the locker room. It's been three days since the audition and I have no idea how I'm going to get noticed. I think back to tennis class and the way Somi and Kyungmi talked to me for the first time. *But that was because of DB's Instagram post. There's no way they'll ever post about me. Will they?*

After we wash up, I follow the twins out of the locker room, nearly coming nose to nose with a boy with floppy brown hair parted straight down the middle and wire-rim glasses. His face is deadpan as he raises a hand in greeting.

"Daeho!" Hyeri says. Her cheeks grow pink as a small smile spreads across her lips.

"Hi." He looks past my shoulder. "Ready to work on our project, Hyeri?"

"You didn't have to come escort me. I could have met you in the engineering wing."

"It's fine," Daeho says. He glances at Juhyun. "I don't mind. How are you, Juhyun?"

"Fine, thanks," Juhyun says. She links an arm through mine, wiggling her eyebrows at me. "Shall I *escort you* to the student lounge while Hyeri nerds it out in the engineering lab? I hear the patbingsu bar is back now that the weather's warmer."

Daeho's ears perk up. "You like patbingsu? I just so happen to be an expert patbingsu maker. I've created a perfect recipe based off a scientifically proven ideal ratio of shaved ice to red bean. I even invented my own ice-shaving machine."

"Uh . . . wow, Daeho. Who knew you had such hidden depths?" Juhyun says. I bite my lip, stifling a laugh while Daeho looks on, beaming at Juhyun's comment.

Hyeri glances between Juhyun and Daeho. "I love patbingsu

too," she offers. "Maybe you could make it for me sometime? Your recipe sounds excellent."

Daeho nods, his hair flapping around the sides of his face. "Definitely."

Hyeri perks up.

"I'll make it for you, and you can share it with Juhyun."

"Oh . . . right. Well, sure. Sounds good, Daeho." She gives us a half-hearted wave as she follows Daeho down the hall. "See you guys later."

I give her a sympathetic wave and glace over at Juhyun, who's checking her eyebrows on her phone, totally oblivious to the love triangle that just played out in front of her eyes. For a smart girl, she can be really noonchi ubssuh.

"Come on," she says, throwing her phone into her gym bag and steering me down the hall. "Patbingsu awaits."

I drag my feet as we walk down the hall, sunlight streaming in through the school's gigantic glass and steel windows. The student lounge is the last place I want to be right now. It's always teeming with students all crowded around big-screen TVs blasting the latest K-pop music videos. I'm really not ready to be bombarded with questions about Jason and Mina.

"How about we go hide in the Stained-Glass Library instead?" I turn around, trying to lure Juhyun to the cavernous library on the other side of campus, so named for the stained-glass replica of the opening scene from *Beauty and the Beast* that an art student did for their senior project years ago.

"What, so you can sulk alone in some library corner?"

"I wasn't planning to sulk," I say. Which is technically true. I was planning to curl up in one of the library's squashy armchairs and watch reruns of *Vampire Diaries* on my laptop.

"Sorry, Rachel, what you need now is tough love. Not Klaus-and-Caroline-shipping emotional therapy."

Damn. She knows me too well.

As we approach the student lounge, I hear the unmistakable buzz of excited students. "Put it up on the big screen!" I recognize Kyungmi's squeaky voice and freeze. Are they putting up the photo of Jason and Mina? I just managed to escape my Instagram shame spiral and I *really* don't need to be sent down another one right now.

"So about the library . . . ," I start, but before I can finish, Juhyun pushes me through the door of the lounge. A big crowd of students is gathered around the flat-screen TV, sitting on plush leather sofas with bowls of patbingsu on their laps, leaning forward to watch . . . a YouTube beauty blogger? Huh. That's not what I was expecting.

Kyungmi turns around to see me and Juhyun approaching. "Look at this new beauty blogger! Some girl down in Suwon. She can do things with eye shadow that I've never even *seen*."

Next to me, Juhyun freezes. "How many hits does she have?" Juhyun asks.

"Oh, it's wild—almost half a million hits in twelve hours. It's totally viral. And she has almost four million followers!"

"But . . . *I* don't even have four million followers," Juhyun stammers in disbelief, stalking away to the patbingsu bar.

I watch as the girl on the screen coats her face in smooth, silvery foundation before transforming her eyelids into a dazzling array of vivid-pink cherry blossoms bursting off tiny branches, each one topped with a small jewel. Juhyun shoves a bowl of shaved ice into my hands, but even as the ice melts, forming a soup with the condensed milk and fruity syrup, I can't look away. This video is mesmerizing.

"Isn't that wild? One second she's just a normal girl, playing around with makeup in her bedroom, and the next she's a celebrity."

I blink, taking in the comment from my classmate. It *is* amazing how much impact one viral video can have. The wheels in my mind begin to turn as Juhyun loops her arm around mine. "Ugh. It sucks here. I'm ready to go to the library."

I laugh, leaning over to kiss her on the cheek. "That girl isn't half the beauty blogger you are. Did you notice the products she was using weren't even organic? Hyeri would have a fit!"

Juhyun smiles, looking mollified, as I dig into the last of my melting patbingsu.

"Delicious, right?" Juhyun says. "Isn't this exactly what you needed?"

"Oh," I say, smiling over my spoon. "You have no idea."

 **Six**

When I first started my training at DB, I was homesick a lot. Whenever it got really bad, Yujin would hide me away in her office and let me cry. She would rub my back and I would breathe in the fresh smell of eucalyptus from the plants that covered her bookshelves and her desk. To this day, the smell of eucalyptus reminds me of home as much as the smell of those sugary roasted nuts that you can find on every sidewalk corner in New York.

"Take a seat," Yujin says, ushering us through her office door after Akari and I bow our heads in greeting. She gestures to the white leather-backed seats in front of her desk. She squints at my face. "What happened to your eyebrow?"

"Oh, uh . . ." I offer her a sheepish smile. "Just trying out a new style." Today's beauty and presentation class was all about the importance of eyebrow grooming. Akari's naturally thick, straight brows fit the teacher's ideal Korean "boy brow" aesthetic easily, but mine required a bit more maintenance and

I might have gotten a little carried away with the tweezers. I rub my left eyebrow, hoping I did a good enough job with the pencil to cover up the slight bald patch.

She frowns and leans back in her seat, crossing her arms. "How can I help you two?" she asks.

There's an unfamiliar frostiness in her voice that makes me uneasy. I glance at Akari, who gives me an encouraging nod. *Right. I can do this.* I take a deep breath and dive in.

"I have an idea that might give me a second chance at singing the duet with Jason," I say. I nod to Akari, who pulls out her phone. She holds it up and presses play on the viral video of the beauty blogger. "Have you seen this?" I ask.

"Of course. The cherry blossom festival was last weekend. This video was everywhere." Her frown deepens. "What are you suggesting? You're going to find some way to make up for your dance audition with some ridiculous eye shadow?"

I wince. I know things are different now that I'm so close to debut age, but sometimes I miss the days when Yujin would just let me sit on her couch and cry. "Not exactly," I say, pressing on. "But you said so yourself. This video was everywhere. And now SKII wants to offer her a sponsorship and she has more opportunities than she could've ever imagined. When a video goes viral, people talk. And other people *have* to listen."

I fiddle with the cuffs of my bomber jacket. I had pictured myself strolling out of Yujin's office like Sandra Bullock at the Met Gala, all mastermind plotter with a specialized team of badass women to back her up. I take a deep breath. "We all know Mina's voice isn't up to a duet with Jason. I was thinking if I could get a video of me singing to go viral, the execs will notice all the attention we're getting and have to give me another chance."

Yujin is silent. Akari and I both lean forward expectantly.

"That is the most ridiculous idea I've ever heard."

My shoulders slump. So much for my *Ocean's 8* fantasy.

"Your audition wasn't just a disappointment, Rachel. It was a disaster," Yujin says, narrowing her eyes. I sink down into my seat, but Yujin isn't finished. "You've been at DB for six years. You know how this works. No one's forcing you to be here. You have to choose it. You have to want it. How can I trust that you can sing a duet with Jason when I'm still getting reports that you can't even get through media training class? And how will you make a viral video when you're still afraid of a camera?"

A lump rises in my throat. She's right. Of course she's right. A wave of shame and embarrassment washes over me. How did I think this would be such an easy fix? I bite my lip and nod, looking down at my lap and trying not to cry.

"Look at me when I'm speaking to you," Yujin says sharply. My head snaps up. "We all had such high expectations for you, Rachel. *I* had such high expectations. Not only did you humiliate yourself, but you humiliated me as well. Since I'm DB's head trainer, my reputation is on the line! Your performance reflected poorly on both of us. So tell me, why should any of us give you a second chance?"

Shame presses down on my chest. "I'm so, so sorry, Yujin.

I know I let you down. But I also know I can do better. Please give me a second chance because . . . because . . ."

Yujin's cold gaze bearing down on me reminds me of the harsh, empty stare of a camera lens, and I hang my head, feeling my words slipping away. What can I say? There's nothing that can make up for this.

"Because you remember what it was like hearing Rachel and Jason sing together." Akari squeezes my hand as she jumps in. She looks Yujin straight in the eye, speaking with confidence. "I know you felt the electricity in the room. We all did. They were meant to sing together. Can you deny that?"

Yujin stares right back at Akari with equal intensity. "And how exactly do you plan on getting past DB's social media rules?"

"It's against the rules for *us* to post," Akari says, smiling mischievously. "But if the video doesn't show up on Rachel's social media, it's technically not her fault. What can she do if a leaked video that she just *happens* to be singing in goes viral?"

Okay, I might not be the Sandra Bullock, but Akari is the Cate Blanchett of this scenario, I think, in awe of her ability to say exactly the right thing at exactly the right moment. *All she needs now is a sparkly, perfectly fitted pantsuit.*

Yujin's gaze shifts to me, and I quickly wipe the tears threatening to spill out from the corners of my eyes, accidentally smudging my eyebrow pencil. Shit. I'm a mess. Maybe I was a fool for thinking Yujin would jump to my aid like she always does. Even my mentor has her limits, and I've clearly projectile vomited right past them.

I cautiously look up and hold her gaze. Her eyes soften and she sighs. "The performance was pretty amazing," she says.

My heart leaps. "I promise if I get a second chance, I won't mess it up," I say quickly. I take a deep breath. "You're the one who taught me to believe in myself. I know I can do this."

Yujin rubs the small bamboo plant on her desk. Then she plucks a business card from a small tray and flips it over, writing something on the back in precise, blocky script. She slides it across the desk. It's some random address in Itaewon.

Akari and I look up at Yujin, and she gives us a mischievous smile of her own.

"Meet me there after training tomorrow night," she says. "Make sure no one follows you. Got it?"

Akari squeals. "Does this mean you're helping us?"

"It means this conversation is over." Yujin nods to the door. I take the business card and slide it into the pocket of my jacket.

"Rachel," Yujin says as we turn to leave. I look back and she smiles. "Do something about that eyebrow by tomorrow, will you? You want to look your best in a video that the whole world is going to see."

Hope balloons in my chest. I bow. "Thank you, Yujin-unni. I won't let you down."

I stand in front of my bedroom mirror, twisting my hair into a high ballerina bun to show off the Peter Pan collar of my lavender top. Ugh. I look like a librarian.

Tugging my hair out of its bun, I toss the shirt into the pile of already rejected clothes on the floor. Should I try all black with the leather jacket and ripped skinny jeans? Maybe the leopard-print maxi dress with the billowing sleeves? I hoist some high-waisted jean shorts up over my legs and throw on a matching oversize denim shirt, glancing at myself in the mirror. *Definitely not.* I want to wear something that says *Hey, you can trust me. You didn't make a mistake choosing me.* Not *Hi, I'm Rachel, the lost Smurf.*

I swing open the closet, rooting around for more outfit options. A bunch of pictures are taped up on the inside of the door, and one catches my eye: I'm with some of my cousins at my first noraebang during a family vacation to Seoul when I was eleven. I had been looking forward to going to the noraebang all summer: the private rooms stocked with microphones and leather couches, the disco ball flashing neon lights against the walls, the tambourines, the endless snacks. Until then I had only ever sung in our tiny New York apartment—I couldn't wait to feel like I was putting on a real show, like a real K-pop star, just like in all the music videos I had been watching for years.

That was the night I met Yujin. I had just finished singing "Style" by Taylor Swift and my cousins were all cheering, when I heard someone clapping behind me. I turned around and saw a woman with electric-blue hair leaning against the open door (my cousin had forgotten to close it when she came back from the bathroom). She asked me what my name was and told me I reminded her of a K-pop star she used to know.

Then she winked and handed me her card and told me to have my parents call her.

I grab a pair of gray grid-print wide-leg pants from the top shelf of my closet, along with a cropped white turtleneck sweater. Shutting the closet door, I poke through the jewelry tray on my desk until I find my big gold hoops, sliding them into my ears as I tug half my hair into a messy topknot. *Perfect*, I say to myself as I grab my bag and slip on a pair of leather clog sandals.

Yujin's been by my side ever since. As a kid, I'd loved K-pop. But she helped me turn my small, seemingly unrealistic dream into a reality. She showed me that there was an entire world of people who felt the same way about this music that I did—and that's why being a K-pop singer is so special. It's about storytelling, connecting with audiences all around the world. She told me how being Korean American would make me special in this industry. She made me fall in love with K-pop in a whole new way. I can't let her down. Not again.

"I'm pretty sure we're lost."

I look down at the business card Yujin gave me. Akari and I have been wandering around the same street in Itaewon for the past twenty minutes, but this address is nowhere to be found. We've walked by the same dak-galbi restaurant so many times that people sitting inside have started looking at us suspiciously through the window.

"Let's try walking that way one more time," Akari says.

She adjusts the collar on her flowy, off-the-shoulder yellow top, and I can see that the back of her neck is turning pink and sweaty the way it does when she gets flustered. "We didn't look behind that Coffee Bean and Tea Leaf, did we?"

"Only about six times," I say. I blow a strand of hair out of my face and sigh, zooming in on my Naver Maps app. "I don't get it. It should be right here."

"Oh my god," Akari says.

"I know, right? I don't even know what we're looking for!"

"No, not that!" Akari grabs my arm, dragging me behind a row of parked motorbikes. She points across the street, where a bearded man with broad shoulders and a stubby ponytail has just stepped out of a squat little brown building with a scratched-up steel door. He slides on a pair of sunglasses and a knit cap that pulls down over his forehead. "It's Han Minkyu from *Oh My Dreams*," Akari squeaks out, aghast.

I stare at her blankly. I haven't really had much time for K-dramas the past six years.

"You *know*. He's the one who kidnapped Park Dohee after she lost her memory falling off her lover's motorcycle. He pretended to be her doctor to sneak into her hospital room. Rachel, he made her believe that she was in love with him the whole time!" Her forehead creases with worry. "We'd better hide. Who knows what he's capable of? He could kidnap us right now if he wanted to."

"Um, Akari, that's just his character. You know he's probably not a kidnapping memory hacker in real life."

"Oh. Right." Akari pauses, narrowing her eyes in his direction as he disappears down the alley. "Still. I don't trust him."

I glance over at the building. It's nothing remarkable—I hadn't even noticed it before: all the windows are tinted so you can't see in from the outside, and the walls are desperately in need of a new paint job. But maybe . . .

Curious, I gesture for Akari to follow me.

I pull on the handle and the door swings open smoothly, revealing a tiny, wood-paneled hallway. We step inside, and the door slams shut behind us. Akari looks at me, face pale. "You want to rethink what you said about us *not* being kidnapped today?" I shush her, straining my ears.

"Do you hear that?" I ask.

"The sound of our imminent death? Why yes, I do," Akari whispers dramatically.

"No, you dork. It's music."

The hallway ends in a thick velvet curtain. I can hear music pouring through from the other side. I turn to Akari. "Ready?"

She looks around nervously. "No?"

I laugh and take her hand, pulling her through the curtain to the other side.

Around us the walls burst to life with ethereal images of gardens that look plucked straight from the French countryside. Above us, pink and purple wisteria vines sweep across the ceiling, hanging heavily from an angular chandelier, all gold and milk glass. The room is filled with people seated in plush jewel-toned booths, chatting and listening to a man playing jazz tunes on the piano atop an impressive stage that covers the right side of the room. The entire place smells like a mix of baked croissants and rose petals. I glance down at the table near me to see a woman sipping her drink with a latte art swan so delicate and perfect that I feel like it might stretch its wings and fly straight out of the mug.

Holy shit. What *is* this place?

A voice calls out, "Rachel! Akari!" breaking me out of my trance. Yujin rushes toward us, her pink hair and dangly bronze earrings flying in a wave behind her. She puts an arm around both of our shoulders, beaming. "It's about time you got here. Welcome to Kwangtaek."

"Where are we?" Akari asks. "Also, do you know Han Minkyu?"

"I could tell you," Yujin says, laughing, as she guides us across the room. "But I think I know someone who would do a better job."

She stops in front of a cozy corner booth where a vaguely familiar older woman is already sitting, drinking from a porcelain tea set. She looks like she's stepped straight out of a 1940s Hollywood movie, with her silver hair swept up in an old-school glamorous updo and the most luxurious embroidered silk shawl I've ever seen draped casually over her shoulders.

"Rachel, Akari, meet my mother," Yujin says, sliding into the booth next to the woman. "Chung Yuna."

Chung Yuna? Did Yujin just say her mother is Chung Yuna?

Next to me I hear Akari gasp. "You're *the* Chung Yuna?"

Akari says. She turns to face Yujin. "Ooh-ahh, Unni, how come you never told us that your mom is the OG K-pop star?!"

I can't believe this. Chung Yuna is truly a legend. Before her, K-pop music didn't even exist. Now, forty years after she retired, everyone still knows her name—and loves her. Electric Flower even did a twenty-minute homage to some of her biggest hits during their last world tour.

I immediately straighten my back and bow at a ninety-degree angle. "Ahnyounghasaeyo."

Akari quickly follows suit. Yuna pats the seat next to her. "Ayy, that was a long time ago. I leave the K-pop to girls like you now."

Yujin grins. "You two look like a pair of fish. Close your mouths before you catch some flies."

I force my mouth closed and smile as calmly as I can, even though this is all blowing my mind. "So, where exactly are we right now?" I glance over at Akari, whose eyes still look like they might pop out of her head.

"Kwangtaek is an underground café I started for the celebrities of Korea," Yuna says, sipping from her teacup. "A place for people to relax and escape from fans and paparazzi, even for just a moment. We didn't have anything like this when I was in the industry, and I always longed for such a place. And then several years ago, I thought: if I want it so much, why don't I build it? It took a while to find the perfect location, but this one has been serving us quite well."

"That's amazing," Akari says, her eyes widening even

more. "I mean, I've heard rumors of a secret café for stars, but I never imagined it was real."

Yuna chuckles. "It's real all right. Now, tell me, what do you think of the wisteria vines? I'm wondering if we should go for more of a minimal look. . . ."

Akari smiles wide as she and Yuna discuss decor. From across the table Yujin takes my hand and stands up. "We'll be back," she says. Akari waves her away as Yuna starts in on the pros and cons of crushed versus panne velvet.

"Yujin," I say as we walk across the café. I try not to stare openly at the celebrities all around me, but—oh my god. Is that Park Dohee sitting over there with Kim Chanwoo? They're lovers on *Oh My Dreams*, but from the puppy-dog eyes they're making at each other over a plate of pastel-colored macarons, it looks like they might be together in real life, too. I look away—after all, they *are* here to escape all the prying eyes. "How come you didn't follow in your mom's footsteps and become a K-pop star? She's so inspiring!"

"I was inspired by her," Yujin agrees easily. "But just in a different way. I knew from a young age that I was never meant for the stage. Instead, I wanted to use what I learned from my mom to guide the next generation of stars." She squeezes my hand. "People meant for the spotlight, like you."

My heart fills up as I gulp down my nerves. *Meant for the spotlight.* I squeeze her hand back.

She leads me to a table close to the stage and pulls a chair out for me. I sit, content to let the biggest stars in Korea sip coffee all around me and talk with Yujin, just like the old days (well, if you replace the glitterati of Seoul for a bunch of plants), but there's one thing I still haven't figured out.

"Yujin-unni, this place is really cool. But um . . ." I lower my voice. "What exactly are we doing here? What about the video?"

Yujin winks. "You'll see. Let me get you a drink. Be right back."

She disappears toward the coffee counter by the stage. My hands are beginning to twitch with nerves, so I grab a napkin and start doodling in the corners. What's Yujin's plan? Maybe she's going to have me sing a song to her mom? That would surely go viral. Oh, or maybe she's getting Dohee and Chanwoo to be in the video? I laugh to myself. Leah's friends would *definitely* be impressed then. When I've filled the napkin with weird little curlicues and flowers, I push it aside and fiddle with the teaspoon on the table and sigh. What's taking Yujin so long?

I glance around the room, looking for her, and see Dohee and Chanwoo sitting at their table, lips locked. Ah-ssa! They are together! Leah is going to *freak* when she hears this. I'm so absorbed in my thoughts, I flip the spoon smack into the middle of my face.

"Ouch!" I rub my nose, glancing around to see if anyone saw that. Luckily, I'm not high on a priority people-watching list at a place like this. I breathe a sigh of relief and settle back in my chair.

"Wow . . . that looked like it hurt."

★ Seven ★

Jason pulls out the chair next to mine and takes a seat. The sleeves of his sweater are rolled up to his elbows, and I can't help but notice how nice his arms are. Tanned and lean and surprisingly smooth. And strong. I gulp as I flash back to him putting his arm around me at the end of my audition. Right before I uploaded a night's worth of soju and champagne onto his shoes.

My cheeks light up at the memory of it all. "What are you doing here?" I sputter. *Must regain composure.*

"You're the one sitting at my regular table," he says. His eyes crinkle as he leans forward, putting his mouth right next to my ear and whispering, "Let me guess. You're stalking me."

I force out a small laugh. This whole thing may be about getting this duet with Jason, but there's no need to inflate his ego any further. He already has the DB rumor mill for that.

He sits back and smirks. "I think I make you nervous."

My face is blazing. "Nope," I say a little too forcefully. "I think you're delusional."

"Really? Because your face is turning red." He presses one of his hands against my cheek. "Warm, too."

I swat his hand away. "Excuse you. I don't remember saying you could touch me."

He holds his hands up, resigned. "You're right. I'm sorry. I just wanted to make sure you were feeling okay. . . . We don't want anyone getting sick in Chung Yuna's fine establishment. It would chase all the K-drama actors away." He lowers his voice into a stage whisper as he waves across the room at Dohee and Chanwoo. "They're notoriously weak-stomached."

Just then, a waitress arrives at our table, carrying a platter filled with two steaming coffees and pastries. Jason flashes his perfect smile at her as he reaches for the coffee. "Wonderful timing. How'd you know this was exactly what I needed?"

She giggles, bowing her head once before skittering away. Seriously, is there anyone he doesn't charm?

"I forgive you, by the way," Jason says to me as he dumps half the sugar bowl into his coffee. "For the puking."

I look over at him nervously.

"I mean, I had to throw away my favorite sneakers, but other than that . . ." He grins, flashing his perfect smile in my direction now.

I feel my stomach swoop in response, but I force myself to ignore it, instead rolling my eyes at him. "Thanks. Glad to know someone is laughing about the most embarrassing thing that's ever happened to me."

His face falls a little and he grits his teeth. "Okay, okay! I was kidding about the shoes. But seriously. I know how nerve-racking those DB auditions can be. I've been there."

If only nerves had been the problem. But I can tell he means it this time. I give a small nod. "Thanks. For real."

He smiles, draining the entire jug of cream into his cup until it's completely empty. He shakes out the final few drops and then gives me an apologetic frown. "Sorry. Did you want some of this?"

"It's okay. I like my coffee black." I wrinkle my nose at his caramel-colored drink. "And you obviously prefer your coffee to taste like a milkshake."

"What can I say? I have a sweet tooth." He winks, sipping his abomination of a drink. We sit in a beat of silence. It's not exactly awkward, but it's not comfortable, either. The whole viral video plan is sitting heavily in my mind. What the hell is Yujin up to?

"So, Rachel, tell me," Jason says, reaching for a pastry. "Other than being a pajama fashion icon and a raging coffee snob, what else should I know about you?"

My mind races around for something to say. I'm a K-pop trainee? But he already knows that. I'll do anything to debut? But he's already done that. I'm here to make a video in the hopes that it will go viral, everyone will see how much better my voice is than Mina's, and Mr. Noh and the DB execs will see it and give me another chance at singing the duet with you? But I clearly can't tell him that. Luckily, at that moment, the waitress makes another appearance, setting a small white tray on the table. A smile spreads across Jason's face. "You'll love this—it's Yuna's most famous dessert." He grabs a small bowl on the side of the tray and begins to pour melted milk chocolate over the clear, spun-sugar orb in the center, which looks filled with strawberries and edible flowers. The orb melts, its contents bursting over layers of blackberry panna cotta and gingerbread crumble. *Um, wow.*

"This really beats the last dessert I had," I mumble to Jason through a mouthful of chocolate and strawberries. "My mom brought home pastries and I grabbed one, thinking it was fruit or something—but really it was sausage! With corn! And some kind of weird sugary sauce."

"Sausage bread masquerading as a normal pastry," Jason says, dropping his spoon. He shakes his head in disappointment. "The worst."

"Why do Koreans have to put hot dogs in everything?" I say, scooping up another spoonful of creamy panna cotta.

"And cheese," Jason adds. "They love adding cheese to everything. Cheese ramyun."

"Cheese kimbap."

"Cheese dak-galbi."

"Cheese sausage."

He laughs. "Can you add extra cheese sausage to your cheese sausage?"

"Of course! This is Korea. You can get a cheese-cheese sausage-sausage."

We both burst out laughing, and for a second I let everything else melt away. There's no DB or Mina, no scheming or final chances. It's like Jason and I are just normal friends with normal lives, drinking coffee and eating fancy desserts. But then the second's up and my laughter dies. I'm not sure how far DB's no-dating rule extends, but I'm willing to bet it would frown upon a trainee giggling and eating pastries with a DB superstar. I look away, self-conscious, reaching up to wipe the sweet sauce from my mouth with my napkin.

Before I realize what he's doing, he reaches out and grabs my wrist. I freeze, my eyes flicking to his. He's looking at my lips. *Oh my god. Is he going to . . . ? But he can't!*

"What's that on your napkin?"

Huh? He tugs the napkin out of my hand and flattens it against the table. *Oh. So he definitely wasn't going to . . .* My cheeks flush.

"That's nothing," I say, trying to grab the napkin away. He pulls it out of my reach, and I sigh, giving in. "They're just doodles. I like to sketch outfits and stuff when I'm bored."

"Outfits?"

"Yeah, outfits. I grew up in, like, the fashion capital of the world. I was always looking at people's clothes."

He says nothing, his eyes skimming over the napkin. I suddenly feel vulnerable, like he's going through my closet.

"Did you really draw these?" he says. His voice is surprised but not unkind. "They're good. Really good."

When he looks at me, his face is open. Genuine. Maybe even a little impressed. I feel like he's about to ask me to sketch *him* or something. Which, no. I swipe the napkin from him and ball it up, swiftly dunking it into his coffee.

His mouth drops open. "You did not just do that."

"It's nothing. Just some silly outfits. And that coffee is way too sweet. I'm saving you from getting diabetes."

He pulls out the sodden napkin with two pinched fingers and groans. "How sad. Perfectly good coffee, ruined by your doodling." He pauses. "That's not a bad line, actually."

I offer him a fresh napkin. "Maybe you should write it down," I joke. "You know, if DB ever decides to let any of you write your own lyrics."

I expect him to crack another joke, but his face is serious. He laughs gruffly, dropping the wet napkin on the table. "You don't know the half of it."

A dark look crosses his face, one I've never seen on him before. All traces of his charming, firecracker energy fade for a moment and his shoulders slump forward, subdued.

"Jason? Are you okay?"

He opens his mouth like he's about to answer, but before he can, the high-pitched squeal of a microphone interrupts him.

A group of four boys have taken the stage next to the piano. One of them is tapping a mic and grinning directly at us. I recognize him. In fact, I recognize all of them. It's Jason's band, NEXT BOYZ, and the guy holding the mic is Minjun. International superstar and the guy who ate fried chicken out of my purse.

"Calling Jason Lee and his lady friend to the stage," Minjun says, his voice breezy and mischievous as it reverberates around the room. "Café rules. If you want free drinks, you have to sing onstage."

Everybody cheers. It's only then that I realize the piano music has stopped and the whole room is buzzing. People are whispering behind cupped hands and shooting curious, starstruck glances in our direction (curious for me, starstruck for Jason, I'm sure), just like I'd been doing earlier with Dohee and Chanwoo. I spot Yujin sitting back in her corner booth with her mom and Akari. She catches my eye and winks.

Jason slips an arm around my chair and grins lazily at me, all traces of his shadowy expression gone. "Eh, ignore them, Rachel. Minjun just wants to get me back for leaving the noraebang early after the party the other night. I'll pay for our drinks."

I glance back at Yujin, who's gesturing discreetly to her phone and tilting her chin toward the stage. I turn to Jason, understanding dawning on me. This is why Yujin brought me here. Not just to make a viral video. To make a viral video *with Jason*. It's now or never.

Mustering all the courage I can, I grab Jason's hand. The room erupts into even more frantic whispers, and his eyes widen in surprise as I stand, flashing him a smile. "Come on.

Everyone's already talking. We may as well give them something to talk about."

For one gut-punching second, I think he might not follow me. Then he smiles back and stands. "You know what they say, Werewolf Girl." His hand grips mine, and my heart sputters into a series of somersaults as I pull him toward the stage.

The whole café is cheering and whistling. Then Minjun hands me a microphone with a bemused expression as the other NEXT BOYZ members are stamping their feet and catcalling in front of the stage.

"We're all rooting for you," he says with a wink.

Jason grabs a mic from another stand. He glances at me from across the stage. "You ready for this?"

I look for Yujin's face in the crowd. She gives me a thumbs-up and turns her phone toward the stage.

I gulp. Cameras on. "Ready as I'll ever be."

"Three twenty-five," he says, turning his face away from the mic so only I can hear him.

I frown in confusion, and he nods down at his shoes.

"That's how much these cost me. Three hundred twenty-five dollars. I let you go last time, but I'll expect full payment if you ruin these, too."

I can't help but laugh right into the mic, my shoulders starting to relax.

The audience quiets down as the pianist begins to play the opening chords of a familiar ballad. Everyone in the café lets out a collective sigh. It's a Chung Yuna classic. A love duet

from the eighties that makes me tear up instantly. A sudden memory rushes into my mind of Umma and Appa slow dancing to this song in the tiny blue kitchen of our New York apartment. I remember sitting under the table watching them, and knowing, even as a kid, that that was what it looked like to live from a full heart. Between Appa's late nights at the boxing gym and his clandestine law classes and Umma working through the weekend to get back on tenure track, it's been a long time since I've seen them dancing like that.

Jason starts to sing the first verse. His voice is a lot like his arms. Strong but gentle, a melody that feels like it's wrapping you up in a warm embrace.

I look out at the audience and see Yujin clutching her phone, pointing it directly at us. I feel a familiar panic start to rise in my chest as I stare into the camera lens. My own thoughts start to buzz in my head, drowning out the music. *What was I thinking? That I would decide to make a viral video and my camera fright would just magically go away? I'm such a fool. I should just vomit on the stage again—that would absolutely go viral.*

Next to me, Jason's voice is building toward the chorus. It's my cue to join in with the harmony, but I freeze. My mouth opens and nothing comes out. I turn to Jason, panic in my eyes. He grabs my hand, attempting to move me across the stage as he continues to sing the chorus solo, but my arms feel locked at my sides. There's a short musical interlude before the start of the second verse and Jason steps behind me, putting his

hands on my hips and spinning me. My training instincts kick in and I lean into the spin, twirling across the tiny stage. A smile starts to spread across my face as I remember how I used to spin Leah around our kitchen floor, shouting K-pop lyrics at the top of my lungs as she would squeal with glee. *I belong here.* A tingle of warmth spreads through my body as I grab Jason's hand and wink. *Just like last time*, I mouth right before the second verse starts. Everyone in the crowd is totally silent. I focus on the feeling of Jason's hand on mine as our voices braid together like fingers interlocking. It's just like that day in the auditorium. We were meant to sing together, and I can see in his eyes that whatever I'm feeling, he's feeling too.

I break gently away from his grip and walk across the stage as I sing my solo verse. I think of six-year-old Rachel listening to K-pop for the first time, feeling special to be Korean for the first time. I think of eleven-year-old Rachel singing her heart out at a noraebang, wishing an impossible wish. They would be so happy to see me here on this stage now. One step closer to living our dream. To sharing our love of K-pop with the world. And then Jason's voice weaves with mine again and we're unstoppable, feeling every rush, every high, every beat of our hearts in the thrum of adrenaline.

He walks toward me until he's right at my side, one hand gripping mine, the other raised like he's about to touch my face, but he pauses. A question. I decide to answer just this once, and as our voices lift into the final line, I press my cheek against his palm for the briefest of moments.

I slowly pull away as the song ends. We look at each other, eyes burning, the energy between us saying everything I can't. Everything I don't even have the words for. *It's magic singing with you.*

Suddenly, the crowd erupts into cheers, jumping to their feet in a standing ovation. We both blink, breaking out of the moment. He smiles and takes my hand, turning toward the crowd. We take a deep bow. Yuna rises from her booth and joins us onstage, embracing me tightly.

"That was absolutely lovely," she says, taking my face in her hands. "The best cover of my song I've heard in years."

I bow my head. "Thank you so much. I hope we did it justice."

She moves to hug Jason. In the crowd, I see Yujin lower her phone, a huge smile on her face. I suck in a breath as I snap back to reality. Part one of the plan is complete.

That night, I lie in bed thinking about Jason's smile and the way our voices melted together in a perfect harmony. I can't help but feel a stab of guilt for using him as part of my scheme, but he said it himself—he's been there. He knows how tough training at DB is. We have to do everything we can to go after our dreams.

Still, I can feel the guilt gnawing away at me. I scroll through my Finsta feed (the one no one but the Cho twins knows about), trying to keep myself distracted. Looks like Hyeri and Daeho got tteokbokki after working on their experiment all day. Cute. I make a mental note to bug Hyeri about her crush later and double tap to like the photo.

There's a knock on my door, and Umma pops her head in. "Rachel, are you sleeping already?"

"I'm just resting," I say, sitting up in bed. "Long day at training."

She purses her lips. "Did you finish your homework?"

I think of the mountain of schoolwork I haven't even touched. "Yes, Umma."

Her eyes scan the room like she's looking for something to disapprove of, landing on the equally large mountain of clothes on my bedroom floor. "Look at this room. It's a disaster! You can't expect me to constantly clean up after you."

"I don't expect you to," I say, sighing and flopping back down on my bed. I close my eyes and go into my dream world instead, where she asks me how training is going and I tell her all about the magic of singing with Jason. Maybe we would even listen to the original Chung Yuna classic together and I'd tell her about my memory of her and Appa dancing in the kitchen. But nope. I can still hear her going at it.

"I'm home," Appa calls from the front door.

"Yeobo, come here and look at this pigsty your daughter is living in," she says.

Appa joins her in my room. There are dark bags under his eyes, and it looks like he's lost some weight since the last time I saw him. Late nights at the gym and night school seem to be taking their toll on him. Maybe I should offer him some of Juhyun's depuffing eye cream.

"Talk some sense into your daughter!" Umma says.

"Rachel, clean your room," Appa says tiredly.

"Yes, Appa," I say. I don't want to stress him out more than he already is. "I'll clean it tomorrow."

"There. Done. Harmony restored to the Kim household," Appa says with a smile that doesn't quite reach his eyes as he drags his feet out of my room. Umma frowns worriedly and hurries after him without closing my door. I roll out of bed to close the door myself, but before I can, Leah pops her head in, talking a mile a minute.

"Hi, Unni," she says, waving her hand in my face. "You'll never guess what happened on *Oh My Dreams* today. Park Dohee's character and Kim Chanwoo broke up! Apparently she had been carrying on a secret love affair with his brother this whole time! But it wasn't really her fault because he had hypnotized her into believing she was a single aerialist who lived with him in Australia and—"

I flash back to Kwangtaek. I can't wait to tell Leah the truth about her favorite TV couple, but now is not the time. She would never leave my room. I steer her over to the door and shove her through it. "Come back later, little sis. It's resting time."

"But I don't have anyone else to talk—"

I close the door and lock it. Sighing, I flop back onto the bed and close my eyes. But it's pointless now. Guilt is coursing through my body like I just pounded a triple-shot espresso. I can't stop thinking about Appa's tired eyes and Leah's sweet face. If I could just debut already, it would all be worth it. They would be able to see that everything they've sacrificed for me—leaving jobs, leaving friends, leaving the States—wasn't for nothing. Debuting would solve everything.

My phone pings with a Kakao message. It's from Yujin.

Check your Instagram.

Oh my god. My hands are shaking as I open the app on my phone. A video of me and Jason singing at Kwangtaek pops up at the top of my feed.

It already has more than two hundred thousand likes.

I keep scrolling through all the major K-pop fan and gossip Instagrammers that I follow, and it's everywhere. Whatever Yujin did to leak it, it worked.

And people are *freaking out*.

I scroll through the comments, not daring to breathe.

Is that Jason Lee's yeochin?

Her voice is amazing. They sound so good together!

#FullMoonLoverReveal?

OMG this song, I'm crying!

Where can I download this??? I need it for my ringtone!

My phone is buzzing nonstop with texts from the Cho twins and Akari (HOLY SHIT, Oh my god! Yujin is our hero!). My Instagram DM pings, and I see a message from Coach Sloat (Congrats, Rachel! Let me know if you and Jason ever want a private tennis lesson!). There's a pounding at my door, and Leah cries, "Unni! Open the door right now! Is this really you?" But I can't focus on any of it.

I lie back in my bed and hold my phone against my chest, a huge smile spreading across my face. Any feeling of guilt I had earlier washes away as I watch the likes rack up and I let out a giddy scream.

I did it. I freaking *did* it!

I'm one step closer to my second chance.

And I'm not going to let it pass me by.

★ Eight ★

Twelve pairs of eyes are locked on me, watching my every move. I straighten out my blazer and smooth out a little wrinkle at the top of my black skinny jeans. Today's look is chic and professional—the model of a picture-perfect K-pop trainee— because that's exactly how I need the DB execs to see me.

Mr. Noh sits at the head of the long rectangular board- room table, his face gleaming in the table's shiny mahogany surface, his fingers steepled together beneath his chin. Yujin and I stand at the opposite end, posture perfect. Just a couple days ago, she was my co-conspirator. Today, it feels like she's my lawyer.

"The video that was leaked has gone viral," Yujin explains. "People love hearing Jason and Rachel sing together. It's the number one most-played video of the week on Instagram and already has over three million hits. There's buzz around them. If Rachel does a duet with Jason, the buzz will only grow. We're guaranteed success."

"Hold on a second." An exec by the name of Mr. Lim holds up a hand. He's even older and more critical than Mr. Noh, with wiry glasses perched on the edge of his crooked nose. "Are you suggesting we give Rachel another chance after she *vomited* on our star? Ms. Chung, with all due respect, I think you're letting your personal feelings for the girl get in the way of your better judgment."

I maintain a straight face, reminding myself to let Yujin do the talking, just like we discussed.

"Jason has clearly moved past it," Yujin says, gesturing to her phone. "Perhaps it's time that we did too."

"Time?" an exec named Ms. Shim says incredulously, the veins bulging out of her impossibly thin neck, her mouth twisted into what I assume is a permanent scowl. "It's only been a couple of weeks. It'll take a lot longer than that for Rachel to earn back our trust, if that's even possible. That was the worst audition I've ever seen in all my years at DB."

Several of the other execs murmur in agreement. I clench my fists by my sides but stay silent. As much as I hate being talked about like I'm not even in the room, speaking without being spoken to is not an option for any K-pop trainee. Not even a viral one.

Mr. Noh holds up a hand and everyone falls silent.

"I think that's enough for today. It's clear the majority of you think that Rachel is . . . not ready," he says. He sounds almost disappointed. "Does anyone have any closing remarks?"

My body temperature skyrockets. *What? No!* I can't let it

end this way. Not when I'm so close. I can feel myself about to explode when Yujin touches my elbow gently. She gives me an almost imperceptible shake of her head. *Don't make it worse,* she's saying. *You're already on thin ice.* My heart sinks. She's right. Better to still be in the program and not be singing the duet than to get kicked out altogether. The plan has failed.

I swallow everything—my tears, my pride, the last shred of my hope. I turn to follow Yujin out of the room when someone stands up abruptly.

"Wait!" he says. We both turn around to see one of the execs—a younger man with a boyish face and freshly styled hair—holding up his phone. "I don't think we can close this conversation without seeing the video in question. Mr. Noh, permission to connect my phone to the projector?"

Mr. Noh pauses and then gives one terse nod. "Go ahead, Mr. Han."

Mr. Han glances over at me and gives me a small wink. *What? Is he really trying to help me?* A spark of hope reignites in my chest.

He streams the video on his phone and casts it onto the projector, and suddenly sounds of Jason singing fill up the boardroom. Some of the execs' faces soften in recognition at the familiar chords of the Chung Yuna classic. To my left, Ms. Shim sighs happily, a faraway smile on her face, her hands clasped to her chest, as Jason continues to sing on the camera. Is there anyone in the world who doesn't have a soft spot for this boy?

I hold my breath, waiting for my part. When I hear my own voice play back at me, I sneak a glance at Mr. Noh. His eyes are hidden behind his glasses, and as always, he's tapping his fingers in time to the music. All the execs are. Some of them even start smiling and singing along. By the final chorus, I see Ms. Shim dab at her eyes. I crack a smile of my own. Tears! Always a good sign.

The song ends and the video fades to black. Everyone claps and Mr. Han whistles. The hope in me is growing, but I don't dare breathe comfortably yet. Was it enough?

"I have to admit, that was quite lovely," Ms. Shim says, almost begrudgingly.

"And people love them together," Mr. Han says, scrolling through his feed. "Social media is quite literally exploding over this performance."

"That may be true," Mr. Lim says gruffly. "But it was never Rachel's talent that was in question. We all know the girl can sing. But can she be professional? We've all seen the media training reports. Can she perform in front of the cameras? Is she devoted to upholding the image of the DB family? That's a completely different matter."

"That's true," Ms. Shim says. "We need her image to be spotless if she's going to accompany Jason. And that display of hers at the audition was not exactly spotless."

"But *why* does it have to be spotless?" Mr. Han challenges. "We know their duet will be a big hit—we've already got the numbers to prove it. It's a strategic business move. Not to mention, the audience these days is more interested in seeing authenticity over spotlessness. Like this video—they want to see real, relatable people exhibit raw talent and discipline. And Rachel has that. Plus, you only need to watch her sing to see she's clearly gotten over her camera shyness."

My face burns at this last comment, but I don't dare open my mouth.

Truthfully, I can't believe what I'm hearing. All K-pop executives, but especially DB, are known for being incredibly strict and set in their ways, accepting nothing less than a performer who will put the needs and wants of DB before anything else. Tradition over innovation. Rote perfection over authenticity. That is the K-pop way. But Mr. Han sounds like he sees things differently. I don't really know what to make of it, but I find myself nodding along to everything he's saying.

"Rachel," Mr. Noh says, speaking to me directly.

I straighten up immediately. "Yes, Mr. Noh."

"Why should we give you a second chance?"

My impulse is to look to Yujin, but I force myself to keep my eyes fixed on Mr. Noh. He only wants to hear from me right now. I take a deep breath, lifting my chin. "Because," I say, "there's no limit to how brightly I can shine. That video was just a taste. If you give me a second chance, I'll work twice as hard and shine twice as bright. Give me three chances and it'll triple. And I know there's no one who can do this better than me."

The room is silent. Mr. Noh leans back in his seat, his mirrored eyes boring into mine. I hold his gaze, standing tall. He nods in approval, a small smile playing on his face.

"Meeting dismissed," he says.

I blink as the execs gather up their things. I glance at Mr. Han and then at Yujin, who both look just as confused as me.

"Wait!" I cry as Mr. Noh heads for the door. I realize I'm breaking all kinds of rules by addressing him, but I need to know. He turns, raising an eyebrow. "Does this mean I'm doing the duet with Jason?"

A wide smile spreads across his face. There's a calculating tilt to it that makes goose bumps rise on my arms.

"Yes, Rachel," he says. "You'll be singing with Jason. But it won't be a duet. It will be a trio. You, Jason . . . and Mina."

A trio. I'm singing with Jason and Mina.

"Oh, and, Ms. Kim."

My head snaps up. "Yes, Mr. Noh."

He eyes turn steely and sharp, and he looks right at me. "I'm not in the habit of giving third chances. No matter how brightly you shine."

On my way home, I nearly skip off the bus, stopping by Dunkin' Donuts to pick up a treat for Leah. I get a box of glazed doughnuts and a strawberry banana smoothie, her favorite.

I feel like I'm in a dream, one that I don't want to wake up from. I'm singing with Jason. I, Rachel Kim, am singing with Jason Lee! There's a huge grin on my face, dampened only a little by the fact that Mina will also be singing with us. She wasn't a part of my original equation. . . .

Whatever. That's a problem for tomorrow.

I race up to the apartment. "Leah!" I yell as soon as I'm through the door. I kick off my shoes. "Unni's home and I have your two favorite things. Snacks and gossip!"

I step into the living room and come to a sudden halt. Umma is sitting on the couch, her phone clasped in her hand so tightly, her knuckles are white. She narrows her eyes at me, her lips pressed into a hard line.

"Umma," I say hesitantly, "you're home early." The look on her face makes my stomach churn. A thought flicks through my mind. Something's happened with Appa. She's found out about his law classes and she's angry we've been keeping it a secret. I scramble for the words to explain, but she speaks first, her voice completely flat.

"Do you want to tell me what this is?" she says, holding up her phone.

I walk forward slowly, Leah's smoothie sweating in my hand. A video is playing on Umma's phone. Not just any video. A video of *me*.

And it's not the one that just went viral.

It's me at the trainee house party, clothes so drenched in what can only be alcohol and sweat that you can see my bra straight through my tank top. I'm totally out of it, laughing at nothing and dancing on the table with a champagne bottle in one hand and a bright-green Tupperware in the other. I notice

Umma's eyes narrow in on the container as Lizzie and Eunji egg me on in the background of the video, whistling and hooting. God. I can't even call it dancing. I'm flailing my arms and legs and making a total fool of myself. I have no memories of this at *all*. What the fuck did Mina put in that drink?

I flash back to the party. To falling asleep on the couch and seeing Mina from across the room, her phone pointed directly at me. I gulp, my throat so tight I can barely speak.

"Umma, where—"

"Someone texted me this video today," she says quietly, her eyes burning.

I swallow hard. I should have known Mina wouldn't stop at just drugging me and ruining my audition. I open my mouth to say something, but Umma holds up her hand. "Before you try to explain yourself. Just tell me. Is this the trainee house?"

I stare down at the floor, completely silent. I nod once.

"And did I or did I not tell you that you are not allowed to go to the trainee house?"

"You did tell me," I whisper, my voice raw.

"So you lied to me when you said you were going to study with the Cho twins. And then you went to a place I explicitly told you not to go. And *then* you got out-of-your-mind drunk and put on a strip show in front of your good-for-nothing K-pop friends?"

I look up, tears in my eyes. "Umma, please, it's not what you think it is."

"Why are you crying?" she snaps, raising her voice. I cower

back. I've never seen her so mad before. "What have you done to deserve to cry? Tears are for the sorrowful, but you're not even sorry."

"I am!" I cry. "I am so sorry for lying. And I'm sorry that you had to find out this way. I never even imagined—"

"What do you think your father will say when he sees this? He's going to be heartbroken." She shakes her head, her voice catching. "I knew this K-pop world would be a bad influence. It's poisoning you."

"It's not," I insist. Tears are streaming down my face now. I desperately try to wipe them away, but I can't get them to stop. "Please, Umma, just let me explain."

"When did my daughter become such a disgrace? How can you live with yourself like this? Huh, Rachel? You're out of control!"

In the midst of my guilt and regret, I feel another emotion swell to the surface. Anger. Can't she even give me a moment to explain myself? She's supposed to be my mother. She's supposed to be on my side.

"Well, maybe I wouldn't have had to lie if you tried to be supportive for once! The whole reason we moved here was so I could train, but you act like it's just some hobby I've had for the last six years." I explode. "You think I wanted to sneak out behind your back? I had to do it because of you and your *rules*. I had to give myself a fighting chance at being noticed by the execs. And I succeeded, by the way. Most parents would be proud that their daughter is going to

Didn't you hear me? I'm singing with *Jason Lee*. Right before the DB Family Tour in the fall. This is just how DB debuted Electric Flower almost seven years ago, Umma. It means everything I've worked so hard for over the last six years is about to happen. It means they're going to debut *me*." I'm begging now, all the anger slowly ebbing out of my voice. I'm desperate for her to see me, for her to believe in me—and maybe even a little desperate for me to fully believe in what I'm saying too.

"Please, Umma. *Please*. I'm so close."

She says nothing as she grabs an onion out of the fridge and starts chopping away at it. The onion fumes mingle with my rising panic, and tears start streaming down my face. I can't hold back my sobs as Umma turns to face me. Her posture is still rigid, but her eyes are no longer snapping with anger—instead, she almost looks sad. "Rachel," Umma says, "there are so many things you just don't understand. That you just can't understand at seventeen." She sighs. "But you are my daughter. Which means you need to try. So, sing this song with Jason and see where it goes."

Just as my shoulders start to relax, she holds up a finger.

"But," she says, her tone final, "you said it yourself. If you haven't debuted by the time the family tour starts, I'm pulling you from DB. End of discussion."

She abandons her half-cut onion on the kitchen counter and walks into her bedroom, slamming the door shut behind her. I collapse into a chair, Leah's smoothie and doughnuts be singing with Jason Lee in his next single." I stop abruptly, out of breath.

A look of surprise crosses her face. "You got the duet?"

"It's not a duet anymore, but yes." I take a deep breath, trying to calm myself. "I did."

"Well . . . congratulations, Rachel. I know how badly you wanted that." She stiffens. "But it doesn't change what you had to do to get it. This industry is toxic."

"It's not *toxic*, Umma. It's competitive. It only accepts the best from people."

Umma lets out a disbelieving laugh in one short breath. "The best from people?" She holds up her phone. "So this is your best? You, drunk and making a spectacle of yourself in front of everyone you train with?"

My face burns with embarrassment, and when I open my mouth, nothing comes out. I want to tell her about what Mina did, about why I was so drunk in that video—but it would only make her think that she's right. And she's not. Not about this.

Umma's glare is unforgiving and her voice is hard and clipped. "I let this go on for far too long. I won't have you be a part of this anymore. Not when training makes you act this way."

She turns her back on me, walking out of the living room. I stare at her in disbelief. Is she seriously going to end things like this?

I storm after her into the kitchen.

"What do you mean you won't have me be a part of this?

wilting on the table. How did I go from feeling on top of the world to crashing headfirst into rock bottom in just a few hours? I choke out another sob. This song with Jason and Mina isn't just the next step on the way to debuting anymore. It is the only step. If it doesn't work, everything I've worked for, everything I've been dreaming of . . . is over.

Nine

Whoever said exercise gives you endorphins had clearly never been a K-pop trainee.

"Maybe you should take a break, Unni. You look miserable—and you're going to give yourself premature forehead wrinkles."

Leah sits cross-legged on my bed, snacking on a bag of honey butter chips. I guess there's one Kim sister who shares Korea's obsession with turning salty snacks into sweet ones.

I frown at her in the wall mirror and lean forward to inspect my reflection, smoothing my hand across my forehead. "What wrinkles?"

"They come with your 'I'm so stressed I look like I haven't pooped in three days' face." She tosses a chip into the air and catches it in her mouth. "Basically, the way you've looked since your trio training with Mina started. You really should relax."

She waves her bag of chips under my nose, but I grimace at the smell.

She's not wrong, though. It's been a week since my show-down with Mr. Noh, and things are crazier than ever before. There are constant weigh-ins and interview drills and nonstop cardio. I'm waking up at 4:00 a.m. every morning to make it to DB by sunrise, training all day, and falling into bed around midnight—only to get back up and do it all again the next day.

It's still only on weekends, but I'm not about to try to renegotiate my training schedule with Umma. Things are tense enough between us as it is; we've barely spoken since her ultimatum. The days keep ticking away until the start of the DB Family Tour and the new girl-group debut, so I can't rest. Not even for a second.

Luckily, Leah's here during the week to whip me into shape. And she's almost as strict as the DB trainers.

"Do it again, Rachel," she says as I get back into formation. "From the top."

Leah hits play on her phone. My muscles scream in pain as I go through the dance routine for what feels like the hundredth time that night, stopping only to watch video playbacks from my rehearsals with Mina. There's this one move in the second verse that I keep messing up, and the trainers' constant critiques play in a loop in my head:

You're never going to debut if you can't get this move right, Rachel!

You're dancing is a disgrace to DB, Rachel!

Your dancing looks like an elephant in a zoo, Rachel!

Rachel!

I practice so late that Leah falls asleep on my bed, honey butter crumbs dusting her chin, and my own eyes start to droop. I tuck a blanket over her and reach for the empty bag of chips to toss it. There's still one honey butter chip inside. I'm so hungry that even this sugary potato chip seems appealing to me right now.

No. I shouldn't. DB weighs us almost every day. And Mina and I are being fitted for our music-video outfits tomorrow.

I kind of freaked out when Yujin told me there was going to be a music video. The trainers with their constant critiques are like a horde of bees swimming around in my head, and I know the execs are going to be watching me like a hawk that day, seeing how I handle being up close and personal with the cameras for an entire shoot. But then she softened the blow with the news that we'd all be getting custom outfits for the video. And a whole day of trying on clothes? Definitely worth it. Now I just need to ensure the execs can't make a single complaint about my body.

I sigh, toss the chip bag in my trash bin, and then press play on Leah's phone one more time.

"Ai-yah! Look at your stomach. Like a cow. Take that off immediately."

I'm struggling to breathe in this purple sequined corset. It pinches around my waist so tight that it physically hurts to suck my tummy in enough to keep the whole thing from popping off.

"Too bad," the stylist, Grace, says, undoing the corset fastenings while her team of underlings helps me step out of my skirt—a lavender leather nightmare with a huge tulle train bursting from the back. "I was really hoping the mermaid concept would work. Next."

Thank god.

She pulls me into a Twiggy-esque orange checkered dress with dramatic bell sleeves, then steps back and grimaces, twirling her finger in the air for the next outfit.

A white leather jacket with matching high-waisted snakeskin shorts.

A golden yellow romper with ruffled shoulders that nearly fan up to my ears.

A floral jumpsuit with a chunky silver belt and sheer lace sleeves that make my arms itch.

Being a Barbie doll isn't as much fun as I'd imagined it would be. I'm in each outfit for less than ten seconds before Grace signals for the next one. Mina is going through the same wardrobe fitting to my left, her face pinched as people zip her up on all sides in a pink latex dress. God, she looks like bubble gum. It would almost be funny if they weren't about to dress me in the exact same thing.

"You know, it's so rare to find someone who looks washed out in every color she tries," Mina says, glancing in my direction. "I almost didn't see you there. You blend right into the wall."

I catch one of Grace's assistants smirking in my direction,

eyebrows raised. My face burns, but I don't back down. I can't. Not when I know there isn't anything Mina wouldn't do to keep me from succeeding.

"Luckily, the people who matter do see me; otherwise they wouldn't have decided you couldn't handle singing with Jason on your own," I say smoothly.

That earns me more than a few snickers from the room, and Mina's mouth drops open in fury. But before she can snap back, Grace swoops in, pulling a tiered black fringe dress from the clothing racks.

"Let's try this flapper-girl look," she says. I step into the dress as she plonks a pearl-encrusted headpiece on top of my hair. She circles around me, tweaking the fringe and scratching her chin. "All right. I can see it. I can see it." She snaps her fingers at one of the wardrobe fitters. "Mark this one down as a maybe. And let's get Rachel to try on some shoes."

Just then Heejin, one of our trainers, whisks into the room, iPad and a bottle of barley tea in hand.

"Rachel, Mina, get over here for your weigh-in," she says briskly. "And quickly. I don't have all day."

The fitting team helps me out of my dress so I can get weighed in just my bra and underwear. I walk over to the scale, where Heejin is waiting for me, Mina following closely behind.

"After you, Princess Rachel," Mina says with an overexaggerated arm flourish.

Ignoring her, I step onto the scale. Heejin squats down

next to the calculating number, watching closely with her pen poised over her iPad.

The number pops up and I'm . . . twelve pounds heavier than last week?

What the hell!? That can't be possible!

My jaw drops and I sputter, "I . . . this is . . . the scale *must* be broken."

"What is happening here, Rachel?" Heejin says, whipping her head to look at me in disbelief. "You know I have to report a weight gain this huge to Mr. Noh! There's no way you'll be allowed to continue with the trio. What did you even do to gain twelve pounds in a week?!"

Mina snickers behind me, and I turn around just in time to see her lift her foot off the back of the scale. I narrow my eyes.

Mina. Of course she was stepping on the scale as I was being weighed to make me look even heavier. This is a new level of petty. My body feels ready to burst with rage. "Pretty pathetic attempt at sabotage, Mina. Seems like you've lost your nerve," I say in a low voice.

"I'm sure I have no idea what you mean, Princess," she replies, her voice sweet but her eyes glinting with hatred.

"All I have to do is tell Yujin what you did to me, and you'll be kicked out of DB forever."

Mina smiles indulgently. "You mean all you have to do is admit to Yujin that her perfect, perfectly behaved Princess Rachel went to a party at the trainee house and—*gasp!*—got drunk?"

"I didn't 'get drunk,' Mina. You put something in my drink! You drugged me! You and the other trainees did it on purpose so I wouldn't—"

"That's a great story, Rachel," Mina cuts in over me, "but I'd love to see you prove it." She smirks at me for a moment, and when I don't reply, she walks away.

I want to storm after her, but there's no point. She's right. I could never prove it, and even if I could, what good would it do me? I would have to admit that I was at a party and that I was drinking. I would lose my spot singing with Jason, and if that video ever came out, I would probably get kicked out of DB altogether.

Instead I turn back to Heejin with gritted teeth. "Please let me try one more time," I ask. "There was obviously a mistake."

Heejin sighs, irritated. "Hurry up, then."

I step off the scale, pause for a second, and then weigh myself again, shooting a death glare behind me to make sure Mina isn't joining me this time. The number that pops up on the screen is the same as last week. I breathe a sigh of relief, and Heejin nods, satisfied.

"Okay, Mina, your turn," Heejin says, typing my weight into her iPad.

Mina steps onto the scale, sucking her breath in. A number pops up and her face falls.

Heejin purses her lips. "One pound over last week's weight," she says, her voice scathing. "Is this also a mistake, Mina?"

"I . . ." Mina looks down at her toes. "I'm sorry."

"Tell me." Heejin's tone is low and scary. "Tell me everything you ate since the last weigh-in."

Damn. A whole food interrogation. I would feel sorry for her if she weren't Mina.

"I had a Greek salad, the smoothies you recommended, and . . ." Mina trails off. When she speaks again, her voice is small. "A pizza."

"How many slices?"

"Three."

I let out a low whistle as if to say, *Wow. Three pizza slices.* Mina glares at me from the corner of her eye, and I feel a split second of shame before remembering all the times Mina has tried to ruin my life—and that's just over the past few weeks.

Heejin shakes her head. "No self-control," she yells. "Absolutely none. If you don't want to do this, just leave. Walk out right now. Do you want to quit? Huh? Do you? Because it seems like you already have."

Mina looks down at the floor in shame. "No. I'm sorry. I don't want to quit." She bites her lip. "I'll do better next week."

"I certainly hope so. Otherwise I'll have to tell your father that his daughter is getting too heavy to be a K-pop star," Heejin says. "If you don't want to disappoint him, I'd stop gorging on those pizzas."

Mina's face goes gray at the mention of her father. She's always bragging about how he and Mr. Noh are such good friends, how her dad hosts parties and dinners for all the trainers and execs at DB, and how she knows them all so well, but she doesn't look too happy about that connection right now.

Mina straightens up, rolling her shoulders back. "There's no need to tell him anything. I won't gain any more weight. I promise."

Heejin grimaces, typing a quick note. Her eyes flick to Mina's legs. "Also, if the dieting doesn't work, we should consider plastic surgery for those daikon legs. All your weight goes straight to your calves."

Damn. I should take lessons from Heejin on how to burn Mina. Heejin flips her iPad case closed and walks swiftly out of the room. Mina steps off the scale, and I smile brightly at her.

"That was fun, wasn't it?" I say.

She scowls and pushes past my shoulder, storming away to grab her clothes.

By the afternoon I'm back in my favorite Adidas sweats for dance practice. Mina's been ignoring me since the weigh-in, which honestly, is fine by me. If only we could figure out a way to get through these next few months without having to speak at all. . . .

As we walk down the hall, I hear a familiar singing voice. "Start again!" someone says. "You still don't have enough control on the high notes."

Mina and I turn the corner, and I see Akari doing a wall sit outside one of the vocal lesson rooms, her trainer standing over her with her arms crossed. Akari starts the verse again, sweat beading on her forehead.

"From the diaphragm!" the trainer yells.

Akari's legs are starting to tremble, but she keeps singing. Suddenly, her voice cracks on the high note and the trainer bends over, slapping her hard in the gut. Akari winces through the blow but doesn't stop singing.

The wall sit is one of the roughest punishments the trainers dole out, forcing us to sing while we sit against a wall, our knees bent at a ninety-degree angle. The continual slaps to the stomach are supposed to strengthen our diaphragm, but mostly they just hurt.

My body aches as I watch Akari's face turn redder by the second; she is clearly struggling to hold in her tears.

The trainer hits her again. Harder. "You're weak. If you can't even get through this, how will you get through anything else? Start again!"

Poor Akari. I sigh and glance over at Mina, but—wait? Where did she go? I look at my watch.

Shit. I'm late for dance practice.

I try to slip in as discreetly as possible, but as soon as Mina sees me, she stares pointedly at the clock on the wall. "Wow, Rachel. Three minutes late, I see." She turns to the trainers, shaking her head. "She clearly doesn't understand how important your time is."

"That's enough, Mina," Yujin snaps at her. I almost smile, but Yujin quickly turns to me, eyes narrowed. "Now that you're both here, let's get started on the dance number, shall we?"

She shoots me another look, and I bow my head in apology

to all the trainers. There are three execs sitting in the back room today, all with iPads glued to their hands.

Fuck, I need to get it together. And fast.

Mina and I take our spots in the middle of the room. The music starts just as Yujin flips on the video camera. Mina shoots me a smug smile, and suddenly the red light from the camera feels like a mosquito that's been launched directly into my brain. But then something unexpected happens. Akari's face—desperate and determined as she pushed out those high notes in the hallway—flashes in my mind. The buzzing doesn't stop, but it gets quieter as I focus on her face and try to ignore the camera that's five feet in front of me.

The song we're singing with Jason is called "Summer Heat," and it's pure energy and fun. An upbeat, catchy pop song about being young, careless, and carefree in the summer.

Ha.

I make it through the first verse, nailing the complicated footwork as Mina and I slide into the chorus. But I start to tense up as we head into the second verse. Even though Leah's been drilling me all week, I just can't seem to get the dance moves down.

I keep my eyes fixed on the mirror. *Come on, Rachel. You can do this.*

I land the first step okay, but as we move into the second, my body is telling me to spin one way while my head insists on going the other way, and I end up missing the beat altogether. Mina, on the other hand, looks flawless. Even I have to admit she's nailing every move. I'm watching her out of the corner of my eye, marveling at the way her legs seem to fly her around the room, when I realize I completely missed the next step.

Shit. I quickly find my rhythm again, but my body temperature is skyrocketing and my head is filled with the noise of a thousand mosquitoes all hungry for their first meal of the summer. I don't know where to look. Yujin? The camera? The execs?

I struggle through the last verse, grateful when the music finally comes to an end.

A second later, the door to the practice room flies open and Jason saunters in, holding a Lotteria takeout bag in one hand and a half-eaten chicken burger in the other. He flashes a smile to the execs, and Ms. Shin's eyes light up as she waves back, the other two execs jumping to their feet to shake his hand. Typical. Jason walks into practice late, eating a freaking chicken burger no less, and the execs are still drooling all over themselves.

"All right," Yujin says. "Now let's hear some singing. We need to decide which one of you girls will sing which parts, so let's have each of you run through it once on your own. Mina, we'll start with you."

I slide my sweaty body into a chair as the instrumentals start up and Mina begins to sing. Even without a microphone I wouldn't be surprised if they could hear her on the roof. Jason scoots into the chair next to me, holding out the Lotteria takeout bag.

"French fry?" he whispers.

I ignore him, trying to focus on Mina's singing.

"More emotion, Mina," Ms. Shim calls out. "You sound good, but I'm not *feeling* anything from you."

Jason presses the bag closer to my face. "I promise there are no secret cheese sausages in it. Go ahead. Have one."

I continue to ignore him, but I can't help myself as the corners of my lips quirk up in a smile. I quickly drop it, but it's too late. He grins.

Damn my own lips for betraying me.

"How cool is it that we can sing this song together?" he says.

"Uh, pretty cool, I guess." I keep my eyes fixed on Mina's performance.

"Mina, your face looks like someone killed your puppy! Is that what being a DB star means to you? Smile!" another exec shouts. I can see the tension in her neck at each of his comments.

"I know I'm excited. You know why, right?" Jason leans in so close I can smell the french fries on his breath. Mmmm . . . it's not a bad smell, actually. I can't even remember the last time I ate a french fry.

I don't respond. He waits expectantly, his big puppy-dog brown eyes staring at me, and I sigh.

"Okay, I give in. Why are you s—"

"Rachel!" a sharp voice hisses. One of the trainers is glaring at me, putting a finger to her lips. "Pay attention. Do you have no manners?"

I flush. Across the room Yujin covers her forehead, looking absolutely mortified. I swivel away from Jason and focus on the song, but inside I'm seething. Why am I being called out when Jason was the one talking to *me*?

After a beat, he leans in to whisper again. "You didn't get to hear my answer."

I stare straight ahead, ignoring him. I'm in enough trouble today as it is.

"It's a good one, I promise."

He puts his head on my shoulder and I shrug my shoulders to shake him off.

"You really don't want to know?"

Enough is enough. I whip my head around to face him, ready to tell him off, but his closeness catches me off guard. We're nearly nose to nose, and his eyes are fixed on mine.

"Huh," he says, his voice hushed low enough that only I can hear him. "I always thought your eyes were brown, but up close they're really brown with gold flecks in them. I bet most people miss that about you." He smiles. "Too bad. They're beautiful. But then again, I kinda like being one of the few who know."

I gape at him, completely speechless. Mina finally finishes the song, and Jason glances at the clock.

"Sorry, everybody," he says, addressing the whole room now. He stands, balling up the Lotteria bag in his hands. "I have a meeting with Mr. Noh to discuss some ah . . . important business. I hate to duck out early, but when Mr. Noh calls . . ."

He gives everyone a knowing glance, and all the trainers and execs chuckle. With one last toothy grin at me, he walks out of the room, the door slamming shut behind him.

⭐ *Ten* ⭐

I'm back in the practice room with Jason, but this time it's only the two of us. He has this huge bag of greasy, delicious-smelling french fries, and we sit against the mirrored wall, eating them and laughing. All of a sudden he turns to me and stares deep into my eyes. "I always thought your eyes were brown, but up close I can see gold flecks in them. I kinda like being one of the f—"

"EARTH TO RACHEL! WAKE UP, RACHEL!"

Huh?

My eyes fly open, and I see Juhyun's and Hyeri's matching dark-brown ones staring down at me from above.

"Oh my god, are you okay, Rachel?" Kyungmi says, her face popping into view between the twins'. "You totally got clobbered by that tennis ball!"

Am I in gym class?

When I put my palms down on the clay court and gingerly sit up, I hear a weird *click, click* sound that seems like it's coming from inside my head.

Oh my god, do I have permanent brain damage?

I turn around to see Coach Sloat grabbing Kyungmi's phone out of her hands. "Get out of here, Kyungmi. Five laps around the court!" She leans down to inspect the bump on my forehead and clucks her tongue. "You need to pay more attention on the courts, Rachel. You should go see the nurse."

"I can take her!" Kyungmi says, still hovering in the distance.

"Kyungmi! Laps! Now!" the coach yells over to her.

"No, it's okay." Juhyun stands protectively by my side. "We can take her."

Hyeri puts an arm around my shoulders and I follow the twins off the courts.

"Thanks, guys," I say as they lead me through the locker room. I catch a glimpse of myself in one of the mirrors. Oof. My eyes look glassy and unfocused and my forehead is a deep, bright-red color. This better not leave a bruise. I can only imagine Mina's delight when I show up at training with a purple forehead.

"Can you guys believe I just wiped out in gym class?" I say, shaking my head slowly.

Juhyun and Hyeri exchange glances. "Actually . . . we can," Hyeri says. "You've been out of it all week."

"Like in botany on Monday when you were singing while trimming your bonsai tree, but then you got so distracted trying to remember the lyrics that there was nothing left to trim," Juhyun says.

"Or remember in the cafeteria when you were practicing

dance moves in line and knocked Daeho's mandu ramyun right out of his hands? He smelled like pork dumplings all day." Hyeri smiles but quickly wipes it off her face and looks at me, concerned.

"Or in drama class when—"

"All right, all right," I say. "I get it. There's just been a lot on my mind these days. You know, training stuff."

And Jason stuff, I think, my mind flashing back to the tennis-ball-to-the-forehead-induced dream I was just having. But I don't mention that part.

"Well, lucky for you we have that school break coming up. You can recharge, relax, refine your bonsai trimming techniques." Hyeri is teasing me, but I barely hear her.

A break. Umma won't let me train on a weekday, even if there is no school, but I don't care this time. This is exactly what I need. No school, no training, no commitments. I can't wait to spend an entire day at home doing absolutely nothing.

"Unni, wake up!" I feel a finger poke against my cheek.

It's a week later and school is officially on break at last. I had big plans to sleep in, eat some fried chicken with Juhyun and Hyeri, then maybe binge *My Only Love Song* on Netflix for the rest of the day.

Another poke.

I groan and open my eyes just a crack. Leah's standing there in a plaid skirt and an oversize cream-colored sweater that looks suspiciously like the one I bought last month. She climbs into my bed and sits on top of me.

"Leah, oh my god, no talking, okay? Just sleeping. Shhh," I say as I close my eyes again.

"Unni, wake up please—it's important!"

"Leah, nothing is more important than sleeping in on your day off. Except maybe your little sister bringing you breakfast in bed in exactly three hours." I smile without opening my eyes and roll over, already dozing off again.

"Okay, Unni, I'll see you later." I can feel Leah moving off the bed, but something in her voice niggles at my heart.

I open my eyes and prop myself up onto my elbows. "All right, what's so important?"

Please say it's a Her Private Life *marathon. . . .*

"Welllll . . ." Leah bites her lip. "I won a contest. To go somewhere. With you."

"You did? But you never said anything—"

"I meant to tell you earlier, but you've just been so busy with training and school and . . ." She trails off, and I sigh as the guilt winds its way around my heart. I open my eyes wide and put on my silliest smile. "Well, that's why this is officially Kim Sister Day! We can do anything you want!" Leah grins, and I grab her feet, tickling her as she tries to squirm away. "Well, don't leave me in suspense! Where are you taking me?!"

"I entered the lottery for the exclusive NEXT BOYZ fan signing and WON!" She gasps as I continue to tickle her. "Can you believe it? We're going to the fan signing! Today!"

My hands (and my whole body, really) are frozen, and I stare at her, waiting for her to say she's joking. Instead, she jumps off the bed squealing and dancing around my room. Oh god. She's serious. Of course she's serious. This is Leah we're talking about. The future Mrs. Jason Lee.

"No," I say. "No way. Nope. We are not doing that."

Leah stops twirling. "Why not? You said we can do anything I wanted!"

I shake my head. "Anything except that. Come on, Leah. I can't go to a NEXT BOYZ fan signing!"

"Why not?"

I can think of a million reasons why not, reason number one being that I'm not so sure I want to see Jason any more than I have to. I get a weird swoopy feeling in my stomach every time he's around, and the more I see him, the more that feeling might come back. Or even worse, the more it might *grow*. I don't want to risk it. Not now—not when I'm so close to debuting. Jason already takes up way more of my brain space than I care to admit. If anything, I need to go on a Jason cleanse. But there's no way I can admit any of this to Leah. I'm already feeling guilty enough. I can't add "crush stealer" to the list of ways I've disappointed her recently.

"It's embarrassing," I say finally. "I'm supposed to be Jason's singing partner, not his fangirl."

"Yes, I thought you might say that," Leah says solemnly. The corners of her lips rise in a mischievous smile. "But did I mention that the fan signing is at Style Dome?"

Holy shit.

Style Dome is Seoul's newest by-invitation-only clothing

store. It only opened last year and there's already a yearlong wait list to shop there. I heard even Kang Jina had to wait two weeks just to get an appointment. The clothes are supposedly a mix of haute couture, high fashion, and vintage, with stuff at every price range and fashions for every style. Even the thought of stepping foot inside the store makes my fingers itch for a doodling napkin.

"I mean, if you don't want to go, I'll just give our spots to someone else . . . ," Leah says, stepping back toward my bed with a mischievous grin on her face.

"Don't even think about it, you demon!" I yell, grabbing her and pulling her back into bed with me. "I *guess* . . . we can go to the fan signing. But it's only because I'm the best sister in the world, understood?"

Leah screams, throwing her arms around me. "Yes, yes, yes, you are the best! I can't believe I'm going to meet Jason!"

And I can't believe I'm going to Style Dome!

Three hours later the excitement has worn off for both of us.

It was still dark outside when Leah and I left the apartment—a fact I hadn't realized when she woke me up at 4:00 a.m. But, according to Leah, even when you have a guaranteed spot at a fan signing, you still have to wake up at the crack of dawn because it's not enough just to *be* there. You have to be at the front of the line when you get there too.

There are already a handful of people in line by the time we get to Style Dome, and we settle in to wait, but Leah's so tired she keeps nodding off and dropping her poster—a giant handmade one complete with a photo timeline of Jason's journey from local Toronto YouTube singer to worldwide K-pop sensation and covered in glitter, pink washi tape, and handwritten notes.

"Here, let me hold that for you," I say, taking the poster from her.

"Thanks, Unni." She stifles a yawn, her eyelids drooping.

The line grows, winding down the block behind us, and I glance at my watch. Still an hour to go before the signing starts. "I'm gonna go get us some drinks at that café over there," I say, pointing across the street. Maybe some sugar will get her energy up. "Be right back, okay?"

She nods, her eyes half-closed.

I sprint across the street, poster in hand. I take a quick scope around as I enter the café. The last thing I want is for Goo Kyungmi to pop up and snap a picture of me holding some Jason Lee fan poster. Luckily, the coast is clear. Just a few early birds drinking coffee and an employee mopping the floor.

I order an iced coffee for myself and a strawberry cream frappé for Leah. Just as I step to the side to wait for my order, someone in a hoodie runs by, knocking right into me. I slip on the freshly mopped floor, the poster falling from my hand as I reach out to balance myself on a nearby counter.

"Are you okay?" a voice says from behind. Wait. Not just any voice.

Turning my head up, I see Jason looking down at me.

"Rachel?" he says incredulously, pushing down the hood of his sweatshirt.

"Hey." I smile, trying to use my foot to slowly slide the poster behind me, but he's too quick.

"Here, let me get that for you," he says as he swoops down and picks it up. He flips it over, a huge cocky smile spreading across his face.

"Is that for me?" he says in delight. "Handmade by *the* Rachel Kim herself?"

This can't be happening to me.

I grab the poster out of his hands, noticing a rip at the bottom of it. "I . . . it's not—" I sputter, tripping over my tongue-tied words. "It's my sister's. She made it. And she's here with me! I mean, I'm here with her. I wouldn't be here if she didn't want to come. It's school break and I said I would."

Oh god. Why can't I stop talking?

"So yeah. Got it? Let's just go through the points one more time so you really understand. The poster is my younger sister's. I'm only here because of her, and now it's ruined and she's going to be so—"

"Order number seventeen!" the barista calls.

Saved by the barista. I turn my back on Jason and grab my drinks, tucking the poster under my arm.

Jason grins. "Well, I gotta get to the signing. I guess I'll see you in line." He winks and jogs out of the café.

I make my way back to the line and spot Leah surrounded by a group of girls. I'm smiling, thinking Leah has made some friends in line, but as I get closer, I see Leah's arms are crossed and she looks like she's about to cry. "If your sister's really DB's 'best trainee' like you're always claiming, why did you have to come to a fansign to meet Jason Lee?" The group of girls around her bursts into a fit of giggles as Leah's face turns a deep red. "Your sister's probably the worst trainee they have—that's why they keep her so far away from the real stars like Jason."

I'm almost at the line, and I get a good look at the familiar heart-shaped face of one of the girls. My heart drops into my stomach. The girls from our apartment.

I march up to Leah, balancing the drinks in one hand and steering her forward with the other. With a smile I turn toward Heart Face. "The line is moving. You girls better get back to your place in the *back* of the line."

She scowls at me but starts to walk away. Suddenly, she whips around, a sickly sweet smile on her face. "By the way, Leah, thanks *so much* for telling us about this fansign. It's just too bad none of us wanted to go with you—although I might have reconsidered if I knew you didn't have any other friends to invite and would have to bring your sister!" She throws her head back in laughter as she runs to catch up to the rest of her friends.

I look down at Leah and her crumpled, tearstained face. "Leah," I say hesitantly, but she doesn't look at me, instead forging ahead through the double doors of the Style Dome. I trail behind her, the weight of what just happened settling into my shoulders like a backpack filled with bricks. Leah was too young to have much of a social life in New York, but I know moving to Korea made things even harder. Everyone at school knows who Leah is because they know who I am—the rumored DB trainee, the future K-pop star. Half of them want nothing to do with her because of it (K-pop fame—really any kind of fame—is way too nouveau riche for some of the snobs at our school), and the other half only want to use her to get the latest K-pop gossip or peddle conspiracy theories about me.

I'm barely paying attention as the line pushes me forward into the Style Dome. But as I look up, Leah's brush with her middle-school mean girls goes right out of my head. A huge glass-and-bamboo elevator cuts through the center of the store, which stretches up seven floors to a giant skylight. Each floor features a different color, from white on the first floor to black on the seventh. All around us, racks and racks of clothes are lined up in a perfect gradient from cream to pearl to ivory to blinding, fluorescent white so bright I can barely look at it.

I want to fling myself in it. All of it.

I'm so distracted that I don't realize we've made it to the front of the line. A signing table has been set up right in front of the elevator, all silky off-white with mini pom-poms and Lucite chairs.

Minjun notices me first. He taps Jason on the shoulder. "You didn't tell us your girlfriend was coming."

Jason smiles just as wide, wiggling his fingers in a wave. "Why, hello there, loyal fans. Fancy seeing you here."

Leah's entire body is vibrating next to me, and she elbows

me hard. I look down to see her face split into a grin so big I can practically see her molars. Looks like the mean girls are forgotten.

"Ouch," I say, rubbing my side.

She ignores me. "Unni, quick, quick, give me the poster!" she says, grabbing at my arm.

"Um . . . about that . . ." I hold out the ripped poster, hanging my head. "I accidentally ripped it in the café. I'm really sorry, Leah."

For a second her face falls. But then she smiles, squeezing my hand. "It's okay, Unni. It was an accident. Besides"—she whips out a roll of washi tape from the pocket of her skirt and starts ripping off pieces—"I came prepared."

She patches up the poster at lightning speed and eagerly slams it down on the table in front of Jason. "Jason oppa, this is for you. I wanted to show you how far you've come from your YouTube days and how you captivated the world with your singing and your glorious hair." She presses her hands together under her chin and beams. "I'm your number one fan!"

Jason pores over every corner of the poster. "I love it," he says in awe. "You even added a sticker of the Toronto Raptors! I need to take a photo with this."

He pulls out his phone and snaps a selfie of him with the poster. Then he smiles and waves Leah over. "How about a selfie of the two of us?"

Leah gasps, pointing to herself. "A selfie? With me?!"

She scrambles behind the signing table and leans in next to

Jason, holding up a finger heart as he snaps picture after picture of the two of them. I hang back, watching the scene. My heart swells. I haven't been able to give Leah much time since I started training to do this song with Jason, and she looks so happy right now—for that alone this trip was worth it.

Of course, it would be even better if I could take a look at some of these clothes while I'm here.

I'm about to slip away when Leah turns to me and says, "Unni, can I borrow your phone? I forgot mine this morning and I want some photos too!"

I hand her my phone and they take a few more pictures. I'm mortified as Leah starts calling out matching facial expressions ("Surprised face! Diva face! Now Jason Lee Number One Fan face!"). But Jason just does what she says, looking amused. Suddenly, he turns to me. "Hey, get in here. We should take a photo of the three of us."

"Me? Oh no. No thanks. Nope." I shake my head, hanging back farther. "This is Leah's day."

"I would love a photo of the three of us!" Leah squeals.

"See," Jason says. "Leah wants a photo and it's Leah's day."

She nods sagely. "He's right. It's Leah's day and I'm Leah." She runs over and grabs my arm, dragging me to stand between her and Jason. Jason passes my phone back to me and snaps a selfie on his own. Leah is cheesing, both her hands posed in finger hearts now. I smile as brightly as I can, but being this close to Jason is making my heart race. This was exactly what I was trying to avoid.

His arm is on mine and I sneak a glance at him, only to catch him looking right at me. He smiles. My stomach swoops.

Shit. Forget about heart racing; it's practically flying out of my chest now. Out of the corner of my eye, I see Minjun smirking at us and I quickly look away from Jason.

"All right, that's enough selfies!" I say a little too loudly.

"I'll send them to you," Jason says. "Let's add each other's numbers." I hesitate, and he raises an eyebrow. "We should have each other's numbers, don't you think? We do work together."

He has a point. Nevertheless, I roll my eyes at him as I unlock my phone and pass it over.

Behind us in line, a girl with green hair raises her voice. "You're not the only ones who are here to see Jason, you know," she says, clearly annoyed.

"Yeah, we want to meet him too!" a fan wearing a black NEXT BOYZ concert T-shirt chimes in.

Her friend, who's wearing a matching T-shirt in white, catches my eye and squints at my face. "Wait, isn't that Rachel Kim . . . from the video? She's the one who was singing with Jason!"

"Oh my god it is," Black T-shirt says. "Rachel, I love your voice!"

I blush, flattered. My first public recognition! "Thank y—"

"Can I get a picture with you and Jason?" White T-shirt asks.

"Wait, I want a photo too!" the girl with the green hair cries.

"Rachel, Rachel! We love you!" The crowd starts to swell forward, people screaming my name from all directions. I smile nervously, taking another step back behind the signing table and putting an arm around Leah.

"Is that bitch really Jason's girlfriend?" another person yells.

"You're not pretty enough to date him!" screams another.

Whoa. This was cool for about two seconds, but it's getting overwhelming real fast. The crowd is pushing even closer around the signing table, hands grabbing out to touch us, when Jason jumps to his feet. "Hey, cool it, everyone! Step back!"

His words get swallowed up in the chaos. One girl gets close enough to rip Leah's poster out of her hands. "Hey!" I yell, trying to pull it back—but it's no use. People are everywhere.

Suddenly, the NEXT BOYZ's security team rushes over, surrounding me and Leah as they guide us through the still-screaming crowd of fans. I look back at Jason, his face crumpled and distressed despite the throng of girls chanting his name, before walking through the Style Dome doors.

"That was so wild," Leah says as we're walking to the subway afterward, her face shining with excitement. "I can't believe some girl stole my Jason Lee poster."

"Aren't you upset about that?"

"What? No! It was awesome! We started a fan riot at the signing!"

More like a feeding frenzy. I grab her hand. "Come on, Leah. Let's go home."

Later that night, I'm lying in my bed, trying and failing to focus on my botany text—there's a big class trip to Jeju Island coming up, and only people with grades above a 90 will be going—when a Kakao message pings on my phone. It's from someone named Sweet Coffee Boy.

Jason.

Part of me wants to delete the messages and put my phone down, but my hand has a mind of its own and instead I find myself with a big goofy smile on my face as I scroll through all the selfies he just sent me. There's a ton of him and Leah and then a whole series of the three of us together.

For Leah's next poster ;)

I smile to myself, excited to show her the pictures in the morning.

My messages ping again.

Oh and . . .

One more photo pops up. My breath catches. Our faces fill the screen. It's a selfie he must have snapped right at the moment we were looking at each other, his lips quirked up in a smile, my lips parted in surprise to catch his eyes on mine. My finger hovers over the delete button on my phone. I

★ Eleven ★

Side step, hip pop, slide, and . . . No. Hip pop, slide, and side step right . . . or was it left?

I blow a strand of hair out of my face and glare at myself in the training room mirror. This is one of the easiest steps in the whole dance routine, so why am I having such a hard time with it?

The room is open to everybody for a block of free practice time every Friday afternoon. Usually I'm at school too late to make use of it, but the twins' driver offered to drop me off on his way to taking Juhyun and Hyeri shopping in Gangnam. It's crowded with trainees, including Mina, who's hanging out in the back, gossiping with Eunji and Lizzie. I hear Mina's loud laugh and look over my shoulder, catching her eye, but I quickly look away. I don't want to interact with anyone today. I just want to nail this move.

I take it again from the beginning. I study my reflection in the mirror, but all I can see is Jaehyun, our lead dance trainer, scowling at me.

know I shouldn't keep this picture—what's the point? What if someone saw it and thought something was going on between us when there is definitely *nothing* going on between us? It's just not worth the risk. But then one last message appears on the screen.

This one's just for you. Good night, Werewolf Girl.

My lips spread into a smile before I even realize it.

"All wrong," he shrieked at me at our last practice. "How can you mess up such an easy move? I don't understand what Yujin sees in you. Again!"

I kept my face stoic, refusing to let his voice be added to the symphony of harsh critiques that were playing on a loop in my head, instead starting again with as much energy as I could muster. He cut the music almost immediately.

"Nope. Wrong already. I can see you overthinking it before you've even taken a step. Start again."

I took a deep breath, trying not to grit my teeth. But Jaehyun noticed the frustration on my face.

"Look, if this is too hard for you, go home," he said, cutting the music again and storming over to me. "You think giving me attitude will make you a better dancer? Get your head out of your ass and try harder. If you can't even get these dance steps, you'll never get anywhere."

I still can't get his voice out of my head. It's like some horrible carousel spinning around and around in my head—the more I fixate on it, the more I mess up, and the more I mess up, the more I keep fixating on it. I collapse on the floor, seething at my sweaty reflection. I see Mina watching me, but for some reason her expression isn't as scornful as it usually is. She looks more annoyed and maybe a little bit . . . pitying?

I cover my face with my hands. I must look truly pathetic if even Mina feels sorry for me. It almost looks like she's about to walk over when the door to the practice room swings open.

The trainees all stare as Mr. Han walks in, and they immediately start whispering among themselves.

"What's an exec doing in a training room during open practice?"

"I bet Mr. Noh sent him to do his dirty work."

"Do you think he's here to kick someone out?"

"Sumin is looking kind of sloppy these days. . . ."

Lizzie straightens up, twirling a strand of hair around her finger and batting her big double-lidded eyes in his direction. I can't blame her. Compared to the rest of the execs, Mr. Han is like a Korean Chris Hemsworth. It would be hard to imagine him sitting around with a bunch of wrinkly old men in power suits if I hadn't seen it with my own eyes.

He strides across the room—oblivious to the fact that half the room is talking about him and the other half is staring at him longingly—and stops right in front of me. I stiffen. Wait—am *I* the one he's here for? The whispers stop as everyone watches us, not even bothering to pretend like they're not eavesdropping.

"Hello, Rachel," Mr. Han says cheerfully. He leans forward and lowers his voice. "You have a call from your mother in the main office."

I balk. "Is everything okay?"

"Oh yes, everything is fine. It sounds like she just wants to check in on you and ask when you'll be home for dinner."

The room erupts into quiet giggles.

I don't know which feeling is stronger at the moment: my need to leave the training room and never come back or my need to go to the main office and destroy their phone. Trainees aren't allowed to have our phones on us while we're on DB campus, so our parents call the office if they need to get ahold of us.

Not that anyone's parents ever do. That's like announcing to all of DB that your parents still treat you like a child. It's bad enough I live at home and go to school when most of the other trainees my age live at the trainee house and train full-time. This is just what Mina and her minions need to torture me for weeks on end.

I slink after Mr. Han, trying not to look at anyone in the face. As I walk past, I hear Eunji whisper, "Come on, guys, it's sweet. Her mom probably just wants to make sure she went potty today." My face burns.

Mr. Han pauses for a brief moment by the door to smile at Mina, who smiles back quickly. Lizzie raises her eyebrows at her, and Mina waves a hand. "He's a friend of my father's. We had him over for dinner last week," Mina says as we walk out the door.

"Um, thank you for coming to get me, Mr. Han," I say, following him down the hall. "I hope I didn't interrupt any important business."

"Not at all, Rachel," Mr. Han says. "I just happened to be in the office when your mother called, and I thought I'd pay you a visit. Don't worry. I understand," he adds, giving a nod toward the training room. "I have a nervous mother as well. She likes to call me five times a day. I keep telling her to text, but she complains the letters on her phone are too small. In fact," he says, hitching up his suit sleeve and glancing at his watch, "I think I'm overdue for a call." He smiles at me and I smile back, taking in the watch on his wrist—it looks vintage, the leather on the strap worn but smooth and the square gold face gleaming with just the right amount of patina.

"I love your watch, Mr. Han," I say.

He looks down at it and smiles. "Thanks. It was my grandfather's. He passed it down to me when I took over his position on the DB board of executives." He rotates his wrist toward me. "See the red rubies circling the outside of the watch face?" I nod. "He had those put in special to represent our family legacy. . . . 'There's no other family like the Hans,' he used to say. But I'll tell you a secret." He gestures to me, and I lean in closer. "I think he's just a huge soccer fan." He throws his head back laughing and I giggle along. I could get used to having an exec like Mr. Han around.

"So how are you feeling about the dress rehearsal on Sunday?" he asks as we continue walking. He raises his eyebrows meaningfully. "All the trainees, trainers, and execs will be there to see the progress you three have been making. Are you ready?"

I flash back to Jaehyun's scowling face. "Not exactly," I admit. At this rate, I honestly wonder if I'll ever be ready. A terrified shiver runs through my body.

"Keep practicing," he says encouragingly. "You'll get it."

I smile weakly. I really hope he's right about that.

The next morning, I brace myself for dance practice with Mina. I'm not too keen to see Jaehyun again, but I'll have to face him sooner or later if I ever want to nail these steps.

I linger at the door before practice starts, not wanting to actually step inside, but when I peek my head in, it's totally empty except for Mina, who's doing stretches by the mirror. She turns around when she sees me, putting her hands on her hips.

"It's about time you got here," she says. "Come on. Let's start."

I drop my bag on the floor, frowning. "Where's Jaehyun? And all the other trainers?"

"Getting massages and soaking in the hydro tubs at the luxury jimjilbang down the block," Mina says. When I raise my eyebrows, she waves a dismissive hand in the air. "I thought we could use some time to practice alone, so I had my dad send them a present for being 'such great support to his little girl.' They totally ate it up."

"But . . . why?" I don't even try to hide the suspicion in my voice. I take one step back toward the door. "I don't understand."

Mina sighs. "You're really going to make this difficult, aren't you? Listen. We both know you're struggling with some of the dance moves. And I haven't had the easiest time with certain parts of the song. So I had this idea." She crosses the room so we're standing face-to-face. I keep one hand on the doorknob in case she tries to pull something nasty, but when she speaks, her voice is earnest and even a little excited. "I was thinking, why don't we switch up some of our parts? Like, you can sing the verse that I'm struggling with and I'll dance the lead in the section you're struggling with. Everybody wins."

"Um, yeah, everybody but the trainers and execs who'll be pissed out of their minds when we go against their decision," I say. "Come on, Mina, you really think I'm going to let you trap me in such an obvious trick? You *drugged* me. You tried to ruin my audition. And you sent a *video* of the whole thing to my mother?! We both know I can't prove it, but you can't tell me you think I'm naive enough to do this. For all I know, I'll go along with it and then you'll tell the execs that *I* drugged *you* and forced you to dance my part. So just . . . leave me alone."

She rolls her eyes to the ceiling, but I see her cheeks go a little pink. "Okay, I did all that. Fine. You're right. I'm not going to apologize for it—"

I blow out a breath. "Big shock."

"But I promise I'm *not* trying to trick you now. I know everyone might be mad at first, but they'll see it's for the best when they watch our rehearsal. We've been training so fucking hard. Why can't we make one small change so that we can both play to our strengths?"

She has a point.

"Please." Mina clasps her hands together. "Can we at least try this?"

I hesitate. I notice for the first time how tired she looks. The usual gleam in her eyes has been replaced by dark, puffy eye bags and she keeps massaging her shoulders like they ache as much as I know mine do. She looks . . . like me. Determined but exhausted. I guess I'm not the only one on this wild training schedule. Everything I've been doing, she's been doing too.

"Okay," I say slowly. "Fine. We can try it out—but just for this practice. Then we'll see."

Mina lets out a deep breath, her shoulders relaxing. "Okay. Great. Come on, let's start with the dance move you're having trouble with. I've been watching you in practice and I think I know what the problem is. . . ."

There was a time when I loved Sundays—when Sundays meant sleeping in and watching cartoons with Leah all day. But this Sunday came too soon, and between the hours of homework I had to cram in and the extra hours of practice with Mina, I'm exhausted by the time the dress rehearsal starts that afternoon. Exhausted and also nervous—because the changes Mina and I made . . . they're really good. At least, I think they're good. The question is, will the execs love them, or will they murder us?

I peek from the wings of the stage, into the auditorium where all the trainees, trainers, and execs are sitting, waiting for Jason, Mina, and me to perform. I spot Mr. Noh in his silvery pinstripe suit and shiny black loafers talking animatedly with a man sitting next to him. Mr. Choo. Even without having spent the last few weeks staring at her face for several hours a day, it's easy to see how much Mina takes after her father. They both have the same wide forehead and sharp facial features.

"You ready?" Mina appears beside me. Her dress is a shocking neon pink, cinched in the middle with a bedazzled silver corset. A black ribbon choker with diamonds spelling out "Summer" is around her neck. It's almost identical to the one I'm wearing, which spells out "Heat."

I nod, clicking the heels of my white suede go-go boots, but my mouth has gone dry. There might not be any cameras here, but a room full of DB trainees and execs is almost as bad. Suddenly, I hear a high, cheerful voice shouting "Rachel!" behind me. I whirl around, and Akari is there, a huge grin on her face. She skips over to me. "It's all happening! I'm so proud of you! This is just the beginning of everything you've been working for—"

"Sorry to break up this little lovefest," Mina interrupts, stepping in between us, "but Rachel has to go now." She looks at Akari and gives a little sneer. "Some of us have futures as K-pop stars to worry about . . . not that you would know." She glances at me, turning her back on Akari completely. "Jason is about to start the fireworks," she says, and walks toward her entrance spot on stage right. Akari is still there, staring open-mouthed at Mina's retreating figure, her eyes lighting up with anger. I feel like it's been weeks since I've seen or even talked to Akari, and all I want to do is stay with her and talk shit about Mina, but I hear the opening notes of the song. "I have to go!" I say with an apologetic smile as I run toward my entrance spot. I cast a quick glance back and see Akari's smile wilt just a bit as she makes her way into the audience.

I shake it off, telling myself there'll be plenty of time later to catch up with my friend, but suddenly the lights are dimmed and Akari is the furthest thing from my mind as I peer out onto the stage and spy Jason's silhouette. The entire auditorium is silent, and I fight the nervous urge to chew on my lip. Can't ruin my makeup now. Then, all at once, the spotlight turns on and the music begins.

Jason spins around, launching into the first verse. He looks so cute in his fitted pinstripe suit and fedora that I have to close my eyes. The audience starts to clap in time to the music. Listening to his voice as it rides the upbeat melody of song, each note like it's as natural as breathing, feels like coming alive. My nerves seem to melt away, replaced by electricity and anticipation that hums in my veins. I want to go out there and sing with him. Just a few seconds longer . . .

Just before the second verse hits, the lights dim in the auditorium and Mina and I strut out, on cue. For a moment the audience is completely silent. I can feel their eyes on me. I can hear them thinking I don't belong here, I don't belong on this stage. And I freeze. But then the lights come blazing on and the crowd erupts—trainees cheering, a few stamping their feet and whistling, and I smile. I can do this. I catch Yujin's eye, and she gives me a wink. I hope she's still talking to me after this performance. . . .

The verse begins, and I do a choreographed catwalk to Jason, feet slinking in time to the music as I walk across the stage singing my line.

My new line, that is. To the trainers and execs, this was supposed to be Mina's moment. I can almost feel them freeze in their seats, trying to process what's happening onstage. I hear a few of them shuffle in their seats, whispering to each other.

"What the hell is going on?"

"Mr. Noh, did you approve this?"

Mina joins in a few lines later, and we step into the move that's been stressing me out for weeks. I glide to the back while she steps into center stage with Jason, and the two of them fly effortlessly through the sequence. Mina and I switch spots while the second verse continues, and I belt out the line that had originally been Mina's, my voice blending with Jason's in perfect harmony. Effortless again.

We launch into the chorus, and the three of us smile at each other. We can feel the energy onstage radiating out into the auditorium like lightning. In the crowd somewhere I hear Akari cup her hands around her mouth and cheer. Even some of the trainers are having a good time, singing along and snapping to the beat. But in the front row I can see Mr. Noh's face burning red as my lipstick.

I gulp. We may be lightning, but I can feel a different kind of storm coming after the performance.

As the song ends, the audience erupts into applause. Yujin shakes her head at me, but even she has an undeniable smile on her face. Mr. Noh simply rises and heads backstage, the execs quickly trailing after him. Mr. Choo follows, his expression unreadable.

Jason, Mina, and I take a bow and run backstage. I scream,

high on adrenaline, and Jason joins in, shouting and throwing an arm around both me and Mina.

"You guys crushed it out there!" he says, squeezing tight. He smirks down at us. "And thanks for warning me about that little switch you two did."

"Sorry," Mina says. "We didn't want you to rat us out to the execs." She rolls her eyes, but I can tell by her smile that she's teasing him.

I blush against the feeling of Jason's arm around me and quickly pull away. "You were great too!" I say. "Both of you were so—"

"Disgraceful. A complete disregard for authority."

Mr. Noh strides toward us, Mr. Choo and the execs marching in behind him, their faces all shrouded in darkness and anger. He looks like he's ready to explode, but before he can say another word, Mr. Han swoops between us, spreading his arms out and gathering me and Mina up in big hugs.

"Absolutely amazing performance! Incredible! We knew we made the right choice making a team out of you three. South Korea's biggest rising stars, right here. Plus the indisputable Jason Lee, of course." He shakes each of our hands with enthusiasm before turning to the other execs. "Their chemistry was killer, wasn't it?"

"It was . . . interesting," Ms. Shim admits hesitantly, glancing at Mr. Noh.

"What I saw was those two girls switching roles and going

against instruction," Mr. Lim says, arching an accusing eyebrow at us. "What is to be praised about that?"

"Nothing, certainly, if they had flopped the performance as a result," Mr. Han says. "But if anything, they made it even better. That's what I call innovative! The next generation of K-pop!"

Some of the other execs murmur in agreement, but most of them frown at Mr. Han's words. I glance at Mr. Noh, holding in a deep breath. The redness has disappeared from his cheeks, but his eyes are still flinty and narrowed in anger. He glances from us to Mr. Han in silence, clearly torn between wanting to scream at us for disobeying him but also not being able to deny anything Mr. Han said.

Finally, he looks right at me and Mina. "Keep practicing. I don't want to see it again until it's perfect," he says, and turns sharply on his heel and walks away, the rest of the execs in tow.

Mr. Han gives us a thumbs-up before following the rest of the execs out the door.

I exhale. I can't believe we pulled that off.

"Ladies, always a pleasure," Jason says, smiling at both of us. "Catch you two later? I just remembered there's something I forgot to tell Mr. Noh."

He waves and jogs off. For a second I stare after him, the minty, mapley scent he leaves in his wake winding its way into my brain, but I snap out of it once I realize Mina's talking to me. "Sorry, what did you say?"

Mina shrugs. "Just that Jason's a brave guy. I would not want to be around Mr. Noh right now."

"Oh, right," I say, desperate to change the subject. "Anyway, we should go change. And maybe get some patbingsu in the cafeteria to celebrate?"

"Uh, I'm not sure I can."

"Come on, we earned it. We must have burned like ten thousand calories on the stage just now."

"You go ahead," Mina says, glancing at the curtains. "I'll catch up."

I follow her gaze and see Mr. Choo still standing there, arms folded across his chest. I bow to him, feeling uneasy, and quickly make my way toward the changing rooms. Once I'm alone, I let out a little scream.

That performance was everything.

For the first time in a long while, I feel like I'm finally, finally on the right track.

My heart is still pumping with adrenaline as I unzip my black-and-white checkered skirt and scramble into my favorite green bomber jacket and black skinny jeans. I head back toward the auditorium, thinking about how I asked Mina to patbingsu. I laugh to myself. Two days ago, celebrating anything with Mina would have felt like a living nightmare. But hey, maybe this is the beginning of a new era.

I sweep my hair up into a ponytail as I step backstage to look for her. She never came to the changing room, so maybe she's still here. I hear a voice coming from the far side of the stage.

". . . absolutely shameful. How *dare* you disrespect the executives and trainers?"

I freeze and duck behind a large speaker. A few meters away from me Mr. Choo is screaming at Mina, his face even redder than Mr. Noh's had been.

"How do you think that reflects on me? If you're going to perform like that, don't even think about coming home or showing your face around me ever again."

Mina hangs her head and says nothing. I've never seen this side of her before. Any minute, I think she's going to snap back or look up with that devilish spark in her eye, but she doesn't. She just stands there and takes it, her shoulders hunched in shame.

"I don't know what I've done to deserve such a disgrace of a daughter," Mr. Choo says. "If you disappoint me like this again, there are no second chances. You will be no daughter of mine. Understood?"

"Yes, Appa," Mina says quietly.

Mr. Choo shakes his head in disgust and storms out of the room, leaving Mina behind him. She stands rooted to the spot, trembling all over.

"Mina," I say tentatively, stepping out of my hiding place. She immediately tenses and whips around, her eyes narrowing into slits. "Hey. Are you okay?"

"Whatever you heard, don't think this makes you better

than me," Mina says, fury snapping in her voice. Her eyes are filled with angry tears. "I don't need your pity."

"I don't think that. I just want to make sure you're all r—"

"It's none of your business!" She wipes at her eyes and pushes past me, heading for the changing room. Then she stops and turns around, a deep scowl on her face. "And by the way, we're *not* friends. So stop acting like we are. Just because we sing one song together doesn't mean I give a shit about you. Or that I want to go eat some fucking patbingsu with you in the cafeteria. This isn't a Disney movie, Princess Rachel. Grow up."

She spits out the last words and walks off the stage, as I watch the start of our new era fade away before it could even begin.

⭐ Twelve ⭐

"Everybody hold on to your loved ones! It's about to get wild!"

I nearly fly out of the Jeep as we go hurtling along the dirt roads through the Jeju mountains. The rough, rolling terrain is almost as up and down as my life has been lately.

After the mob at the NEXT BOYZ fan signing and the dress rehearsal on Sunday, I could barely bring myself to even think about training. By some miracle of late-night studying, though, I qualified for the botany field trip, along with Juhyun and Hyeri. So instead, I've been whisked away to the beautiful island of Jeju to marvel at the wonders of nature. . . .

And apparently, fear for my life.

"You're right. That was . . . ahh . . . bumpy," I say, laughing nervously at the driver next to me. Juhyun, Daeho, and Hyeri are sitting in the back seat, clutching the car handles.

The driver bursts into hearty laughter. "That wasn't the bumpy part. Here we go!"

Okay, so maybe this ride is more up and down than my

life. In fact, it probably makes my life look like a kiddie ride at Lotte World, spinning around in carefully engineered circles. I scream as we go racing down the road. The twins shriek in the back, totally exhilarated. Daeho looks like he's about to throw up.

The car swerves sharply to the left, and Juhyun bounces out of her seat, both her legs splaying up into the air, and lands right across Daeho's lap. I look into the rearview mirror and see Hyeri's face fall as Daeho blushes furiously. Juhyun giggles, rolling her legs back over to her seat.

"This ride is wild!" she shouts.

"Certainly the wildest," Daeho agrees, red to the tips of his ears.

Hyeri leans forward to the driver. "Ahjussi, you could go a little slower, you know."

"Don't you worry. I'm a veteran driver," he responds cheerfully. "Now, look to the left, everyone. Horses!"

I catch Hyeri's eye in the mirror and give her a sympathetic smile. She sighs and stares out the Jeep, resting her chin in her palm. My phone buzzes in my pocket, and I fish it out to see a new Kakao message from Jason. My own face goes as red as Daeho's.

Jason: Enjoying island life?

He adds a sticker of Ryan, the Kakao character of a lion without a mane, sitting on a beach chair and flipping on a pair of heart-shaped sunglasses. I grin. I happen to have the same pair of sunglasses perched on top of my head right now.

I snap a photo of the wild horses we drive by. They look content, flicking their tails as they munch on an overgrown field of grass and wildflowers.

Me: The best, obviously. Meet my new friends.

Jason: Jealous. Your friends are way cooler than mine.

He sends me a picture of Minjun making a peace sign as he fits an entire burger into his mouth. I laugh. Jason and I have been texting more since we exchanged numbers. I keep thinking I should stop, I should keep my distance, I should not turn into the next cautionary tale the DB rumor mill uses to scare newbies about how dating will get you kicked out of the program, and more than anything, I should not text back that Apeach emoji right now. . . .

But everyone knows that when you have the perfect Kakao emoji to send, you have to send it. And besides, texting isn't dating. It's harmless. It's meaningless.

I press my phone against my chest and smile as we bounce along the road.

Jason: Fun fact: I've been all over the world, but I've never been to Jeju.

Me: You're kidding. Does that mean you've never had the magical experience of eating a hallabong??

Jason: Had it, just not on the island where it's from. It's not the same, is it?

Me: Nope. You gotta have it on the island.

Jason: Are you eating one right now? If you are, I need a play-by-play. I'm talking peeling-the-orange-and-eating-it-one-slice-at-a-time-level play-by-play. Got it?

Me: No hallabong yet, but we're about to meet some haenyo divers. Almost as cool as eating an orange, right?

Jason: Just almost.

In true Seoul International School fashion, the students had their parents insist that the school put us up at the most luxurious hotel on the island for our field trip. It's the nicest I've ever stayed at (by *far*), with, like, five saltwater pools and a tropical garden on the rooftop, plus daily barbecues hosted on the hotel's private stretch of beach, all cabanas and cozy chairs for people to eat their juicy, perfectly well-done gogi in style. Inside, my classmates are bouncing in their seats, eager to check out the PlayStation arcade and the gourmet bakery in the lobby, but truthfully, of all the things on the field trip roster, I've been most looking forward to meeting the haenyo.

There are only a few of these legendary female divers remaining—the mermaids of Jeju, people call them, deep-sea diving every day, hunting through the ocean for abalone, clams, and seaweed—and we're meeting three of them here today. As they walk in, I watch them closely, taking in their graying hair, the deep lines that stretch across their faces. They're all in their late seventies and early eighties, but they seem to radiate a special kind of strength. They start to speak, and I lean forward, hanging on to every word.

"It is difficult to do this work," one of the haenyo says, looking at all of us with her hands spread wide, her words radiating across the room. "But we do it to support our families, to make a living, and to carry on a legacy. We are the last generation of haenyo, and we carry that proudly."

"Through freezing-cold waters and exhaustion that seeps through our bones, the most important thing for us is to remember that we are strong," the second haenyo says. I feel my body come alive with goose bumps. "We are courageous. We are powerful. When we feel like we cannot do this any longer, we remember that we already have, and we will again."

The third haenyo lifts her chin. She is a smaller woman with a curved back, but she exudes authority with every word she speaks. "It is crucial for us to remind ourselves of our own strength, especially as women in Korea. Who else will tell us this? Nobody. It's up to us to be independent, to tell ourselves the truth of what we are capable of, and to do everything we know we have the strength to do."

Unexpected tears well up in my eyes. I wipe them with the back of my hand and carefully store their words away in my heart.

Jason: Any pearls of wisdom from the haenyo?

Jason: Get it? Pearls? ㅋㅋㅋ

I roll my eyes but smile at his pun, then pause, fingers hovering over my phone. All of our conversations so far have been lighthearted at most. I'm not sure how to express anything deeper to him, and honestly, I'm not so sure I want to. It's one thing to send Kakao emojis and jokes about eating tangerines.

It's another to be vulnerable about something that's made a lasting impression on my heart. Something that feels so much like it was meant for me to hear at this very moment in my life.

I click my phone off without responding to Jason and turn to Hyeri, who's sitting in the beach chair next to me, gazing at the honeymooning couples lounging around us.

"They all look so happy, don't they?" she says, sighing. "Do you think Juhyun and Daeho will come here for their honeymoon one day?"

"Oh, come on," I say, trying to keep my voice light. I give her a playful nudge on the shoulder. "You know Juhyun doesn't like him like that."

"But Daeho *does* like her like that, and with his charm, it's only a matter of time before she falls for him too." Hyeri slides down in her beach chair, covering her face with her wide-brimmed hat. "I'm just a ghost to him."

"A ghost with top-notch computer programming skills!" I say, pinching her cheek for a smile. I think of Daeho's floppy hair and creased slacks and the way he keeps a laser pointer in his pocket at all times—even using it to give us an impromptu flower lesson during breakfast. *See that flower over there?* he had said, brandishing the pointer like a light saber and directing it across the hotel garden. *That's a rhododendron, the official provincial flower of Jejudo. Neat, huh?* Not exactly what I would call charming, as Juhyun had barely looked up from her phone, instead checking her YouTube stats for the island-themed makeup video she had posted the night before.

"To be honest," I continue diplomatically, "I really don't think he's Juhyun's type."

"Who's not my type?"

I glance up to see Juhyun walking toward us, looking stunning in a halter top and a pair of cargo capri pants, her long ponytail swishing behind her head. Only Juhyun could make capri pants look fashionable. I would just look like somebody's mom.

"Um, Kim Chanwoo from *Oh My Dreams*," I say quickly. "So not your type, right?"

"Yeah, he's way too Prince Charming for me," Juhyun says, wrinkling her nose. She peers down at Hyeri's hat-covered face. "Hyeri? Is that you?"

"Yes," Hyeri says, her voice muffled and miserable.

"Well, c'mon, I've been looking everywhere for you two." Juhyun lifts the hat off Hyeri's face and tugs her out of the beach chair. "I'm starving! Let's hit the buffet!"

The hotel buffet stretches down the entire length of the main banquet room, and we devote ourselves to it, piling our plates high with freshly caught salmon, asparagus, sautéed bok choy, and steaming heaps of wild rice mixed with chestnuts. I spy a bibimbap bar in the corner and make a mental note to leave room for seconds. Juhyun, Hyeri, and I settle into a table next to a young couple sharing a bottle of wine with their salmon dinner. Juhyun glances at the wine and whistles softly.

"Romantic," she says.

"Yeah," Hyeri agrees, casting a longing look in the couple's direction. "So romantic."

I sneak a glance, and it looks like the perfect romantic scene. The couple is dressed casually, both in soft-looking sweats and T-shirts. I can tell the woman has no makeup on behind her huge Chanel sunglasses, but even with ssaengul, her skin looks absolutely flawless. I'm kind of in awe. She's pulling off that effortless chic look that so many celebrities aspire to have.

I'm mortified when I realize that I'm staring openly at her face, and I look away quickly, but she hasn't noticed—probably because she's arguing with the man sitting across from her. Damn. Maybe it's not a perfect romantic scene after all.

"Why can't we just have a nice meal together without you bringing this up all the time?" she says, her voice full of rage despite the fact that she's talking in a whisper.

"Because you never want to talk about it. When are we going to have a real conversation about our future?" the guy presses. He's wearing a dark-gray T-shirt and has a buzz cut that would make most guys look intimidating, but somehow it makes him look softer. Or, at least, it makes the back of his head look softer because that's all I can see right now.

Their voices rise, and Juhyun and Hyeri glance over with concerned eyebrows. Suddenly, Juhyun gasps, clapping a hand over her mouth. She turns her head to us, dropping her own voice to a hush.

"Don't make it obvious, but look at that girl's nails. See the seashell-swirl patterns with the French tips? That's Samm's design."

Hyeri and I blink at her, and Juhyun sighs. "Seriously guys? Samm? The most popular nail designer in Seoul? She's so exclusive only the biggest stars can get an appointment with her! I would recognize her style anywhere."

Hyeri leans out of her seat to look at the nails, and Juhyun pokes her in the ribs. "I told you not to make it obvious!"

I turn my head more discreetly to sneak a look as the couple's conversation escalates.

"Now is the best time to talk about this," the guy insists. "It's been seven years. Your contract is ending. Negotiations are coming up. You don't have to keep living this way—the long hours, the labor, the constant stress. Now is the time to ask for what you want. What you deserve. Please! They treat you terribly. Why is this even a question for you?"

"You know our contracts don't work like that. Besides, K-pop is all I know. I can't risk what they might do if I make those kinds of requests. And I can't just think about myself! What about the fans? I can't let them down."

My ears perk up. K-pop?

"You'd rather let yourself down than your fans?" the guy says, shaking his head.

"Don't you dare make it sound so simple," she responds fiercely. "I can't just waltz out of Electric Flower like it's nothing. How can you ask me to do that? I would expect you of all people to understand."

Electric Flower? Suddenly a light bulb switches on over my head.

Holy shit. It's Kang Jina, the lead singer from Electric Flower. No *wonder* she's pulling off that effortless celebrity shabby chic look so well—she *is* a celebrity! I turn my attention swiftly to the guy. His voice sounds familiar, but I can't place it. For a second I think he might be her manager, but I look at the way he reaches for her hand, his fingers intertwining with hers. Wait . . . is he her boyfriend? My brow furrows.

Kang Jina has a boyfriend?

I think back to the Electric Flower interview Leah and I watched together just a couple months ago. As part of the no-dating policy, DB drills us girls on the party line: we're too busy to date; we're not looking to get married until we can dedicate our lives to our husbands—and like all of us, stars and trainees alike, Jina went with the program. I close my eyes, trying to recall her exact response.

Do you feel like you're missing out? the interviewer asked.

Not at all, I distinctly remember Jina saying. *I love being single! All I really need are my Electric Flower sisters. How could I be lonely with them by my side?*

Jina drops her napkin on her now-empty plate and pushes her chair back. "Come on, let's go outside. I need some air." I hear Buzz Cut say something about paying the bill as he moves away from the table and walks toward the front of the restaurant.

Jina sits for a moment, staring after him, and then pushes

back from the table. As she walks past us, she glances down at our table and I see her eyes go wide. She stops, cocking her head at me.

"Hey. Rachel Kim, right?"

Hyeri stares at her with her mouth open. A piece of bok choy falls from Juhyun's fork.

"Uh . . . that's me. Hello." I gulp and force a bright smile.

She grins back, lifting her sunglasses and winking. "I'm Kang Jina."

Duh.

"I recognize you from your viral video. Genius move." She laughs, laying her hand over mine on the table. "I wish I could have seen all the execs' faces when they saw it blow up."

My shoulders relax and a genuine smile spreads across my face. "It was epic. But terrifying. Please tell me how you survived DB for all these years."

Jina turns back to us, her smile fading quickly off her face. She leans in, lowering her voice and looking me directly in the eye. "You want my advice about DB?"

I lean forward, noticing Juhyun and Hyeri unconsciously leaning their bodies toward Jina as well. Jina's eyes flick back toward Buzz Cut's retreating figure.

"Never get a boyfriend."

I gape at her. Do I have *I can't stop thinking about Jason Lee* stamped across my face or something?

"What are you talking about?" I ask.

"Just trust me. You can't be a K-pop star and fall in love.

Having a boyfriend isn't just difficult; it's dangerous. Mr. Choo has Mr. Noh wrapped around his finger, and neither of them will ever shell out money for a female star that's anything less than perfect. Single and perfect."

Mr. Choo? Mina's dad? What does he have to do with anything?

Before I can ask more, Buzz Cut approaches the table, putting his hand on Jina's shoulder. "Come on, jagiya. It's almost time for your flight."

She smiles at him. "I'm coming." Jina gives me one last grim nod before disappearing behind her sunglasses and walking out of the restaurant.

As the two of them leave, I look over at Juhyun's and Hyeri's faces. They both look dazed, like they've been sitting out in the sun all day. Hyeri turns to us and grins. "I can't believe we just met Kang Jina!"

Juhyun lets out a breath and laughs. "Kang Jina?! I can't believe we just met Song Gyumin!"

"Song Gyumin?" I say incredulously. "Like, the lead singer of Ten Stars, Song Gyumin? Like, currently rumored to be recording a K-pop/American pop crossover duet with Ariana Grande Song Gyumin? What are you talking about?"

"Rachel," Juhyun says, shaking her head. "Didn't you see the guy Jina was with?"

I'm still stuck on the weirdness of the whole interaction later that day. All my classmates are on the beach in front of the hotel, playing volleyball as the sun is setting, their laughter ringing across the sand. I'm perched on a striped lounge chair near them, one eye on Hyeri and Daeho splashing around in the waves, one eye on my phone.

Jason: Still waiting for my hallabong play-by-play . . .

Me: I ate it too fast. I'm sorry! I only ate one. Okay, maybe three. Fine, four, I ate four.

Jason: Wow. I may have to change your nickname from Werewolf Girl to Hallabong Monster.

I pause typing, thinking about Jina's words. Is it really so dangerous for a K-pop star to fall in love? She makes having a boyfriend sound like one of Leah's movies with The Rock. . . . Also, how dangerous could it be if she's here on vacation with her boyfriend right now? And her boyfriend is also an international K-pop star? Ugh. My head is spinning. I don't know how to make sense of any of this.

I jump as my phone pings in my hand, breaking me out of my thought spiral.

Jason: Hello? You still there, Hallabong Monster?

Me: Still here. Just thinking. A lot on my mind. Things have been hectic lately.

Jason: Hmm. You know what you need? A self-care day.

Me: Self-care day?

Jason: Yes! A day to recharge and take a break from thinking about all the things you're thinking about. C'mon, you're from America! They're all about that over there.

I laugh.

Me: A self-care day sounds like exactly what I need.

A stretch of time passes before his next message pops up.

Jason: So let's take one. You and me.

Wait . . . he wants to take a self-care day? Together?

He adds a sticker of Ryan and Apeach rolling around in a field of grass, totally carefree. I bite my lip. I know I should say no. I've already gone too far just with all the texting. And now Jina's words won't stop swirling around in my head. *It isn't just difficult; it's dangerous.* I start to type "sorry, I don't think so" when he sends another message.

Jason: And obviously it wouldn't be a self-care day without Leah.

I pause. Leah's invited? She would never forgive me if she finds out I turned down an opportunity for her to spend a whole day with Jason. I think back to the day of the fansign and how desperate Leah was for someone to go with. All the times she's asked me to hang out and I've shut the door in her face because I needed sleep or I needed to practice. And now there's finally something I can give to her. Something that would make all my training worth it for her. Besides, if she's there, I don't have to worry about anything between me and Jason. I'll just be there for her. Not for him. I repeat this over and over to myself until I start to believe it, quickly typing back "yes" and hitting send before I can change my mind.

"Hey, Miss Viral Video!" Juhyun plops down next to me, handing me a coconut with a swirly straw stuck into it. "This field trip isn't going to last forever. Come have some fun with us, will you?"

I laugh as she pulls the phone out of my hand and tugs me up. I take a big sip of coconut water and follow her onto the beach. She's right. This part of my life won't be forever, and I'm going to enjoy these Jeju waves and this time with my friends while I can.

★ Thirteen ★

"Unni, hold me! It's getting bumpy!"

"Leah, we haven't even left the tarmac yet. . . ."

"Oh, right. That's just me." Leah stops bouncing around in the cushy beige seat next to me, her eyes continuously swiveling in her head to take in every inch of the private plane we're in, on our way to our self-care day with Jason. He wouldn't tell us what we're doing today. He just had a driver pick us up at 8:00 a.m., and next thing we knew, we were on this plane, with flight attendants waiting on us hand and foot, bringing bottles of sparkling water, cozy blankets, and charcuterie boards piled high with fresh fruit and Brie.

"This is officially the coolest day of my life," Leah says, popping a grape in her mouth after the plane takes off.

I laugh while my stomach does flips. Lucky is definitely part of what I'm feeling (not to mention unbelievably glam), but the longer we're up in the air, the more my nerves are getting out of control. A whole day with Jason. I've spent the last few days trying to convince myself that it's no big deal, that I'm really here for Leah, but who am I kidding? The butterflies in my stomach are clearly saying otherwise.

A few hours later the pilot's voice comes on over the intercom. "Hello, folks. We're about twenty minutes from landing." Leah looks over at me and squeals in excitement as the pilot drones on.

"The weather is one hundred percent sunshine. Thanks for flying with us and welcome to Tokyo."

Did he just say . . . Tokyo?!

As soon as we get off the flight, we see Jason waiting for us, looking effortlessly cool in sunglasses and a black tee. Leah breaks out into a run, throwing her arms around him in a hug. "Jason, this is unreal!" she cries. He laughs, hugging her back.

I approach more slowly, a cautious smile spreading across my lips. "Is this really Tokyo?"

He grins, opening the door of the car. "Find out for yourself. Get in."

We pile into the car, and the driver pulls us smoothly out of the airport and onto the highway. Leah rolls down the window and sticks her head out. We zoom past tall buildings with bright neon signage and blocky, minimalist-style houses on quieter residential streets. I can't believe it. We're really in Tokyo.

I pull out my phone to text Akari and tell her where we are, but Jason swipes it from my fingers. "Hey, hey, no phones on self-care day. Today is all about relaxing."

I feel guilty, but I let him pocket my phone. Between training and the school trip to Jeju, I still haven't had time to catch up with her since the dress rehearsal at DB, but I vow to take a mental snapshot of everything I see and add it to the massive list of things I can tell Akari about when we finally get to have our epic catch-up session.

Jason smiles at me like an excited puppy, and I find myself smiling back. "All right, self-care master. What's on the itinerary?"

"What else? Lunch!"

The car pulls to a stop. Jason climbs out, holding the door open for me and Leah. "Have you two ever been to Japan before?"

We both shake our heads, and he grins. "Well, then, you're in for a treat. Welcome to Harajuku."

I'm speechless. Everything is popping with color, from the Technicolor shop signs to the rainbow spun cotton candy people are eating as they walk down the street. And the outfits! I suddenly feel basic in my yellow sundress. Everyone here is striking in pink tulle skirts, retro knee socks, and dresses covered top to bottom in enamel pins. I admire a girl with ombre violet hair sporting a metallic varsity jacket and a purse in the shape of a Coca-Cola bottle.

It's official. I love it here.

Jason takes Leah's hand and pulls her into a restaurant as I follow behind them. It feels like we've stepped into a box of Crayola markers. A waitress with long sparkly eyelashes, wearing a bright-green wig, ushers us inside with a big smile and a grand sweep of her arm. "Welcome to the Kawaii Monster Café!" She leads us into a room with candy-colored chandeliers and pink-and-yellow striped walls. All around us there are giant plastic macarons and furry blue and purple lamps.

Leah squeezes my hand. "Unni, I think we're in paradise."

We scroll through the touch-screen menu and order way too much food: pasta with rainbow-colored noodles, chocolate chicken, sandwiches with multicolored dipping sauces, drinks bursting with edible glitter, and an incredible parfait topped with a slice of colorful roll cake and an upside-down ice-cream cone. I glance at Jason, laughing as the two of us order more and more food, convinced that he's going to transform into the Mad Hatter at any moment.

"I feel like I'm eating a unicorn," Leah says, digging her spoon into everything. "Should I feel bad?"

"Don't worry. It was most likely made by unicorns, not from them," Jason reassures her. I smile at him as Leah digs into her food, charmed by how good he is with her. There aren't many guys who would be up for spending an entire day with a thirteen-year-old girl.

Next to me Leah is polishing off one sandwich and starting on a second. "Slow down," I say, nudging her. "You're going to get a stomachache."

She dutifully puts down the sandwich and starts munching on some pink fries.

Through all the excitement of seeing Harajuku for the first time, I had completely forgotten about my nerves. But as I sit there with Jason's elbow mere inches from mine, my whole body starts to tingle—like that feeling you get when the blood rushes to your foot after it's fallen asleep. Or when you're doing something that you know you absolutely should not be doing but you can't bring yourself to not do it.

"So what do you think of this place?" Jason asks. When I don't answer right away, he pretends to look upset. "Don't tell me they have the exact same café in New York. After I tried so hard to find somewhere unique."

I tease him to cover up my quivering voice. "Oh yeah, I used to go every weekend. I basically grew up on rainbow carbs."

"You know what that makes you?" He leans in, dropping his voice to a conspiratorial whisper.

"Part unicorn?" I whisper back.

"Actually, I was going to say a leprechaun."

I burst out laughing, my nerves slowly ebbing away. Maybe I'm overthinking things. DB might control almost my entire life, but even they couldn't say that me and Jason watching my little sister gorge herself on food that looks like unicorn poop constitutes a date. Today can just be a fun, relaxing day with Jason. Jason, whose company I enjoy. Jason, who looks really cute digging into that glittery mac and cheese . . .

Get a grip, Rachel.

"Where are we going next?" Leah asks as Jason leads us down the busy street after lunch.

"Ever played Mario Kart before?" Jason asks.

Leah and I exchange glances. "A couple of times," I say. "Why? Are we going to an arcade?"

His eyes gleam with mischief. "Not exactly."

Fifteen minutes later, we're gearing up to get into actual go-karts to drive around the city for a real-life Mario Kart tour. Jason's even come prepared with hats: one in the shape of Yoshi's head, a giant Toad mushroom hat, and a blond Princess Peach wig with a crown fixed to the top.

"Princess," he says, placing the wig on Leah and bowing his head. She giggles, running off to inspect the go-karts. I grab the Yoshi head out of his hands.

"Hey!" Jason shouts, reaching for it.

"Sorry, I just can't pull off the mushroom look," I say.

He sighs and smiles, plopping the Toad hat on his head. "Oh, and I can?" He catches a glimpse of himself in a nearby window. "Actually . . . I look awesome," he says, shifting his head from side to side while adjusting his hat.

"Not even a giant rubber Toad can damage your ego," I tease, swatting at his head. Jason runs for his go-kart. "Let's see if the Kim sisters can catch me now!" he shouts as he slams his foot on the pedal.

Leah and I scramble into our kart, me strapping Leah into the seat in front of me. Just as I'm about to race after Jason, Leah rubs her stomach, turning her head to look at me with a grimace on her face. "Unni, I don't feel so good."

"Really?" I unbuckle my seat belt and lean forward to check on her, my forehead creasing in concern. "Should we stop and—"

Before I can finish my suggestion, Leah's cheeks puff up and—oh my god, I know that look—she unloads a wave of rainbow-colored vomit all over my dress.

Her face has turned to a pale green, and I quickly pull her out of the kart and onto the sidewalk, ignoring the barely digested remnants of mac and cheese and french fries stuck to my skin. A passing stranger shoots us a sympathetic glance, and I imagine we must look like quite the pair: a girl in a Yoshi hat with a big blond wig in her arms, squatting on the streets of Tokyo with vomit on our clothes. What a sight.

"Are you okay?" Jason pulls up, parking his go-kart next to mine. "I looked behind me and you guys were gone!" He glances from me to my dress to Leah, assessing the situation. For a second, I wonder if he's going to bring up my own puke disaster, but he simply pulls off his hat and puts an arm around Leah, rubbing her back.

"I'm okay," Leah wheezes. She presses her hands against her flushed face and leans in so only I can hear.

"Did I really just throw up in front of Jason?" she whispers to me through her fingers, mortified.

"Don't worry," I say, winking at her. "It's nothing I haven't done before."

"Come on, Leah," Jason says as his hands move to Leah's back, cradling her as he helps her gently to her feet. For the thousandth time that day, my heart catches in my throat. Jason turns to me and smiles before looking down at Leah, his eyes filled with such caring and protectiveness I would have previously thought only capable of existing in some K-drama universe. "I had them put the newest movie from The Rock on the plane for the return flight."

I'm going to need a self-care day to recover from my self-care day, apparently.

An hour later, we're back on the plane, the two of us wearing cheap cotton Mickey Mouse pajamas we grabbed from a street vendor. Leah's wrapped in a fuzzy blanket, sipping ginger tea and watching The Rock tear his way through downtown Manhattan on one of the plane's portable Blu-ray players.

Leah takes off her headphones for a moment and turns to us. She pauses, twirling the cord in her hands, looking embarrassed. "Sorry about go-karting, Jason. And extra sorry you had to see me throw up."

He gives her a warm smile and ruffles her hair. "Don't even worry about it. What else are oppas for?" Leah's face bursts into a wide smile and she snuggles down into her blanket. I pick up my Blu-ray player and start scrolling through the movie choices.

"Oh, *Kiki's Delivery Service!*" I say. "I used to love all the Ghibli movies. In New York, my best friend and I had a tradition of watching them with a bowl of chocolate pretzels." I smile, a wave of nostalgia hitting me.

Jason grins. "My friends and I loved the Ghibli movies too.

We used to fight over which was the best one—*Spirited Away* or *Howl's Moving Castle*."

"Definitely *Howl*!" I say, laughing.

"For sure," he agrees. "Calcifer is the best."

I try to imagine a Jason before K-pop, one who filmed YouTube covers in his bedroom and watched movies with his friends on Friday nights.

"Do you wish you could go back?" I ask.

He cocks his head to the side and arches his eyebrows. "In some ways, yeah. I mean, I was born in Toronto. No matter how long I live in Korea, there's always this part of me that feels like I don't fully belong, you know? I'm not Korean-Korean. I'm Korean Canadian." He pauses and looks at me, like he's wondering if he should keep talking. I give him a small smile. "And also, you know, half-white, which is this whole other thing." I nod in understanding and he continues, speaking faster, like these thoughts have been building in him for a long time and he needs to get them out. "I feel like I'm constantly straddling two worlds. Too white to be Asian, too Asian to be white. It's like I'm tricking everyone on both sides, trying to convince them that I belong, when truthfully, I'm not even sure exactly where I fit." He laughs, running his hand down the back of his head. "Sorry. Am I making any sense?"

"Total sense," I say. "I'm not half-white, but I feel the same way being Korean American. Sometimes it's like Korea doesn't fully accept me as Korean because I'm from America, but on the flip side, America doesn't fully accept me as American because of my Korean heritage. It's weird. It's like I exist in the in-between."

I don't think I've ever voiced these feelings out loud. At first I feel self-conscious, but Jason is looking at me and slowly nodding his head, like he understands exactly what I'm saying. Like he feels it too.

"I don't regret it, though," he says. "Coming to Korea and starting this whole K-pop thing." He pauses and flashes me a small grin. "Though I do wish I could have gone to summer camp at least once."

"For me, it's road trips," I say.

"Drive-in movie theaters on summer nights."

"Pep rallies."

"Part-time jobs at the mall with all your friends."

"Prom."

He laughs. "Yes! Prom! Why is that not a thing in Korea?"

"I know, right? People go all out in the States. Here, give me your phone."

He obliges, and I scroll through the promposal hashtag on Instagram. Leah's obsessed with these and we've spent more than a couple late nights watching videos of people asking each other to prom through flash mobs, balloon-filled lockers, and elaborate scavenger hunts.

"This one's my favorite." I show him a photo of a box of letter-shaped doughnuts that spell out "PROM?" Just looking at it makes me feel happy. "Total classic. Who expects anything other than regular doughnuts to be inside a doughnut box? It gets me every time."

"Seriously?" Jason cracks up, his nose crinkling with laughter. "Of all the romantic, over-the-top promposals, you like the one with the doughnut box?"

"What? It's genius in its simplicity! Plus, if they say no, you have an entire box of doughnuts to console yourself with."

He grins, shaking his head. "My mom would have been all over this kind of stuff. She'd probably hire a wedding planner to help me plan my promposal and then show up to videotape it herself. She was super extra like that."

My heart squeezes at his words. Everyone knows that Jason lost his mother when he was twelve. I look over at Leah, who's sleeping in her seat next to me. She's snoring softly, and I brush her hair off her face. Twelve. That's practically the same age she is now. I can't imagine Leah losing our mom at this age—much less having that fact broadcast to the entire world. I have the sudden urge to wrap my hand around Jason's, but I resist.

"She would be so proud to see you today. I know it," I say.

He pauses, turning toward me with a sad smile on his face. "You know, I think my mom would have really liked you," he says. His words surprise me, and I blink, trying to find the right way to respond.

"Why do you say that?" The moment feels fragile, tender, different from the ones we've had before. I search my head for something—anything—to tell me to change the subject, to not get too serious with Jason, too vulnerable. But I can't find it. Instead, I hold my breath, not wanting to break this moment between us.

He considers this. "Remember in the practice room, when I said I'm excited to sing with you? And I asked if you wanted to know why?"

I nod, at a loss for words. My heart is moving faster than my reason can keep up, and I don't want to say anything that I might regret tomorrow.

"I feel like I can be myself when I'm with you." He looks at me, and before I know it, he's wrapped my hand in his. "Whether we're singing or just talking like this." I can feel the warmth from his palm radiating throughout my entire body. He takes his thumb and rubs it softly over my knuckles. "I don't have to put on a show for you. . . . It just feels good to be around you."

By now my heart is speeding so far ahead of my brain I can't even see it anymore. Something about Jason's words have burrowed into my mind: *I don't have to put on a show for you.* With a slight start, I realize how true this feels for me, too. How much I've been putting on a show for everyone around me—the twins, Leah, Yujin, my parents, all the DB execs. Constantly being perfect Rachel, well-behaved Rachel, talented Rachel, sister Rachel, daughter Rachel. But with Jason, today, for the first time in months I feel like I've just been me. Rachel Kim. And it feels good.

I want to say all this to Jason, but something holds me back. Saying those words feels like heading down a path I wouldn't be able to turn back from. A path that would jeopardize everything I've been working toward for the past six years. My life with DB might not be perfect, especially now, but it's still my life. My family's life. And I can't turn my back on that. On everything they've given up for me. On everything I've wished for myself. Not yet.

"Your mother may have liked me, but what about your father?" I say lightheartedly, steering us back into joking territory. "I hope my impression is good enough to woo the whole family."

He laughs, but a strained look flashes across his face for the briefest of seconds. "He's a little harder to win over, but if anyone could do it, it would be you." His face softens again. "Rachel. I have to tell you something. I think—" He pauses, shaking his head and straightening the collar of his shirt. "I think . . . I mean, do you—"

Suddenly, Leah wakes up, yawning and stretching her arms across my body. "Unni, are we there yet?"

"Not yet," I say, grateful for the interruption. Whatever Jason was about to ask me, I know I'm not ready to answer it right now. "Keep sleeping."

She dozes back off, and I glance at Jason and smile. "We should get some rest too. Long day."

"Right." He gives me a half smile back. "Well, rest well."

I can see disappointment mixing with some other feeling

I can't quite pinpoint in his eyes. I turn my body away from Jason, half hoping he'll grab my hand and ask the question that he was going to before Leah interrupted us—but he doesn't. He doesn't say anything for the rest of the trip.

⭐ Fourteen ⭐

Kakao!

My phone pings with a message from Leah: Break a leg! followed by a whole cast of Kakao characters waving flags in the air.

I grin and send her a selfie of me sitting in the dressing room backstage, my hair sleek and shiny with hair spray. The room is buzzing as stylists, wardrobe fitters, and trainers rush around, preparing for DB's summer pop-up concert, featuring Electric Flower. It's also where Mina, Jason, and I will be filming the live music video for our single. It's hot in the crowded dressing room, but my skin prickles with goose bumps. When Yujin first told me we were going to film a music video, I didn't realize it would be a live recording. That means if I screw up, it will live forever on the internet. No retakes. No do-overs. I swallow. Nope. I'm not going to screw up. I won't let myself.

But maybe I could use a little luck.

"Just about done." The hairdresser smiles at me in the

mirror as she pins my floral headpiece into place. "Nervous for your performance?"

"No." I laugh. "Yes. Maybe a little?"

She smiles at me. "I'm sure you'll be great. You're singing with Jason Lee, after all! You're so lucky."

I gulp. "Um, right. Actually, would you somehow be able to add this to my hair?" I slip a sparkly red scrunchie from around my wrist and hold it up to the hairdresser. "It's kind of a good-luck charm."

I feel ridiculous saying it, but the hairdresser laughs, amused. "I think I can fit it into your updo."

Juhyun and Hyeri got me the scrunchie this past week in Myeong-dong. We were walking through the bustling streets, sandwiched between hundreds of shops and street-food vendors. Juhyun was on a mission for the perfect hair accessory that would put her YouTube following to over three million.

"I still can't believe Jason flew you and Leah out to Tokyo on a private plane," Juhyun said, shaking her head. "That is some next-level courting."

"It wasn't courting," I said, flushing. "It was self-care."

"How long are you going to sseom ta with him?" Hyeri asked, eating a twisty green-and-white ice-cream cone the length of her arm. "There's no point in denying that you guys have chemistry."

"It's not like that," I insisted. But even I know I'm not telling her the whole truth. Ever since our flight back from Tokyo, I can't stop thinking about Jason. I've gone through four bonsai trees in botany class, and Juhyun insists on being my doubles partner in gym every day, which really means I stand there while she runs around the court hitting every single ball. I've been so preoccupied. To be honest, even when I'm thinking about Jason, I'm not really thinking about Jason.

I'm thinking about Kang Jina.

More specifically, I'm thinking about everything she said to me in Jeju. *Having a boyfriend isn't just difficult; it's dangerous.* No one ever proved that Suzy Choi was cut from the program because she had a boyfriend. (In fact, just last week some newbie trainee whose mom works in the DB admin office swore that Suzy was cut because of a botched eyelid surgery). And then there's Song Gyumin. I mean, Jina was holding hands with him. In public! So how exactly is having a boyfriend so "dangerous"? It's not that I don't believe her. Or that I do. But . . . I just don't know what to think. And even if I did, I still wouldn't know how I felt about Jason. *And* even if I knew how I felt about Jason, I still wouldn't know what to do about it. How could a cute boy who loves Leah and says it feels good to be around me be a "danger"? But how could I risk my entire career—my whole future as a K-pop singer—on a boy?

Basically, everything is a mess.

"I shouldn't even be thinking about this," I said, waving my hands at the twins. "The music-video performance is coming up this weekend, and I'm freaking out. Do you *know* how many cameras are going to be on me at once?"

Juhyun paused, plucking up a sparkly red scrunchie off a

rack in the accessory store we were in. "Here. A good-luck charm, from us to you."

She slipped it around my wrist while Hyeri fished out her wallet. She winked at me as she paid. "We better see you working it onstage!"

I look at the scrunchie in my hair now. It actually looks pretty good with the rest of my outfit. It matches my lipstick perfectly and adds a pop of color to my checkered pants and black crop top. I'm K-pop meets the Queen of Hearts.

I snap another selfie, tilting my head to show off the scrunchie, and send it to the twins. I send the photo to Akari too, typing, Almost ready for the stage! With a little gift from the Cho twins. What do you think?

All the trainees are required to be at the concert, but I haven't seen Akari yet. In fact, I haven't seen her at all since I got home from Tokyo. It feels weird to go so many days without talking—and even weirder that she doesn't know I went to Japan for the first time last week.

I look at my phone and see the read receipts notification on the Kakao message, but Akari's reply doesn't come. I sigh, chewing on my lower lip. Maybe she's mad at me for not making more time for her lately. I'll have to make it up to her in some way.

"Rachel, this just came for you." Mr. Han appears by my side, holding a pink cardboard box tied with a glittery ribbon. He smiles knowingly. "Someone had it delivered to the dressing room."

For me?

I take the box, curiously untying the ribbon and opening the lid. Inside, a row of pale-pink frosted doughnuts in the shape of letters spells out GOOD LUCK, with an extra heart-shaped doughnut at the end.

A bubble of laughter bursts from my lips. Jason. The promposal. I can't believe he remembered.

"Who's that from?"

I clutch it closer to me as Mina peers over.

"I don't know," I lie.

She narrows her eyes suspiciously. A few of the trainers and execs are also staring at me with questioning looks. Jaehyun, our dance trainer, raises his eyebrows and says, "That's cute, Rachel." He comes over and peers inside the box. "Is that a . . . heart?"

For the millionth time in the last few weeks, Kang Jina's words spring to my mind. Despite all the conflicting thoughts swimming around my brain, a nervous pit starts to form in the bottom of my stomach. I'm about to go onstage and sing with Jason. I'm about to make a music video with Korea's most popular K-pop star. Now is not the time to give any of the trainers—or anyone at DB—a reason to doubt me. Not when I'm so close to my goal. The goose bumps on my skin fade away, replaced by a deep flush that stretches from my face down to my feet.

Shit, shit, shit. What do I say?

"They're from me," a voice says. I turn my head to see

Akari walk into the room, a breezy smile on her face. "A good-luck present for my best friend."

The execs and trainers relax, their smiles brightening and the suspicion fading from their faces. Mina shrugs and turns away. I look to Akari gratefully, rushing over and wrapping her in a hug.

"Akari, it's so good to see you! I've missed you!"

"It's so good to see you too. It feels like it's been forever." She hugs me tight and then steps back, a curious tilt to her smile. Nodding to the doughnut box, she lowers her voice. "So who's it really from?" she asks.

I hesitate, caught off guard by her question. "I'm, um, not too sure," I stumble to answer.

I'm still not ready to talk about Jason out loud. Not until I can untangle this knot of emotions inside of me, which only seems to become more tangled every time I think about him.

"Got it," she says. There's an awkward beat between us. Her arms hang by her sides and she touches her elbow, look-ing away. Then she looks back at me and smiles, her tone light again. "There's a card," she says, pointing to the box. "Maybe that'll solve the mystery." Her fingers move as if to take it, but I grab it quickly, clutching it in my hand. My fingers shake a little as I open it. There's no signature, only a short message: *Meet me backstage.*

He wants to see me. Here, right now. My stomach flips into my heart, and I know I want to see him too.

"Sorry, Akari, I just have to . . . check on Leah real quick,"

I say, flashing her an apologetic smile. Her own smile fades, and I feel a stab of guilt as I rush out of the dressing room. One more thing to make up to her.

Electric Flower is starting their performance as I run across backstage. From behind the curtain, I catch glimpses of the crowd waving glowsticks in the air with Leah right up front, singing along and recording everything on her phone. I see Kang Jina, center stage, looking flawless in a metallic blue jumpsuit. Her words from Jeju start to bubble up again, but I push them back down.

And then I see him. Jason.

He's standing in a secluded corner backstage, watching the performance. He's dressed in his costume, relaxed black joggers, paired with a perfectly fitted, light-gray sweatshirt. As if sensing me, he turns his head just as I approach him. He smiles, and there's a nervousness in his face that I've never seen before.

"Hi," I say.

"Hi." He bounces his fists against each other, looking down at the ground and then back up at me with a shy smile. "Did you like the present?"

My heart swells at his uncertainty. Inside I'm screaming, *Yes!* But instead, I just nod. "I did. I loved it."

His face lights up. "I'm glad." He takes a deep breath and steps forward, lightly touching my hand. When I don't pull away, he slips his fingers through mine, pressing our palms together. "Listen. I don't want to pressure you if you're not ready to talk about this. About us. On the plane, it just seemed like . . . like you knew what I wanted to say but you didn't want me to say it."

In that moment, with his skin touching mine, I can almost feel my worries melting away. I want so badly to choose him. For a moment it seems possible, as all the threads in my mind start to untangle, but instead of making my choice easier, they're pulling in opposite directions and I don't know which way to follow. I glance toward the stage, at Kang Jina and Electric Flower, out at the audience to Leah, and then back at Jason. For the last six years, being a K-pop star is all I've dreamed of. All I've wanted.

But what if that isn't enough anymore? What if the endless hours of training and sacrifice, the tired bags under Appa's eyes, the strain in Umma's voice, the sad look on Leah's face just aren't worth it? What if I need more from life than a stage and a song? I look at Jason and I know. "You're right. I wasn't ready then. But I am now." My voice is raw. He squeezes my hands, unfiltered hope shining out of his eyes. "I want to take a chance with you."

And yet. I pull away as Electric Flower launches into their most popular single of the year, "Starlight River." I might be ready to take a risk by dating Jason, but I'm definitely not ready to do it publicly. "Just . . . not here, not with all these people around."

He takes a step forward, closing the gap between us. He's so close, I can feel his chest rising and falling with each ragged breath. "What are you afraid of?"

All of a sudden, everything goes dark as a giant black cover floats down over the stadium, enveloping the whole place in an inky nightfall. LED starlight explodes across the cover as Electric Flower continues to sing onstage. The audience lets out a collective gasp, waving their glowsticks in wonder as the entire stadium is blanketed in pinpricks of sweeping light.

Jason doesn't take his eyes off me. And other than the faint touch of starlight on his cheekbones, we're cloaked in darkness where we stand. He cups one hand gently against my face, and I let my eyes close as I lean in.

I feel his lips press softly against mine. Warmth floods through my entire body as he moves his hand to the back of my neck, sparking in my stomach and out to my fingertips.

If I thought singing with him was magic, this is something else entirely.

My breath hitches as his hands slide down to my waist, pulling me in closer, and I wrap my arms around his neck. His lips part, and the scent of him pins itself to my heart as I open my mouth to breathe him in. Maple and mint.

I barely register the sound of the audience screaming with applause as Electric Flower ends their set. The starlight cover lifts and daylight streams back into the stadium. I pull away from Jason just as the light floods the space between us. He looks as dazzled as I feel.

"We're up next," I whisper.

"Right," he says, his voice raspy.

"There you two are!" We both turn to see Mina marching

toward us, her stilettos clicking rapidly against the stage floor. "Come on, come on, let's get ready."

My lips still tingling as I hurry to join Mina, I turn my focus to the performance, but my mind is lingering on that kiss.

The kiss. Holy shit. I just kissed Jason.

The MC's voice booms out across the stadium. "Introducing the first-ever performance of their new single, 'Summer Heat,' please welcome Jason Lee with Rachel Kim and Choo Mina!" I can hear Leah from her front-row seat, cheering and applauding along with the rest of the audience. Mina saunters out, basking in their adoration, and I'm about to follow when I feel a hand on mine. I turn to the side, and Jason smiles at me, giving my fingers a squeeze. I squeeze back and quickly drop his grip as the two of us walk out onto the sunlit stage.

In this moment, I feel like I could face a thousand cameras.

✦ Fifteen ✦

For most families, summer in Korea means swan boating in the Han River, fireworks at Haeundae Beach in Busan, and watching the parade of lanterns on Buddha's birthday. But for my family it means one thing: naengmyeon.

Four bowls of the ice-cold noodles are spread across our table, each one topped with thin slices of pear, cucumber, beef, and half a hard-boiled egg, except for mine, which is cucumber-free. Umma rings the buzzer on our table to ask the waiter for extra pear slices for Leah like she always does. Appa fishes out the excess ice shavings floating in his broth and plops them in my bowl like he always does. All that ice makes his teeth chatter, while I like mine extra-chilled.

"Rachel, you've been glowing lately," Appa says, beaming at me from across the table.

"I'm not surprised. Her performance last week was amazing," Leah says. She squeezes an extra shot of vinegar into her bowl before slurping up a huge helping of noodles. "It was the highlight of the whole concert! And I'm not just saying that because we're sisters. Unni was born to be onstage."

I grin. "Thanks, Leah."

Umma says nothing as she jabs at her naengmyeon with a pair of scissors. Truthfully, she's barely said a word to me since that day Mina sent her the video of me drunk at the trainee house. A small lump forms in my throat when I think of Leah bursting into our apartment after the concert, screaming about how amazing it all was—how we hit every note, every step, and had the entire stadium on their feet clapping along. But Umma didn't even smile or say congratulations. She just looked at me and said, "I imagine DB will be announcing the Family Tour any day now."

I swallow hard, forcing down a bite of egg.

Just then, my phone buzzes, and I peek at the screen under the table.

Hey, are you tired? 'Cause you've been running through my mind all day. A gif of an exploding heart pops up next to the message.

I snort. It turns out, unsurprisingly really, that Jason is the prince of cheesy pickup lines. He sends me ridiculous texts like this at least three times a day, but I'd be lying if I said I didn't love it.

Appa raises his eyebrows. "Everything okay, Rachel? You're smiling like you won the lottery."

"It's nothing," I say. But he's right. My smile is so big my cheeks hurt. I tuck my phone away and try to focus on my family. It's been a while since Appa's come home early enough to eat dinner with us. Between late nights at the gym followed by even later nights studying, the dark bags under his eyes have reached ultimate panda level. I can tell Umma is worried about him by the way her eyebrows pinch together every time she glances over between bites of naengmyeon. Like she wants to make sure he hasn't floated away in the middle of the meal.

As tired and stressed as they are, they're both smiling and nodding along at Leah, who has somehow mastered the skill of carrying on a conversation without missing a beat while simultaneously scrolling through her phone, liking Instagram photos and reading her favorite K-pop gossip blogs. It's disturbingly impressive.

While Leah jabbers on about Kim Chanwoo's recent bout of amnesia on *Oh My Dreams*, my mind wanders to a couple days ago, when Jason and I snuck away to a movie theater he'd rented out for us for a few hours after practice. (One great thing about Korean culture is that it makes secret relationships pretty easy to maintain—there are private movie rooms, private karaoke rooms, and private dining rooms at most restaurants). We could select whatever we wanted to watch. Jason suggested *Train to Busan*, but I've never been a huge fan of the zombie apocalypse and convinced him to watch *Say Anything* instead. It came out before I was even born, but it was Umma's favorite movie and we used to watch it together in New York. I've seen it thirty times, at least. Thirty-one now, with Jason—and I'm still a sucker for John Cusack holding a boom box outside Ione Skye's window.

"Do you want me to serenade you like that?" Jason asked, his arms wrapped around me on the couch as he bent down to kiss the tip of my nose.

"Of course," I said, deadpan, giving him my most serious look. "But do you think you'd be able to pull it off? I mean, holding a boom box and standing still. That's not easy. It's a whole league above K-pop dancing."

He deadpanned back at me. "You doubt my serenading abilities? You sure know how to cut a guy to the core, Rachel Kim. Come on, let's go right now—I'll serenade you in the street."

I burst out laughing, sure he was joking, but he was already up and dragging me toward the door. "Jason, stop!" I almost shouted. "We can't go outside together! Why do you think I insisted on meeting here in private? You know how strict DB is about the no-dating rule!"

Jason laughed, brushing it off. "Those rules aren't really enforced. They just say that to scare us and keep us on track. Trust me." He squeezed my shoulders. "We'll be fine."

I raised an eyebrow skeptically. Part of me wanted to believe him and cast aside Kang Jina's warning, but I have six years of DB media training and dance practice and the endless hours of wall sits we've all endured on my side. Just being there with Jason was risky enough. I couldn't afford to take any more.

"Jason," I said, "I'm not sure what world you're living in, but I really don't think DB would—"

"Rachel," Jason cut in, giving me a smile that made my stomach feel like it was floating away. "I don't want to go anywhere else. Why would I? When I could be here. Alone. With you." He took a step toward me, and we tumbled back onto the leather couch, Jason's hands tangled in my hair as he leaned in to kiss me. . . .

"Unni, hello? Did you hear me?"

"Huh?" I snap back to the naengmyeon restaurant, where Leah is looking at me with wide eyes. Her face has gone completely pale, like she's just seen a ghost.

"I said, did you know about this?" She holds up her phone. "Kang Jina is leaving Electric Flower!"

The goofy smile drops off my face. "What?"

I grab the phone from Leah's hands and scroll through the articles she has open on her screen. Every headline is the same: KANG JINA SAYS GOODBYE FOREVER TO ELECTRIC FLOWER. KANG JINA LEAVES DB ENTERTAINMENT. WHAT'S NEXT FOR DIVA QUEEN KANG JINA?

Leah grabs her phone back from me and clears her throat. "Listen to this, Rachel." She starts quoting one of the articles. "Kang Jina has made the difficult, but necessary, decision to not re-sign with legendary K-pop girl group Electric Flower at the end of her seven-year contract, which is the legal maximum term for entertainment contracts in Korea. While the rest of her Electric Flower bandmates have signed new three-year contracts, Jina is reported to be leaving K-pop behind for good. 'The luxury, the clothes, the wealth,' says an anonymous source and close friend of Jina's. 'It was all going to her head, and she realized she had to step down now before she got too out of control. She said she couldn't even recognize herself anymore. She was becoming a K-pop monster.'"

"Can you believe this?" Leah says, lowering her phone. "What's Electric Flower going to be like without Kang Jina?"

I shake my head. I'm speechless. My brain rushes back to Jeju and the first time I met her. She didn't seem like she was an out-of-control diva. If anything, she seemed pretty low-key, just a girl trying to enjoy a glass of wine on vacation. But what do I know? Maybe after that one bottle of wine, she went out and bought fifty more.

Still, I feel a sour taste in my mouth as Leah continues reading about Kang Jina and Electric Flower, and it's not from the naengmyeon.

Hey, Werewolf Girl. If I remember correctly, you should be starting free period right about now. True or false?

I lean against my locker and grin, typing back quickly. Jason's pretty much memorized my school schedule so we can talk on the phone during my breaks. It's even better than that time last year when the school brought in puppies during finals week to help us relax between exams.

True. Want to FaceTime?

I actually had a different kind of "FaceTime" in mind.

My phone pings again, and I look, expecting another text

from Jason, but it's a message from Hyeri. Could you come out to the rose garden?

The rose garden? Sure, I type back, worried that I'll find her there crying over Daeho.

I run through the school's outdoor lounge and across the soccer field, searching for Hyeri as I approach the empty gardens that border the school's property lines. My phone pings again. It's Jason.

Turn around.

I whirl around and see him standing underneath the rose archway. As soon as he sees me, he lifts his phone into the air, holding it horizontally with both hands like a boom box.

A huge smile spreads across my face. "Jason," I say, walking toward him. "What are you doing?"

"Serenading you," he says, and hits play on his phone. "In Your Eyes" starts playing, and then he's John Cusack and I'm Ione Skye and this is officially the best moment of my life.

He grins. "Am I dreamy or what?"

I laugh, my heart skipping several beats in my chest. Suddenly, though, I hear the bell ring for next period, and I realize that Jason and I are completely out in the open. Where anyone could see us. A nervous sweat begins to build on the back of my neck, and I grab Jason's hand, forcing him to duck behind the rosebushes.

"Jason! This was a very bad idea. What if someone sees us?" I whisper-shriek, the sweat now spreading down my back.

"Don't worry about it! Hyeri is standing guard at the door,

telling everyone the rose garden is closed for a private assembly," he says as he wiggles his eyebrows at me.

I resist the urge to giggle and instead roll my eyes. "Okay, but that doesn't mean that people aren't still out here. Or that they can't see us from the second- and third-floor windows. Come on," I say as I pull him up. "Follow me."

I lead him into the school, glancing around the corners of the hallways. The coast is clear, and I hurry him to the music room. It's always empty this time of day.

Only when the door is safely closed behind us and I've drawn the curtains that look outside do I let myself step into his outstretched arms, pressing my face against his chest, nearly melting into him. This is so much better than FaceTime.

"I can't believe you're here," I say.

"Well, I never did get to go to high school." He smiles and tucks a strand of hair behind my ear before spying a guitar in the corner of the room.

"Perfect. Now I can serenade you for real," he says as he grabs it, looping the strap over his shoulder. "Taking song requests on Jason Jukebox. What would you like to hear?"

I shake my head and giggle. "Ooh, how about that great song 'Love Letters Start With U,'" I tease, naming NEXT BOYZ's classic debut song. I take a seat on the piano bench and cross my legs, waiting expectantly as he finishes tuning the guitar.

He strums the chords and starts to sing. "Let me write a letter, baby, and seal it with a kiss. It starts with U and ends with U 'cause you're the one I miss ooooooh."

He's hamming it up, making goofy, exaggerated facial expressions as he sings, but he still sounds amazing, especially with the guitar. I almost forgot that he played. He used to sing with it all the time when he did his YouTube covers, but now he mostly just sings and dances with NEXT BOYZ, sans guitar. It's wild how effortlessly good he is, strumming like he doesn't have to think twice about it.

"Next song on Jason Jukebox!" I say. "Something sweet and classic."

He seamlessly transitions into the next tune. "I'll be your dream, I'll be your wish, I'll be your fantasy, I'll be your hope, I'll be your love, be everything that you need."

I crack up. Of course, what's more classic than Savage Garden?

"I don't know if you can top that one," I say between my laughter.

A gleam lights up in his eyes. "Okay. How about this one?"

He slows down, strumming a melody that I've never heard before, but it hooks me instantly.

"I'm back and forth, the push and pull, I'm falling fast and floating free. I'm a glass half-empty or half-full, caught in between two galaxies."

The music is soothing and grounded, and the lyrics more indie than anything he's played so far.

"Am I a sandcastle king or a lost boy from the sea? I'm none and everything, a me that's only me. I am the shore."

He strums the final chord, and I let out a deep breath.

I feel like I'm coming out of some sort of trance. "That was really beautiful. Who's it by?" I ask.

He smiles shyly, placing the guitar back on the stand. "Actually, I wrote it. Ta-da. It's a Jason Lee original."

My mouth drops open. "I didn't know you wrote songs." Even as I say it, I remember how Jason reacted when I teased him at Kwangtaek about K-pop stars never being allowed to write their own lyrics. "How did I never know this?"

"Songs like this aren't really DB's style." He shrugs like it's meaningless, but the tightness in his smile gives his true feelings away. "To be honest, though, it's the kind of music I really want to sing. Something that has meaning to me, that reflects my real-life struggles. Like this song and how I always feel torn between these two identities." He pauses, glancing at me. "Not that I don't appreciate NEXT BOYZ or DB or everything they've done for me. It's just not the same, you know?"

"Jason, you don't have to explain—"

But before I can finish responding, the door flies open. Jason and I jump as the Cho twins burst into the room, both of them gasping hard and holding their phones.

"See, I told you she'd be in here," Hyeri says triumphantly, wheezing as she tries to catch her breath.

"How did you two find me?" I say, shocked.

"Well, you weren't in the rose garden, so we thought maybe you guys had snuck in here, K-pop stars that you are." Hyeri grins. "You're both welcome, by the way." She gives a small

bow. "Jason, my skills at subterfuge texting are always at your disposal."

Jason grins back.

"Okay, okay, okay, that's not what's important right now," Juhyun says, pushing past Hyeri. She passes her phone to me, her face lit up with excitement. "DB dropped the 'Summer Heat' music video an hour ago, and it already has over twenty million hits. Everybody loves your song."

Holy shit.

I had no idea this was coming out today, and judging by the expression on Jason's face, he didn't either. We crowd around Juhyun's phone to watch. There's Jason in his sweatshirt. And Mina in her pink dress. And me.

Me! In HD video! ("That scrunchie looks so damn good on you," Hyeri says. "You're welcome again!")

Even as we're watching, the views are ticking up. I can't believe this. Is this real life?

"It's already soaring through the Top 100 list," Juhyun says.

"No," I say quietly, stunned into disbelief.

"Yes!" she says back.

I'm frozen. Around me, the twins start dancing to the music, singing along and cheering. Jason hugs me, lifting me right off my feet and swinging me around.

People love the music video. They love us. *Me*. I've worked so hard for six years and finally, *finally*, it's paying off. As Jason lowers me back down, an unstoppable smile spreads across my face.

"We need to celebrate!" Jason says, putting his hands on

my shoulders and looking me right in the eye. "You and me. A real date."

The twins stop jumping and stare at us like they're watching a K-drama.

I hesitate, the happiness I was feeling popping like a soap bubble. Of course I want to celebrate with Jason, but . . . how? It's just not possible. I shake my head slowly. "Jason, we've talked about this. We can't. If we go out in public together, people will definitely recognize us. Especially now." I nod toward Juhyun's phone.

"Okay," Jason says, giving in to the skeptical look on my face. "So what you're saying is, we can go on a date as long as people don't recognize us?"

"Jason," I say with an exasperated sigh, "you're, like, the most famous person in Korea. How do you imagine no one will recognize us?"

He grins at Juhyun, whose face lights up with understanding. She grabs my shoulders and plops me down in a chair, already rooting through her purse. "Just leave it to me," she says with a wicked smile. "You two won't even recognize yourselves when I'm done with you."

★ Sixteen ★

Our first stop at Lotte World is the toy stall where they sell balloons, bubble wands, and inflatable hammers that squeak as you bounce them off other people's heads. Not that I would even recognize which head belonged to Jason, as Juhyun was absolutely true to her word, and I do another double take at Jason's heavily made-up face (all pure white foundation covered in large black and red polka dots) as he buys two hammers from the unsuspecting young woman working the stall.

"Bam," he says. "Disguised and souvenired. Ready to have fun now?"

I grin through my own makeup—streaks of rainbow-colored lightning stretching from the corner of my chin to the top of my forehead, bursting with metallic stars covered in shimmery glitter. "Ready."

I take in the smell of spun sugar, the lights glittering at us from the Camelot Carousel, the music blasting out over the speaker, and smile to myself. I haven't been to Lotte World since

I was a kid and we would visit Korea during the summers. Leah and I both thought it was the best place in the world. We would ride roller coasters all day, bouncing back and forth between the indoor theme park and the outdoor Magic Island area.

I grab Jason's hand, marveling at how amazing it is to be out in public with him like a regular couple. I feel myself start to relax, leaning my body into his as we walk along the stone pathways toward my favorite roller coaster, the Atlantis.

"Hey," Jason says as we stand in line. "Do you hear that?"

I listen and hear "Summer Heat" playing over the amusement park speakers. My face breaks into a smile, and I turn to Jason, speechless.

"Rachel?"

I laugh, realizing I'm staring at him with my mouth wide open. "Yeah. I'm good—I'm great! This is just so surreal."

Jason laughs, quietly singing along with the song. Suddenly, he grabs my shoulders. "You know what would be fun?"

"No, what."

"You'll see."

He turns to a group of girls standing behind us in line. "Hey, what do you think of this song? Total hit, right?"

I giggle, swatting him on the arm.

The girls look around our age. Each of them is sporting a cute Lotte World headband with giant, brightly colored polka-dotted bows, Minnie Mouse style.

"It totally is. I'm obsessed," Purple Bow says. "I already know all the lyrics."

"You saw the music video, right?" Red Bow pretends to swoon, draping her hand against her forehead. "Jason is looking seriously fine."

Pink Bow pops up the music video on her phone, zooming in on Jason's face. "Seriously, can I just have his babies already? How can someone be so cute and talented at the same time?"

"Imagine hearing that sweet voice say good night to you every day," Purple Bow says. All three girls giggle. They seem to have totally forgotten that Jason and I are still here, chattering among themselves with the music video playing between them.

"He's single, right?"

"What kind of girl do you think he would like?"

"Someone beautiful, obviously, and probably ridiculously talented and mature."

Jason laughs, taking it all in stride. I force out a laugh too, but my skin is starting to itch. This conversation has taken an uncomfortable turn.

"Nothing like those two girls he's singing with. Can you believe them?" Pink Bow says with a sneer.

"Right? Totally slutty." Red Bow rolls her eyes. "Look at their outfits. You can see everything. It's gross. Don't they know little kids are watching this?"

What? My cheeks flame underneath my makeup. The outfits were hardly revealing at all! And it's not like we get to choose our own clothes. And even if we did, who are they to judge me?

"This one doesn't even have the body to pull off a dress like that," Purple Bow says, pointing to Mina. "Hello, put those daikon legs away. No one wants to see that."

"And this girl singing the harmony with Jason," Pink Bow says as my face pops up on the screen. She snickers. "She totally looks like the desperate type. She's probably trying to seduce Jason behind the scenes. Just look at the way she's staring at him. Obvious much?"

"They're lucky to be so close to Jason," Red Bow says, shaking her head. "But honestly, DB should have picked someone else. These girls aren't even pretty enough to make up for their lack of talent."

I've had enough. "I don't think I want to go on this ride anymore," I say, tears threatening to leak out and ruin my makeup. The girls are so absorbed in their conversation that they don't even notice as I duck out of line, Jason chasing after me.

"Hey, hey, hey," he says. I'm walking so fast he has to jog to keep up with me. He catches hold of my elbow. "Is everything okay?"

Is he serious?

"Do you really have to ask? Didn't you hear what those girls were saying?"

He nods sympathetically. "Yeah. It's tough hearing other people's opinions about your performance. It never really gets easier." He puts an arm around my shoulder and steers me toward the food stalls. "But I know what'll cheer you up. Caramel popcorn!"

Huh? I blink, thrown off by how quickly he's moved on from what those girls said. Doesn't he understand—it's not about their opinions; it's about how sexist and inappropriate they were being, gushing over Jason and shitting all over me and Mina. I open my mouth to say something but close it again when I see how hard he's trying to cheer me up, talking excitedly as he orders the biggest bucket of caramel popcorn on the menu. So far it's been the perfect day, and I don't want to ruin it. This is our first official date, after all.

So I swallow my words and grab the popcorn instead.

"I need to introduce you to the other woman in my life."

"Sorry, what?"

Later that night Jason and I are strolling around a quiet neighborhood that I've never been to before—and where he swears no one will recognize us even after we wash off our faces. He leads me into a pojangmacha where the owner, an ahjumma wearing a matching red apron and hairnet, is serving up odeng, tteokbokki, mini kimbap, and soju. The air inside the small red-tented bar is thick with the cozy smells of classic Korean street food, and my stomach rumbles as I inhale deeply.

"Ah, my favorite customer," the ahjumma says brightly, coming forward to pinch Jason's cheeks. "You haven't been to see me in weeks! You look too skinny."

"Ahnyounghasaeyo," he says, bowing. He halts, looking at her face incredulously. "Eemo, I swear, you're getting younger every time I see you. What's your secret? If you keep going on like this, your tent is going to be filled with handsome young boys asking you out on dates."

She laughs, ushering us onto a pair of plastic stools and handing us a plate of tteokbokki and steaming skewers of odeng. "Ah, you flatter me. Go on, then, eat with your pretty girlfriend."

Jason winks at me before turning back to her. "Girlfriend? You think she's my girlfriend? Oh, Eemo, you hurt me! You know I only have eyes for you."

She rolls her eyes. "Aigoo, silly boy. I know what you're after." She reaches for a platter of tuna kimbap—the roll bursting at the seams with spicy canned tuna fish, perilla leaves, imitation crab sticks, yellow radish, carrots, eggs, spinach, and burdock root—and lowers it ceremoniously onto our table. "Now eat, you two." She gives Jason a warm smile before returning to her spot behind the makeshift counter.

I take a huge bite of odeng, the fish cake filling me with warmth from head to toe. Jason grins. "What do you think? It's the best, right? Try the kimbap next. It's the best in Seoul."

I smile back and nod. But even with the warmth of the odeng, I still can't forget what happened at Lotte World. It wasn't just about what the girls said. It was Jason's reaction to it. Or rather, his nonreaction. I shake my head and take another bite of odeng. *Forget it, Rachel. Just enjoy the day. Don't make this into a thing.*

"Ahjumma!" a voice at the table next to us yells. "Another bottle of soju!"

Jason and I glance over in the direction of the voice. Three girls are sitting around a table eating plates full of dalkbal and gyeran mari, but one of them is clearly wasted, chugging soju straight from the bottle, her delicately polished seashell-swirl nails digging into the green glass.

I freeze. Where have I seen those nails before?

✦ Seventeen ✦

I remember right before we moved to Seoul, I took Leah to the ice-cream shop down the block from our apartment. It was winter, and Umma thought we were going across the street to the library, but Leah had begged for "one last ice cream to remember New York by," and I had given in like I usually did. We had only a few minutes before Umma expected us back, but Leah ordered the largest cone they had and gobbled it up instantly, strawberry ice cream smearing all over her face.

This is the image that flashes to mind as I watch Kang Jina jam a piece of dalkbal in her mouth, the spicy sauce dribbling down her chin. She's chewing so ferociously I can almost feel the crispy *snap!* of boneless grilled chicken feet—more delicious than any chicken wing New York could ever dream of—between her teeth. She washes it down with a swig of soju, wiping her mouth with the back of her hand. Her two friends sitting across from her try to slow her down, but she swats them away. I can't quite believe it, but it's definitely her.

"Is that . . . ?" Jason's voice trails off, his shocked expression mirroring my own.

At that moment, Jina turns her head and looks right at me. Or more like right through me—her soju-weary eyes seem to be having a hard time focusing on anything around her. One of her friends tries to take the bottle out of her hand, and she snaps, "It's mine! You can't take it away." Her eyes are wild now as she scans the room, and her gaze falls on Jason. She rises from the table, the bottle slipping out of her hands with a clatter, her eyes swinging back to me as she sways toward us like a drunken tiger.

"You," she says, pointing a finger at me, her speech slurred. "I know you. Rachel Kim. You look like you're on a date. Didn't I warn you about dating?"

At this, she jabs a thumb in Jason's direction. He raises his eyebrows in confusion, eyes swiveling between me and Jina. I have no idea how to respond, so I do the first thing that comes to mind. I pull out a chair.

"Please sit down," I say. "How are you? Have you . . . been well?"

She lets out a bark of laughter. "Oh please. Don't give me that pity bullshit. I know you know I got kicked out of DB. The whole fucking world knows. Or no, I'm sorry." She flops down onto the chair, crossing her legs and nearly falling off before regaining her composure and smiling widely. "I 'chose not to re-sign.'" She makes air quotes with her fingers. "That's the story they're telling everyone, isn't it?"

My brow furrows. "What do you mean that's the story they're telling?"

"Come on, Rachel," Jina says, the smile wilting off her face. "You of all people must know how two-faced the K-pop world is. DB controls everything about our lives, and all of a sudden I'm the one who can't handle this lifestyle? Everything I ever wore or ever said or ever did was because they told me to! All this shit"—she flashes up her fancy nails, her voice rising—"the expensive clothes, the makeup, the beauty products, it's all so DB can turn us into whoever *they* want us to be, make us look perfect for public consumption. And they're saying I'm the one who's a diva?"

She scoots her chair near mine, leaning in so close that I can smell the soju on her breath. "Listen, Rachel. Know what you're getting yourself into. When you sign that contract, you're losing ten years of your life—"

"Wait, I thought K-pop contracts only last for seven years? Isn't that the law?"

Jina's eyes widen, her mouth curling in another maniacal laugh. "Oh, you naive child. You think DB doesn't have a way to get around whatever laws they want? Somewhere in some bank in Switzerland, in some secure vault, are the three-year-extension contracts DB forced me and the rest of Electric Flower to sign the same day we signed our original contracts. Postdated, of course, so everything will hold up in court." Her eyes focus in on me, an almost pitying look now mingling with her soju-fueled rage. "Didn't anyone ever tell you? This glamour? This fame? It's all an illusion set up by the label. The execs. And then they'll take everything away from you, framing you as an irresponsible, high-maintenance diva, so that no other label will want to touch you with a ten-foot pole." She laughs, but it comes out as a sob. "They'll fucking ruin you and make it seem like you're the one who destroyed yourself. Look at me. My career is over."

"But why?" I say. My mind is whirring as I try to make sense of what she's saying. "Why would they do this to you?"

"What did I tell you, Rachel?" Jina stabs a toothpick into our tteokbokki, holding my gaze. "*It's dangerous to have a boyfriend as a K-pop star.*"

My stomach sinks. "The guy you were with in Jeju? Song Gyumin?"

She nods and her voice grows soft. "The great Song Gyumin. When his first seven years were up, he renegotiated for a better deal. More money. He thought it would be the same for me. He said he was taking me on a 'secret getaway' to talk about it all. Some fucking secret, right? The honeymoon capital of the fucking country? And now . . . well. Secret's out. DB's cut and run. And so has he." She takes a shaky breath as I process her words.

"You mean . . . Wait. You mean he broke up with you?"

Jina covers her face with her hands. Then suddenly, she lets out a scream and smashes her fist onto the plate, tteokbokki sauce flying everywhere and spraying me in the face.

"Of course he broke up with me! That's how all these

stories end. We get boyfriends, we let them ruin our lives, and they get away, scot-free and blameless. You think his label gives a shit about him having a girlfriend? Of course they don't. It's one set of rules for them and another set of rules for us. DB talks about us being a family. But they don't care. They don't care about me. About you. They don't care about anyone. All they care about is making us into perfect K-pop machines that will do everything they say and rake in the money for them. Well, DB can go fuck themselves. Mr. Noh, Mr. Choo, everybody. Fuck them! I know secrets that would set the K-pop world on fire!"

Jina's friends appear at her sides, each of them taking an arm and lifting her from her chair. "Jina sweetie, time to go," one of them says.

As they lead her out of the pojangmacha, Jina locks eyes with me again and shouts, "Watch out for Mr. Choo, Rachel. Don't get any more mixed up with him or his precious daughter than you already have. You hear me?"

She disappears from the tent, her shouts fading into the night. I don't realize until then that I'm shaking. What did she mean she knows secrets that would set the K-pop world on fire? And why did she keep talking about Mr. Choo? I want to forget it, along with the rest of this terrible date, but the look on Jina's face, the sound of her scream—it's all permanently burned into my brain. Suddenly, my whole body starts to ache, the kimbap and tteokbokki I ate curdling into a hard pit at the bottom of my stomach.

I look across the table at Jason, who's mopping up the tteokbokki sauce. "Poor Jina," Jason says, shaking his head. "It really sucks what she's going through. She's obviously distressed."

Something about the way he says it makes me look at him sharply. "Well, of course. You heard everything she said, didn't you? How could she not be distressed?"

He nods. "I heard. But also, I don't know. There are two sides to every story. It's true that DB doesn't pay us well, but like Jina says, they also provide us with clothes and apartments. It's not that hard to make ends meet if you're careful." He shrugs. "I mean, I've always been treated pretty well by them."

"That's because you're Jason Lee," I say, frustration building in my chest as I think of what Jina said about Gyumin. "Of course they treat you well! The worst thing you've ever done is steal Romeo's custom orange hair color!"

"What?" Jason looks at me, perplexed.

I sigh. Now is not the time to get into the DB rumor mill. "It's not important. But don't tell me you haven't noticed the double standard in the industry. It's different for girls than it is for guys."

His brow furrows and I blink, my doubt from earlier in the day rushing furiously back.

"You *have* noticed, haven't you?" I say, flashing back to practice a few weeks ago, Jason strolling in late with an armful of Lotteria, smiling casually at the execs.

"To be honest, not really." He frowns. "At the end of the day, DB is a business. It doesn't really benefit them to treat the guys differently than the girls."

My throat is tight. Is he for real? "What about the girls at Lotte World? You heard for yourself the praise they had for you versus the nasty things they had to say about me and Mina."

"Rachel, that's just a couple people's opinions. Everyone deals with it—even me. It doesn't mean the whole industry is sexist or biased or whatever."

I suck in a breath.

Oh. Wow. He *is* for real. I laugh in disbelief, wiping my hands against my face and shaking my head. "For someone who lives and breathes K-pop, it's amazing how little of it you really see."

His frown deepens. "What's that supposed to mean?"

The red tent flaps open and I turn my head, looking at the couple who's just walked into the pojangmacha and is glancing at Jason and me with curious expressions. Panic rises in my throat like bile. Do they recognize us?

A sinking feeling starts to spread throughout my body, and I realize it's been growing inside me ever since that day eating naengmyeon with my family. Ever since Leah told me about Jina not re-signing with Electric Flower.

I was wrong.

But so was Jina. She told me that being with Jason wouldn't just be difficult; it would be dangerous. And it is. But it's also unjust. I gave my life to DB, and in the end this decision—a decision we *both* made—will destroy me. And only me. In the end I will be the only one who's forced to walk away from everything I've worked for—the fans, the music, the magic. For the first time in a long time, I can feel the threads of my life start to weave together with perfect clarity. And they're all pulling me toward one obvious conclusion: I might want to be with Jason, but I *need* to debut. And being with Jason could cost me my career before it even begins.

The pressure builds in my chest, making it hard to breathe. "I can't believe I let things go so far between us. This will ruin me."

Jason's face softens. He reaches across the table and grabs my hands. "Hey, don't talk like that. Whatever happened with Kang Jina and her boyfriend, it's different between us. We'll tell Mr. Noh that we really care about each other and he'll understand. In fact, he'll probably be happy for us."

"Happy for us?" I snap, pulling my hands away from his. "Open your eyes, Jason. They might bend the rules for you and Song Gyumin, but not for me. One more misstep and I'm out of DB. Kang Jina was one of their biggest stars and they didn't just kick her out—they *ruined* her. And they didn't look back. Imagine how dispensable I am as a trainee!"

"Please, Rachel, you know they're not like that," Jason pleads. "They would never do that to you just because you're dating me."

I stare at him and I realize that nothing I say is going to

make him understand that things are different for me than they are for him. Jason might be the "Angel Boy" of DB, but I've had to fight every step of the way, and I still feel like I'm barely hanging on. DB would have no problem cutting me the moment they find a blemish that could tarnish their squeaky-clean, picture-perfect reputation. And a relationship with Jason would be an irreversible blemish.

"It's over, Jason," I say, standing up from the table. "I can't do this anymore. I've worked too hard for my dreams to let anything stand in my way. Even you."

Jason stares at me, completely in shock. "I can't believe how badly you're overreacting."

My heart splinters at his words. Whatever I was hoping he would say, that wasn't it. I walk out of the pojangmacha without looking back. I can hear Jason calling after me, but I don't care. Once I'm outside, I break into a run. I don't stop until I'm on the subway, out of breath and broken-hearted.

I swallow the lump in my throat, refusing to cry. I did the right thing.

I think of Yujin and how she put her career on the line to help me make a viral video, how she supports me even when it gets her into trouble. I think of my family. I feel ashamed of how I almost let them all down again. How I almost threw away everything I've been working toward for the last six years.

I was so swept away by my emotions, but no more. There's

only a few weeks left before DB will announce the Family Tour, and I need to get back on track. From now on I'll be more focused than ever.

Just me, regular trainee life, and completely avoiding Jason Lee.

✦ Eighteen ✦

My plan for avoiding Jason was simple: Turn the other way when I see him walking down the hall, don't make eye contact during training, and most importantly, imagine his face on the punching bag at Appa's gym.

And it *worked*. Five days later, I've clocked more hours at the boxing gym than I have in the last six months. "Oof!" Appa groans as I land a hard punch, the bag digging into his stomach. "Careful—your old man isn't what he used to be."

"Sorry, Appa," I say, taking a minute to wipe the sweat off my face but quickly getting back into my punching stance.

"How about we take a break? I'm worried you're going to crack a rib."

"My ribs feel fine," I say.

"I didn't mean one of yours." Appa grins and pats the floor beside him as he sinks down, groaning with exhaustion. "So," he says as I sit down next to him. "Anything on your mind?"

I sigh. There's plenty on my mind but nothing I want to

talk about. With anyone. "No, Appa. Everything is fine."

Appa narrows his eyes, taking in my tired face and the forced smile on my lips. After a moment, though, he seems to accept my answer. "Okay. If you say so."

"I do. Now . . . why don't you tell me what's going on with you?"

"Actually, I do have something to tell you." Appa reaches into the pocket of his hoodie and pulls out a crumpled white piece of card stock, handing it to me with a shy grin. Curious, I take it, slowly unfolding the paper. As I read, my eyes light up.

"Appa! This is an invitation to your law school graduation! It's next week!"

"It is. And I'd like for you to be there."

I nod, tears forming in the corners of my eyes as Appa reaches out his hands and pulls me into his chest. "We're going to be okay, Rachel. Everything is going to be okay." And for a moment, I let myself believe him.

A week later I'm smiling as Appa walks across the stage at his graduation, beaming as he accepts his law school diploma. He waves at me and I wave back—but, unfortunately for me, he can't see me. All he can see is the camera that's streaming video of the ceremony, which I'm able to watch due to in-flight Wi-Fi. Because—*surprise!*—the day after Appa invited me to his graduation, DB announced they were sending us on a last-minute promotional tour for "Summer Heat" in Toronto.

That's right. Me, Jason, and Mina. Together. For five straight days.

The thought of spending that much time with Jason made my heart drop into my stomach, but there was no way to say no to DB and still expect them to debut me.

So here I am.

Mina insisted on flying over on her dad's corporate jet, and it's even more luxurious than the one Leah and I flew in to Tokyo. We're all sitting on full-length velvet sofas, and everyone has their own pair of thickly padded monogrammed slippers, along with silk eye masks and wireless headphones.

Mina is in the yoga studio at the back of the plane, having a lesson with her personal instructor, while Mr. Han, who's accompanying us on our trip, is sitting at the wine bar, a glass of merlot in his hand and his headphones clamped tight over his ears, tapping away on his iPad. I'm hunkered down in my seat, a stack of extra-credit homework piled on the table in front of me (that, plus the fact that we're on a two-week summer break from school at the moment, is the only way Umma agreed to let me go on this trip). Normally, I'd breeze through my English assignment, but this one is turning out to be a bit more of a challenge—

"You really couldn't leave the Shakespeare at home?" Jason says, plopping down on the sofa next to me, spooning up a huge mouthful of chocolate soufflé. Jason clearly didn't adopt the same "avoid at all costs" plan that I did after our disastrous night at the pojangmacha. If anything, it's like he's gone out of his way to always be around—unfortunately, the sweet, sensitive, boom-box-holding, promposing guy I dated is gone and I'm stuck with the cocky, snarky guy I met outside the trainee house a couple months ago.

I ignore him, turning my eyes back to Macbeth's big soliloquy.

"I suppose you do have a thing for dramatic storytelling," he says. "Though I've always found his plays to be a bit of a drag. Do you even understand what they're saying? Or do you just pretend to understand and look everything up on SparkNotes later?"

"Can you please just let me focus?" I snap, losing my cool.

He takes his time licking the chocolate from his spoon before dropping it in his empty bowl with a loud clatter. "Oh, sorry." He lifts his eyebrows in mock surprise. "Were you trying to concentrate?"

I suppress the urge to throw my textbook at his head.

Suddenly, Jason looks at me, his expression sheepish. "Rachel, I really am sor—"

But he quickly turns away as my phone pings with a Kakao message, and I pick it up, grateful for another excuse to ignore Jason. I look down and see that Appa's sent me a selfie of him holding his law school diploma with a big cheesy smile on his face.

Your old man's finally graduated!

My heart squeezes and I type back quickly.

I'm so proud of you!

I sigh and lean back in my seat, wishing I could be there with him. I settle for sending as many heart emojis as I can find. He deserves them all. He's worked so hard—hustling to night classes after long days at the gym and keeping it all a secret from Umma and Leah, just so he doesn't get their hopes up. I wonder if he'll finally tell them now that he's graduated, or if he'll wait until he secures a job. Knowing Appa, it'll probably be the latter.

Almost by reflex my hand reaches for my phone again, wanting to share the good news with Akari—but my fingers curl up into a fist before I even start typing the message. Between practice and school and Jason, we have barely spoken in weeks.

I mean, the last time I saw her, it was like I was talking to a stranger.

It was last weekend and Yujin called me into her office. Akari was already there, watering the plants on the windowsill. In that moment, I wanted nothing more than to sit on Yujin's couch and eat Pepero and drink banana milk and talk to her for hours, just like when we were kids. I wanted to tell her about Tokyo and Jeju and Kang Jina and Jason and even those girls at Lotte World. But before I could say anything, Yujin grabbed me.

"Your song with Jason and Mina has been such a hit, DB is sending you to Toronto to promote it!" Yujin announced. "You're going international!"

"Wow, what great news," Akari said, with a smile that didn't quite reach her eyes. "You must be so excited."

"Excited. Yes." I forced a laugh, pumping my fist in the air. "So excited! Woo!" There's no way I could tell Yujin what I was really feeling. At best, she would tell me to suck it up and not let Jason stand in the way of my career. At worst, she would go to Mr. Noh herself and have me kicked out of the program. So I smiled until my cheeks ached and let Yujin toast me with a glass of sparkling raspberry juice.

It wasn't until later, as Akari and I were leaving Yujin's office, that the smile slid off my face. I turned to her, biting my lip. "Akari, listen, I need to tell you something."

She hesitated outside the door. "I should really get back to training . . . ," she said, looking down the hall.

"Please?" I begged her. "I need to catch up with my best friend. There might even be some free food in it for you."

She turned to me, a small smile playing on her lips. "I'm not the one who can never say no to free food, goof."

I clasped my hands under my chin, giving her my best puppy-dog eyes.

"Okay, okay." She laughed. "Ten minutes. You know, I have something I wanted to talk to you about too—"

"Rachel Kim!" A voice rang out in the hallway, and we both turned to see Grace marching toward us. "You better be prepared to lose a few more inches off that thigh gap! Fitting room! Right now! And do some jumping jacks on the way."

I turned back to Akari. "I'm sorry. I guess I . . . have to go." I said, my voice laced with guilt.

"Right," she replied. But her voice sounded flat, hollow. "Of course. We all have important things to do."

"I'll text you tonight?" I said hesitantly, but she was already walking away and didn't seem to have heard me.

We haven't spoken since.

I scroll through my phone, looking at the days' worth of messages I've sent her, all unanswered. Tears unexpectedly fill my eyes. Since the day Akari came to DB, we've been best friends. Our lives have always been hectic, but we would find time to catch up between training sessions, and at night we'd stay up texting each other. I know I've been busier than ever recently, but if anyone should understand that, it's Akari. That's just how it is when you're a trainee. But ever since this whole song thing started, it's like there's this wall between us and I don't know why.

My phone beeps again and I look down.

I love you too, daughter.

"Everything okay?" Jason's looking at me, his expression softening. He seems to have noticed the shift in my mood. For a moment, I contemplate showing him Appa's photo. "You know," he says, before I can reach for my phone, "*Macbeth* isn't really that complicated. Just the story of an innocent guy who gets fooled by a pretty girl." I see a flash of hurt in his eyes, but it's quickly replaced by his signature cocky smile as he jumps up and heads over to the PlayStation console on the other side of the plane.

I blink. Moment gone.

Rolling my eyes, I jam my headphones onto my ears, dialing up the volume and blasting *Lemonade*, letting Queen Bey reel me in before I lose my mind.

We've barely touched down in Toronto before we're sucked into a nonstop whirlwind of hair, makeup, and outfit changes. "We've got a solid list of press and performances lined up for you three here, and then we head north to perform at a music festival," Mr. Han says, running through our schedule. "By the end of this tour, everyone in the country will know your names."

"I'm sure everyone already knows our names," Jason says. A confident grin spreads across his face. "Now they just won't be able to forget them."

It's day four of the tour, and the three of us are in a brightly lit studio, filming an interview for a local morning talk show. The host is a middle-aged man who reminds me of our media trainer at DB. All grease and sleaze, only with whiter teeth and an uneven spray tan. Mina and I are perched on stools in leather jackets and camo skirts while Jason sits between us in an armchair, decked out in coordinating camo pants and a black tee. It feels like there are cameras on us every hour of the day, but truthfully, I can't keep track of them all. Maybe it's because all my energy is going into avoiding Jason when Mr. Han has us practically glued at the hip, or maybe it's because of the kinds of questions the interviewers insist on asking Mina and me.

"Mina and Rachel," the talk show host simpers at us, and

I have to clench my face muscles to keep from wincing. "Who takes longer to get ready for a show?"

I resist the urge to roll my eyes, and beside me I can feel Mina stiffen. It's been like this all week. Just yesterday during a radio show, a fan had called in to talk to us.

"Rachel, your English is so good," they had said. "You must be really proud of that!"

"Well . . . I'm from America," I had answered with a polite laugh in my voice, but inside I was boiling. If I had a dollar for every time I've heard "your English is so good!" on this tour, I'd probably have enough money to buy my own private plane.

At least it's better than the female magazine reporter who couldn't stop mooning over Jason. We were in the DB suite at the Four Seasons hotel in downtown Toronto on our first day, and she was practically drooling, asking question after question about his meteoric rise to success and how he continues to challenge himself creatively. When Mr. Han stepped in and suggested she direct some questions to me and Mina, she could barely tear her eyes away from Jason before asking us if we ever fight over who gets more attention from him.

I open my mouth now to respond to the host's question with DB's preapproved answer (*We get ready together, of course, like all best friends do!*), when Jason puts his hand on my leg and flashes a quick half grin my way.

"I think I'll take this one if you don't mind," Jason says, turning toward the host. "The answer is . . . me!" The host laughs appreciatively, flashing his too-white teeth, as Jason continues. "I am obviously the most high-maintenance member of this group. Especially when it comes to my skin-care regimen."

The host laughs again as Jason mimes scrubbing his face in the mirror, but he quickly gathers himself. "Jason," he asks, "what's it like being back in your hometown?" A somber look covers his face. "Does it make you think of your mother more than usual?"

Beside me I can hear Jason's breath hitch in his throat as he's totally caught off guard. Interviewers rarely bring up his mother. I look over at him and my heart immediately swells. His face is open and vulnerable—it's the Jason that played me his original song in the music room, the one who held my hand on the plane back from Tokyo.

But he recovers in a flash, clearing his throat and smiling widely. My heart snaps shut. "It feels great to be home," he says, expertly dodging the question. "There's no place like Toronto! I only wish we had more time here. We'll be heading to New York City soon for the second leg of our tour." He glances meaningfully in my direction. "It's another special place for us because it's Rachel's hometown."

Mina and I swivel our heads to look at him, both of us trying to mask our shock. New York? No one told us we were going to New York.

"How exciting!" the host says. "I'm sure all your fans in New York are dying to meet you. What a wonderful surprise for them!"

It's a surprise all right, and not just for the fans.

After the interview wraps up, Mr. Han comes up to us. "Rachel, Mina, I'll need your passports for some more paper-work before we head to the States," he says, all business.

I stand there, unable to move. "Our passports?" I say slowly. "But no one ever told us—*ow!*" I cry out as Mina discreetly stomps down on my toes with her heel.

"Oh yes! Seeing that your song is doing so well, we decided to add another city to the tour," Mr. Han says, rubbing his hands together. "The fans have really been loving you three. So after your performance at the music festival in Brantwood tomorrow, we're flying to New York!"

Jason grins, giving Mr. Han a fist bump. "I'm so stoked. I haven't been to New York in forever."

Mr. Han grins back. When Mina and I don't react right away, he looks at us, a flicker of annoyance crossing his face. It's an unwritten rule that K-pop trainees aren't permitted to complain about anything they're asked to do. Not only that, but we're expected to be thankful for everything—for extra-long practice sessions, for punishments doled out to us in the hallways, for the strict diets enforced on us, and especially for surprise trips to New York City. "Aren't you thrilled? This is great news."

Mina opens her mouth like she's about to say something, but quickly closes it again. She smiles widely instead and says, "Of course I'm thrilled! I've always wanted to go to New York!"

She laughs, clapping her hands together.

⭐ Nineteen ⭐

"According to Google, Brantwood is a small, upscale resort town north of Toronto, famous for its Blue Mountain summer music festival," Leah recites as we FaceTime the next morning.

I groan as I brush my teeth. I couldn't sleep last night, so around 5:00 a.m. I gave up and called Leah, who's been catching me up on her K-dramas and reading me facts about Brantwood for the last hour.

"It should take about three hours to get there from your hotel," she chirps happily. "Three hours in the car with Jason! You're so lucky."

"Uh-huh. That's me." I haven't told Leah about anything that happened between me and Jason, of course. As far as she knows, we're still just the best of friends who take her on day trips to Japan.

I pick up my phone and head to my suitcase, grabbing a pair of slouchy sweatpants and an oversize orange T-shirt. "Unni, omg!" Leah's voice shouts over the phone.

"I knew you would be excited!" Mr. Han says, his face relaxing as he joins in her laughter.

New York. I should be thrilled, like Mina and Jason. But at this moment all I can think about is everything K-pop has asked of me: move across the world to a new country, miss your dad's graduation. Train 24/7. Never stop smiling. Even when you have to break up with your boyfriend. The one boy who got it. Who knew what this life was like. Whose dreams were your dreams. I've dreamed about going home for years—but now, in this moment, I don't see home. I just see another thing that K-pop is asking of me. Go to another city, with no notice and no say. I should be jumping up and down with joy, but it just doesn't feel the way I thought it would. Nothing does.

All three of them turn to face me, and I quickly convert my face into a bright smile, beaming at them like they're all my very best friends, just like the rest of the world believes.

"That really is amazing news," I say. "A dream come true."

"What?"

"Isn't that the T-shirt you wear when we stay in and watch movies? You need to put on something cuter!"

"What, stop! No. It's fine. Mr. Han said we can dress down for the car ride," I say defensively. "Besides, it's comfortable and I've spent the last four days in heels and tight skirts."

"Okay," Leah says skeptically, raising her eyebrows.

She looks ready to start another lecture on the importance of grooming, so I quickly change the subject. "Hey, aren't you going to Everland today? Umma said some girls from school invited you."

Leah's eyes swivel to the side of her head. "Oh, um. I was going to go, but . . . I'm . . . not. Anymore."

I frown at her. "What do you mean?"

"Well," she says slowly. "Everyone was planning on sleeping over here afterward. But then they found out that you weren't gonna be here and . . ." Her voice trails off. "It's fine! Maybe you and I can go when you get back?"

There's a lump in my throat, and I have to squeeze my eyes shut to keep the tears at bay before I can answer. "Of course! The minute I get home, it's you, me, and the T Express."

This of course sends Leah into a delighted monologue of all her favorite Everland rides, and after a few more minutes, I can hear Umma telling her to hang up and do her homework. I end the call and head downstairs, quickly stuffing two chocolates that were left on my hotel pillow into my tote bag, thinking I'll eat them in the car later.

As I near the lobby, I spot Jason only a few feet away, pacing by some windows, talking on the phone. I groan inwardly. I was hoping he wouldn't be here yet, but I guess I'm not the only one who couldn't sleep. I'm about to sneak past him so he doesn't notice me, when suddenly I hear his voice, tense and angry as he grips his phone to his ear. I quickly duck behind a huge potted plant.

"I just don't get it. The last time we saw each other was two years ago, and I could barely spend one day in Toronto. You didn't even come to Seoul when I won—no, I know you had to work . . . *I know* . . . But tonight's my last night here."

I hesitate. I shouldn't be eavesdropping, but if I move now, he'll see me. He stops just inches away, running his hand through his hair as he speaks.

"What the hell do you mean you won't step foot in Brantwood? Aren't you supposed to be the grown-up here? You know what, don't answer that. . . . Yep, I get it. Understood. Okay. Bye."

He hangs up and lets out a short, frustrated exhale. Whoever he was talking to, it sounded intense. Way too intense for 6:30 a.m. A huge banana leaf pokes me in the face, and I realize I'm still hiding behind the plant. I quickly move around it, hoping to hop on the elevator back to my room, when Jason turns suddenly, nearly bumping against me.

His eyes widen in surprise. "Rachel. Hey. How long have you been down here?"

I swallow. "Um . . . not that long. I just . . . couldn't sleep."

He eyes me suspiciously. "Right." I look up at him inno-cently and he shrugs, his body deflating a tiny bit. "Yeah, me neither. I couldn't sleep, I mean." His voice is soft, but there's an edge to it that I've never heard before. He opens his mouth and then closes it again, like he wants to say something else. Instead, he takes a step back and shoves his hands in his pockets.

Just then Mina sweeps into the lobby, her hair perfectly done up in a high glossy ponytail. With her metallic rose-gold crop top and amber-studded earrings, she looks more like she's ready for a shopping trip in Paris than she is for a three-hour drive out of the city. I sigh, glancing down at my sweats. Maybe Leah was right.

"Oh good, you're both here," she says. "I'm ready to go. And I'll need breakfast on the way. These continental hotel break-fasts make me sick." She glances around the lobby. "Where's Mr. Han?"

"He's over by the front desk," I say, pointing to where Mr. Han has gathered with some other members of the DB crew, organizing things for today's performance.

"Well, let him know I'm ready to go," she says, looking at me. "Otherwise we'll have to eat scrambled eggs for breakfast. Seriously, it's like people at this hotel only know how to cook eggs one way."

"I have a better idea," Jason says. "Let's rent a car and drive up just the three of us. I'll tell Mr. Han we'll meet him there."

Mina and I stare at him. "What are you talking about?" I say.

"I need to blow off some steam," Jason says, his head swiveling around the hotel lobby like he's about to jump out of his skin.

"Um, are you kidding?" Mina says. "You think we're allowed to just wander off on our own? Besides, Mr. Han's already arranged a ride for us."

"We're not wandering off on our own. We're just meeting him there." He leans against the counter, rolling his eyes. "You worry too much. It'll be fine."

How many times have I heard Jason say that before? "What about our outfits for the performance?" I ask. We dropped them off with the hotel's dry-cleaning service last night and they won't be ready to pick up for another half hour.

"Look, I'll go ask Mr. Han right now." He strides across the lobby floor. Mina and I watch as Mr. Han puts his hand on Jason's shoulder, nodding sympathetically. After a few minutes, Jason returns, grinning. "There. Mr. Han says it's cool and he'll take care of the outfits. I'm getting a car. You guys coming?"

Mina purses her lips together. "Fine. If Mr. Han says it's okay, I'm in."

From across the lobby, Mr. Han shouts in our direction. "Rachel, Mina! There's still room in the DB car if you want to ride with us. Jaehyun sent me some simple dance exercises for you two to do on the trip."

I close my eyes, weighing my choices. Three hours with

Jason while he drives and makes asshole comments and Mina spends the whole time making fun of my clothes, or three hours doing leg exercises in a cramped car with Mr. Han.

"Rachel?" I can hear the note of desperation in Jason's voice. He needs this. Whoever he was talking to on the phone has clearly shaken him. Maybe some time on our own will get him back on his game before the performance.

"Okay, I'm in," I say, opening my eyes. "Let's go."

"Can we please turn on the air-conditioning? It's so freaking hot." Mina wipes the beads of sweat off her forehead, wrinkling her nose in disgust.

"No way," Jason says, laughing and hanging one arm out the open window of our rental Camry. It's the only car the hotel had available to rent on such short notice. He looks totally relaxed behind the wheel, and I get the impression he's missed this. Like all the DB stars, he's either chauffeured everywhere he goes in Korea or he takes the subway, which means there aren't many opportunities to drive yourself. "There's nothing like driving with fresh open-window air."

"Yes, there is," Mina says begrudgingly. "It's called air-con." She eyes me in the rearview mirror. "Come on, Princess Rachel. I know you're sweating too."

Normally Mina's constant complaining would bother me more than the temperature, but my arms are practically sticking to the upholstery on the back of the seat. I carefully peel myself off as I sit up. "It is a bit hot."

Jason sighs, rolling up the windows and cranking the air-conditioning. "Happy now?"

"I'd be happier if I knew where we were going," Mina says, squinting at her phone. "This doesn't look like the right way."

"Relax," Jason says. "I used to drive here all the time. I know where I'm going."

The farther north we drive, the worse the roads get—we're definitely not in the city anymore. Suddenly, Jason veers off the main road and heads straight onto a muddy dirt path. Mina sits up straighter in her seat, grabbing Jason's arm.

"What the hell are you doing?" she cries.

"I told you, I know where I'm going," Jason says. "This is a shortcut. Just trust me." I bite my tongue, not wanting to get in the middle of their squabbling. As long as we get to Brantwood, that's all that matters. I just need to focus on tonight's performance. I close my eyes and start going over the dance steps in my head one more time.

Suddenly, my back slams against the seat as the car lurches to a stop.

My eyes fly open. "Why aren't we moving?"

The tires squeal. Dirt and mud go flying, but we don't move an inch.

Oh no.

"Huh," Jason says. "Looks like we're stuck."

Oh no, no, no.

"No shit, genius," Mina says, her voice dripping with annoyance. "It's fine. My dad's concierge service is international. They'll come give us a tow." She pulls out her phone. "Oh my god," she says, her voice inching from annoyed to panicked. "I don't even have reception."

I sit upright. "What? Let me check my phone." I pull it out of my tote and my heart leaps into my throat when I see I don't have reception either.

We can't call for a tow. We can't even text Mr. Han.

I feel like I'm going to be sick.

Jason revs the engine again, but it's no use. He taps his fingers on the steering wheel, thinking. "Okay," he says finally, turning off the car. "Stay calm and hang tight. I'll go get help."

"What do you mean you're going to get help? We're in the middle of nowhere!" Mina cries.

"I saw a gas station a few miles back. I'm sure someone there can help us."

"Jason," I say, trying to maintain my cool. "There's no time to go get help. We need to be on the road, like, now."

"So I better get going," he says, giving me a wink. "Don't worry, ladies, your knight in shining armor will be back soon!"

"What are you talking about? You're the one who got us into this mess in the first place!" Mina shouts after Jason as he walks back toward the main road.

Mina and I sit in the stifling heat of the car. "I knew this was a bad idea," she says, gritting her teeth. "This is a fucking disaster." She gets out of the car, slamming the door shut behind her. I sit still for a moment, debating whether I should continue to suffocate in the car or join her outside. In the end, Mina wins over suffocation. Though not by much.

We both stand outside, watching the road for Jason and saying nothing.

My stomach grumbles. We never did end up getting breakfast. I reach into my tote, searching for the hotel chocolates. They're a little melty but still good. I knew these would come in handy.

As I unwrap one, I see Mina watching me intently. I stare back at her.

"Do you want one?" I ask.

"No," she says. "It's just rude of you not to offer me one when we're both standing here hungry."

"I literally just offered you one," I say, exasperated. "Here." I throw the other chocolate at her, and she catches it by reflex.

"It's melted," she says, making a face.

"Fine, give it back, then."

She hesitates, her fingers tightening a little around the chocolate. "Are you going to give it to Jason instead? Because if you are, I'd rather just eat it." She scowls and mutters, "This is all his fault, but they'll never blame him. He doesn't deserve chocolate."

I laugh, her scowling reminding me of the way Leah's face looks whenever they kill off a character she likes on one of her K-dramas.

"What?" she says stiffly.

"Nothing," I say, straightening my mouth. "It's just, you know, you're right. He won't get in trouble. If anything, people will probably applaud him for being gracious enough to drive us himself."

"Ha." Mina snorts. "Tell me about it. If people found out about this, they'd probably call *us* reckless and give *him* a free car and make him the new face of Canadian tourism." She pauses, like she can't believe she just said that many words to me in a row without also insulting me.

"Yeah, the way they treat us compared to him, it's like night and day." I roll my eyes. "Like those interviewers. Can you believe one of them asked us how long it takes us to get ready?"

Words tumble out before she can stop herself. "I thought I was the only one who noticed that!" Mina says, her eyes wide. "Why can't they ask us a question that's half as interesting as the ones they ask Jason?"

"Right? And what about sending us to New York? I mean, not that I mind going to New York obviously, but they could have at least told us. What's next? Surprise, we're sending you to Antarctica!"

"In stilettos!"

"And you better have a smile on your face the whole time!"

We laugh and then she sighs, leaning against the trunk and folding her arms across her chest. "Honestly, I should be used to it by now."

I pause, flashing back to Mr. Choo's livid face after our dress rehearsal. "With your family, you mean?"

"Yeah." She shrugs, not looking directly at me. "'No need

to make your own choices; just smile and do as you're told' is basically my family's motto. I don't know why it still surprises me. It's been that way forever." Mina's cheeks have turned bright pink, and she lets out a big exhale. "Sometimes I don't even know why I'm still doing all of this."

"Yeah, I know what you mean," I say, thinking of the past few weeks, letting the frustration and sadness build up inside me. Losing Jason. Missing my dad's graduation. Not speaking to Akari. Leah not going to Everland. "It's like, how much more are they going to ask us to sacrifice before letting us debut? My whole family just up and left our life behind in New York for me and it's been six years and nothing. And now my mom is breathing down my neck about college, and it's like no matter how hard I work, nothing I do will ever be good enough for her." I trail off, staring at the ground to avoid eye contact with Mina.

Mina clears her throat. "Sounds a lot like my dad."

I choke out a small laugh as I realize how much Mina and I actually have in common. "Yeah. She's not the kind of person you ever want to disappoint. Even my dad is too scared to tell her he's been going to law school for the past two years. He just graduated and he's sworn me to secrecy until he gets a job."

Mina lets out a low whistle. "Wow. I'm sure he'll get a job soon, though. I mean, if he has the same work ethic as Princess Rachel, he's gotta be the best lawyer in Seoul." She darts a mischievous smile my way.

I let out an unexpected laugh. I never thought I'd hear

Mina use that nickname in any other way but to torture me.

"So, do you think Jason's dead or just tied up somewhere?" Mina asks, half laughing, half sighing. She raises her wrist to glance at her watch, the rubies embedded in the face glinting in the sun. "If he doesn't get back soon, we'll never make it."

Just then, a horn honks from down the path, and we look up to see Jason sitting in the passenger seat of a rusty white tow truck. "Hey!" he shouts, sticking his head out the window. "Help is here!"

"Finally!" Mina shouts back at him. "I was starting to think we'd die out here."

As the three of us watch the car get hooked up to the tow truck, my stomach starts to rumble. I guess one square of chocolate wasn't enough to relieve my hunger. "Once we're back on the road, can we stop for some food?" I ask.

Jason perks up. "No need!" He walks over to the tow truck, signaling the driver to stop, and then reaches in and pulls two boxes from the front seat. "I brought provisions!"

"Oh goody," Mina says. "I'm dying for a pain au chocolat and an espresso." As she reaches for one of the red-and-yellow boxes, her smiles fades into a look of horror. "This is *not* what I had in mind," she says, brandishing the contents of the box at me. "Are these . . . doughnut holes?"

"Of course not," Jason replies with an easy smile. "They're Timbits."

"What is a *Timbit*?" she asks, her face twisted in disgust.

"It's a Canadian delicacy."

Mina makes another face, and I laugh, popping a honey-dip Timbit in my mouth. "Come on, they're not too bad. Here." I nudge her double-cream, double-sugar coffee toward her. "You'll like this."

"I doubt it."

"Ooh, and remember to save your cup when you're done," Jason says enthusiastically. "You can roll up the rim and win a prize!"

Mina rolls her eyes, but her stomach rumbles and she reaches for the cup. "It tastes way too cheap," she says, shuddering.

"Here, wash it down with this." Jason holds out the Timbits box, shaking the doughnuts toward her.

She picks up a powdered one with two fingers and takes a small nibble. "I can't believe I'm eating this," she moans.

"I can't believe it either. We should take a video," I say.

"Don't you dare," she says, eating the rest of the Timbit in one bite.

The car is back on the main road, and we toss our empty cups into a trash bag the tow truck driver gave us.

"Mina," I ask, "do you want the rest of these Timbits?"

She walks over and peers into the box. "Maybe one or two," she says quickly, stuffing several of the powdered and glazed ones into a napkin in her hand. "You know, for the road. In case we get stuck again."

I grin. "Of course. For the road."

⭐ *Twenty* ⭐

All the sugar and coffee seemed like a good idea when we were stranded in the middle of Ontario, but by the time we get to Brantwood, I feel like my heart is going to burst out of my chest. Next to me, Mina is practically buzzing out of her skin. We've just emerged from the car when Mr. Han comes bearing down on us.

"There you are! Do you know how many times I called you three?"

"We just got reception again," Jason says apologetically.

"Well, hurry up and get ready. You guys are on in an hour! Do you have your outfits?"

Our outfits? I frown at Jason, who's frowning at Mr. Han. "Didn't you say you were going to take care of them?" he asks.

Mr. Han stares at Jason like he can't tell if he's kidding or not. "No," he says, speaking very slowly. "I said you can come on your own as long as *you* waited to pick up your outfits from the hotel's dry-cleaning service."

There's a moment of stunned silence. Mina looks back and

forth between the two of them, her face growing pale. "Does this mean no one has our outfits?"

Mr. Han shakes his head in dismay. "It looks like it."

"This can't be happening." She advances on Jason, her face contorted in a mixture of panic and rage. "Our performance is ruined because of you! You were too busy planning your joy-ride through Canada to bother paying attention to our outfits! Does anything get through that pea brain of yours?" Jason's mouth falls open, but he says nothing. At least he has the good sense to look ashamed.

Mina presses her hands against her face, her voice rising. "Our performance is ruined. Oh my god. What's my father going to say?"

"It's all right. We'll think of something," Mr. Han says, but his voice is unsure. Panicked tears start to fill Mina's eyes, her hands shaking as she wipes them away. "But what is my father going to say?" she half whispers, half cries.

I bite my lip. Maybe it's the fact that for the first time since I met her, I feel like I finally understand where Mina is coming from, or maybe it's my own need to do anything I can to save this performance, but I turn to Mina and say, "Don't worry. I came prepared."

Reaching into my tote, I whip out a pair of strappy high heels and a sparkly orange minidress. "Ever since the trainee house incident, I always carry backups," I joke. She flushes, actually looking embarrassed as I hold the dress out to her. "Here. Take it."

"What will you wear?" she asks.

I grin and do a ballerina twirl. "This outfit, of course." I laugh, tugging on my oversize orange tee. "At least we'll be color coordinated. That's what matters, right?"

Mr. Han glances at Jason, who's wearing all black. Jason lifts the cuff of his pants, revealing orange socks. "It's like it was meant to be," he says.

Mina snorts in his direction. "Just do me a favor and don't talk to me."

Mr. Han nods grimly at the three of us. "It'll do. Let's go."

After hair and makeup, I wander out of the dressing room for some fresh air, taking in the mountains all around me and the huge lake that faces the concert venue. It was a journey to get here, but this town is really breathtaking.

"Aigoo! They haven't been feeding you properly over there!" I startle at the sound of someone speaking Korean behind me, and I turn toward the voice. But they're not speaking to me.

They're speaking to Jason.

He's standing with a group of three older women, all with curly pama hair who are taking turns hugging him and patting his face. As if sensing my stare, one of the women turns and looks right at me. She's wearing a lightweight neon jacket and vest over hiking pants like she's just come back from hitting the trails. I quickly look away, but it's too late. She waves me over. I take a step back as if to say, *No, it's okay; I don't want to intrude*, but before I know it, she's by my side and grabbing my hands. "Hello, friend of Jason! I'd recognize you anywhere from your music video! Come, come, say hello," she says, guiding me to the others.

Jason smiles sheepishly. "Rachel, these are my aunts. You've met Chaerin Eemo, and this is Saerin Eemo, and Yaerin Eemo. Eemos, this is Rachel. She's my . . ."

His voice trails off and my cheeks warm. There's a beat of uncomfortable silence, and then he finally settles on "Co-singer. She's my co-singer. One-third of our singing trio."

Jason's aunts all glance at each other, raising their eyebrows as the two of us laugh awkwardly. I'm cringing on the inside.

"You will have dinner with us after the show, yes?" Chaerin Eemo says, grasping my hands again.

I'm about to politely decline when Mr. Han appears. "Jason, Rachel! You're up next."

Jason hugs his aunts goodbye, and they disappear to find their seats.

"You know, you don't have to come to dinner," Jason says as we walk toward the stage.

"Oh, okay."

"My eemos are just excited to see me. They can be a little . . . overly welcoming."

"Right," I say. Something pinches inside my chest, but I push it away as we reach the backstage area. Mina is twirling in my orange dress and heels. She smiles at me and I smile back.

"Okay, my stars! Time to make DB proud!" Mr. Han

wishes us all luck as we take the stage. The lights are down as Jason sings the first line of the song a cappella, and a hush falls over the crowd, his velvety voice weaving its way through the room like a magic spell, taking everyone with it.

Suddenly, the stage is lit up in white light and music as the spotlights come on and the band behind us starts playing. As Mina and I both join Jason in singing the chorus, I spot Jason's aunts dancing and cheering in the front row. And they're not the only ones. The entire crowd has come alive, waving their glowsticks in the air and chanting our names.

Mina's solo comes up, and for a split second as I watch her, I completely forget where I am. She glides effortlessly across the stage, her moves perfectly in time to the music, her voice full and throaty as she belts out her lines. She approaches me and winks, grabbing my hand and pulling me down into a silly little shimmy move with her. The crowd eats it up. I can feel the stress of this day melting off me. Even our improvised outfits don't seem like such a disaster. Aside from Jason's eemos, the crowd is mostly white people. But they love us. As I look out into the audience, I can see most of them mouthing along the words to the song—even the ones in Korean. The crowd is full of people filming our performance with their phones, but for the first time, I feel myself relaxing in front of all the cameras. A rush of warmth fills my body as I remember why I love K-pop so much. How special it is to be able to share my language and my culture with people all over the world and have them truly see it. Understand it. Love it. I feel my smile

stretch on my face and my heart feels light and free for the first time since this tour started. I remember why I'm here. Why I love this.

Mina's across the stage from me as we start the final verse. She starts off strong, singing as she spins into Jason's waiting arms. But just as he reaches out to grab her waist, I see one of her heels wobble. I barely have time to register what's happening when the heel snaps off the shoe, and Mina goes tumbling down, her palms scraping against the stage. The crowd lets out a collective gasp, but Mina rolls over onto her side and strikes a pose. The audience cheers, and she leaps back up to her feet, kicking off her heels. She doesn't stop smiling, but there's pain flashing in her eyes and I can see her favoring her right leg as we take our bows to a roaring crowd.

Backstage, she whirls toward me, pushing my shoulders. "You bitch! You did this on purpose!"

"What?" My voice catches in my throat.

"You gave me your broken heels. You tried to sabotage me!"

"I didn't!" I say, stunned. "Mina, I'm so sorry. I didn't realize—"

She pushes me again, and I stumble backward. Jason jumps in, holding her back.

"Mina, chill," he says.

"Get the fuck off me!" She pushes him away, seething, turning to me again, fury sparking in her eyes. "I should have known you would pull something like this."

"Mina, are you all right?" Mr. Han rushes toward us, put-

ting an arm around Mina for support. His eyes widen at the sight of her ankle, which is now swelling rapidly. "That looks serious."

She winces, her anger ebbing away to the pain. "It—it hurts." She chokes out the words like she can't stand to admit it. "But I'm okay," she adds. "I just need an ice pack."

"I think we should go to the hospital," Mr. Han says grimly, already guiding her toward the door.

"No! It's fine!" Mina argues. "I just need to . . . walk it off or something." She straightens her back and attempts to walk a few steps, stumbling as soon as she puts any weight on her right foot.

"Hospital. Now," Mr. Han says firmly. She shoots me one last glare as he guides her toward the stage door.

Inside I'm spiraling. *Why did I give her those shoes? Or why didn't I check them before putting them in my bag this morning? Or just wear them myself? It should be me headed to the hospital right now. . . .* But before I can fall deeper into my rabbit hole, Jason's aunts appear backstage, pulling us both into tight hugs.

"What an amazing performance!" Chaerin Eemo says. "We must celebrate you both over dinner!!"

"Oh, please go ahead," I say. I glance over at Jason, who refuses to meet my eyes. "I don't want to interrupt your family time."

"Don't be ridiculous," Yaerin Eemo says, adjusting her black velvet headband with the signature Chanel double Cs outlined in diamonds. "Jason never comes to visit us anymore these days. We must take advantage of it and feed you two—you're both skin and bones!"

"Plus, I know the perfect restaurant," Saerin Eemo agrees, holding up her iPad to snap a quick selfie with me. "Five stars. Best restaurant in all of Brantwood."

I'm swept up in a classic whirlwind of Korean aunts, their guilt-tripping mixing seamlessly with their genuine compassion and reminding me of every single Kim family get-together. I glance at Jason, and this time he's looking right at me, shrugging helplessly.

"If my aunts say eat," he says with a small but pained smile, "there's nothing to do but to eat."

Downtown Brantwood may be the cutest place I've ever seen. The streets are all cobblestone and the buildings look like candied gingerbread houses. Even the most ordinary shops look delightfully quaint, like something straight out of a fairy-tale picture book. Chaerin Eemo tells me how in the winter, the snow makes everything look even more like a magical wonderland.

As we walk toward dinner, Jason's aunts seem to know everyone we pass, stopping every few feet to call out a name or have a quick chat with someone. When we arrive at the restaurant ("Best Caesar in all of Canada! They make them extra spicy!" says Yaerin Eemo), we're immediately ushered to what seems like the best spot in the house, a cozy mahogany table with high-backed leather chairs. All around us are windows that give way to a sweeping view overlooking the mountains.

I glance over at Jason, impressed by the VIP treatment, but he doesn't seem to even notice it. A wave of annoyance washes over me. Typical. I roll my eyes and at the last second he looks over at me, confusion flashing on his face.

"What's your problem?" he whispers, leaning away from his eemos.

"I don't have a problem. I guess I'm just not used to being doted on by adoring fans wherever I go."

His eyes narrow at me. "You have no idea what you're talking about."

Now it's my turn to act confused. "What do you mean I have—"

Suddenly, the waiter sweeps over with a bottle of white wine. "So good to see you all!" he says to Jason's aunts, pouring them each a glass. "Good timing, too. We just got in a new shipment from our wine supplier and we've been saving this bottle for you. We know you're all partial to the 2001 vintage."

Saerin Eemo giggles, picking up her glass. "Of course! All the best things were made in 2001." She winks over at Jason, and he blushes. I smile to myself as I realize Jason was born in 2001.

"She's right!" Yaerin Eemo chimes in before taking a sip. "This is absolutely wonderful."

"Only the best for you ladies," the waiter says, pleased as punch.

My eyebrows knit as I try to fit the pieces together. Maybe

they're not fans of Jason but fans of Jason's aunts. Are his aunts famous too?

"So, Rachel," Yaerin Eemo says after we order. "What's it like working with Jason? Does he hog the spotlight? He would always cry as a kid when he wasn't the center of attention."

"Please, Eemo, when did I do that?" Jason says, his cheeks turning pink.

"Our Jason is handsome, isn't he?" Chaerin Eemo says, looking at him with fondness. She gives me a hearty wink. "He got the good family genes."

I smile politely, this time successfully resisting the urge to roll my eyes. "Yes, he's very popular in Korea."

Saerin Eemo leans forward, looking at me. "Tell us about you, Rachel. What do your parents do?"

"Eemo." Jason groans.

"What? I'm just trying to get to know your friend."

I smile hesitantly and start telling them about my family and our old life in New York, but truthfully, I'm relieved when the food comes. Up until a few weeks ago, meeting Jason's family would have felt like a dream come true, but now it's just another reminder of everything I've lost.

Not that his aunts seem to realize that, with all the heart eyes they keep shooting at us.

"You spoil us!" Saerin Eemo says when the waiter returns with more wine and five plates of free tiramisu.

"Nothing but the best for the Lees," the waiter says cheerfully.

My fork stops in midair as suddenly the pieces click

together. The Lees. I think back to walking down the sidewalk earlier and all the picturesque shops we passed: Lee's Pharmacy, Lee's Grocery, Lee's Dry Cleaners. The special treatment we're getting at this restaurant. How Jason's aunts knew everybody we walked by. They're his mom's sisters, and everyone knows Jason changed his last name after his mom died, so their last names must be Lee as well. . . . I turn to Jason, lowering my voice.

"Does your mom's family own this town or something?" I whisper, half expecting him to laugh out loud at the ridiculousness of my question.

"No."

"Oh right, sorry, I just thought—"

He looks over at me and sighs. "I mean, not that it's any business of yours. But if you must know, it's not the whole town. Just . . . most of it."

My jaw drops. "Seriously? But how come you've never—"

"A toast!" Chaerin Eemo says, interrupting me. She raises her glass. "To Jason and Rachel and a fantastic performance!" Her eyes mist over. "Your mother would have been so proud of you, Jason."

"Hey, hey, party pooper. No tears," Yaerin Eemo says, grabbing her sister's glass. "You've had too much to drink. You're getting weepy."

"You're right, you're right," Chaerin Eemo says, dabbing at her eyes.

"Cheers!" Saerin Eemo says. She looks at me and smiles.

"Rachel, please come back and visit us anytime."

Jason and I lift our glasses, and I see that his eyes are a little misty too. "Cheers!"

Jason and I sit in silence on the back steps of the concert venue as the DB crew loads up the tour vans. Each of us has a huge bag of leftovers from the restaurant, which his aunts insisted we take to have something to "snack on" during the ride. Part of me wants to ask Jason more about Brantwood and his family, but I don't—and he doesn't say anything. It's like we're both trying to put a little distance between us after that dinner.

"Looks like they're back from the hospital," Jason says, standing.

Mr. Han is walking toward us, and Mina follows slowly behind him, propped up on a pair of crutches. My heart sinks as we rush over to meet them.

"She twisted her ankle," Mr. Han says tiredly. "Which means she won't be able to join you for the New York leg of the tour. We'll be sending her back to Korea tonight so she can rest at home." He walks away to supervise the crew.

Mina turns her head slowly to look at me, her eyes shining with angry tears. "I hope you got what you wanted," she says.

It's like a hammer to my heart. How could she think this is what I wanted?

"Mina, I never meant for this to happen—" I start to say, but I'm interrupted by her phone ringing.

At first she ignores it, but it rings again and again and again until she finally gives in and picks up. She barely says hello when Mr. Choo's voice comes bellowing through the other end.

"Shameful! Absolutely shameful! You can't even finish one song without tripping over your own feet? Are you stupid? Because that must be the only explanation for this level of disgrace. You are not a Choo. You are not my daughter." Mina just listens, her head hanging heavily over her chest, tears streaming down her face. Jason and I look away, but inside, my heart feels like it's breaking. When she finally hangs up, she turns her phone off and shoves it deep into her bag, rapidly blinking back her tears.

"Mina," I venture again. But it's no use. She lifts her chin, ignoring me, as she pivots and heads over to get a seat in one of the tour vans.

"Hey," Jason says as I start to follow her. "You can ride with me in the rental car. You know, if you want some distance between you and Mina."

I pause. It's tempting. But Jason is unpredictable right now. And there are too many unpredictable things in my life to pile on one more. Mina may hate me, but at least I know exactly what I'm going to get when I'm with her.

"Thanks, but I think I'll go with the vans," I say. "See you back in Toronto?"

"Okay." He nods and lifts his hand in a wave. "See you."

I walk to the vans and climb in. When I twist around to buckle my seat belt, I see Jason is still standing there, watching me.

⭐ Twenty-One ⭐

"So what's the big deal about this place?" Jason asks. Our faces are almost touching as we sit on the edge of Bethesda Fountain. Behind us, pigeons perch on the Angel of the Waters statue, watching us with a disturbing amount of interest.

"Well . . . ," I say, "it's a beautiful historic landmark at Central Park." I wrap one of my arms around his shoulders and squeeze. "Also, it's perfect for Instagram photos. You can even check your reflection in the water before you take a selfie. Say cheese!"

I whip out my phone and snap a picture of the two of us sitting at the fountain, holding up peace signs.

"Cut!!"

Jason and I freeze in place, as the director and camera crew reframe the shot. "Let's go again, people! And this time, please, a little tighter on Jason's face—let's use what works, people!"

I lower my phone, grimacing. I'm not sure what I thought

our time in New York would be like, but this certainly wasn't it. It's noon on our first day here, and I've been in front of the cameras for eight hours already, filming a promo video DB decided they wanted at the last minute, where I show Jason around the city and take him to all my favorite spots.

Only we're not going to any of my actual favorite spots. They entire day has been scripted for us, including where we go and what we say. The only upside of this whole day is that between my exhaustion and my starvation, I don't even have the energy to feel nervous in front of the cameras.

"Let's get her in another outfit for brunch," the director says.

Another outfit? Argh. Every time we move to a new spot, they have me in hair and makeup all over again. I'm all for carefully curated outfits, but this is ridiculous. Meanwhile, Jason's been wearing the same pair of jeans all day. The only thing he has on rotation is his sunglasses. And no one got into a twenty-minute argument on whether a topknot or a fishtail braid goes better with aviators.

After they curl my hair and put me in an ice-blue wrap dress ("Perfect for a casual brunch!"), we head to what is supposed to be my favorite childhood restaurant—but what is actually a French restaurant that's so fancy I can't even pronounce its name.

"Remember, you'll take a long time staring at the menu and settle on the onion soup," the director says, looking at me. "Jason, get whatever you want. And action!"

I would have much preferred the duck confit waffles—

or even better, Alice's Tea Cup, this amazing old *Alice in Wonderland*–themed tea shop where Leah and I used to celebrate our birthdays, eating scones and drinking tea with our pinkies up and feeling like princesses. I'm usually too busy to feel anything but tired these days, but suddenly a pang of homesickness hits me so hard that I almost fall off my chair. I grip my legs to the seat and pretend to peruse the French brunch items for an unnecessary amount of time as Jason goes ahead and orders the duck confit waffles. Of course. I'm almost tempted to ask him for a bite, but after dinner in Brantwood, things between us are weirder than they've ever been.

The director gestures for me to hurry up and say my line. I lift my glass and smile. "Cheers!" I can only bring myself to look him in the eye for a split second as we clink our glasses. As I do, my stomach growls in hunger and I hear Jason snort with laughter. I look away quickly, taking a sip of my drink (I'm not even sure what's in mine. Pink lemonade? Grapefruit juice?) to cover up the fact that I am about two seconds away from dumping my bowl of soup all over my costar.

"Jalmukesumneda," Jason says, even though he's already inhaled half of his waffles.

"You have to say it like the French do," I say primly, smiling at the camera. "Bon appétit!"

I've barely lifted the spoon to my lips when the director yells, "Cut! Perfect. Let's head to the next spot."

"But I haven't even eaten," I say, blinking.

"We'll get it packed up to go," the director says, distracted.

"We need to get a move on if we want to finish filming today." He turns to his assistant. "Can we get another outfit change for the girl?"

I look sadly down at my onion soup. Suddenly, Jason looks at me in concern.

"Here," he says, nudging his plate toward me. "Eat the rest."

I'm too hungry to argue, and I grab the plate from him, gulping down a few bites of waffle so quickly I can barely taste it, and before I know it, I'm being shoved into a pair of skin-tight leather pants and stilettos and deposited into the middle of Times Square. The sun is beating so hard that I can't even touch the top of my head without my fingers burning. Whoever decided that leather pants and stilettos were a good combo for the most crowded place in New York City should seriously question their fashion choices.

A group of girls stops a few feet away from us, gasping and reaching for their phones to snap a photo. "Oh my god, it's Jason Lee from NEXT BOYZ!"

"Ugh, but he's with that Rachel Kim girl." One of the girls sneers in my direction. "Isn't South Korea known for their plastic surgery? If I were her, I would get a whole new face." His fans have been following us around all day. Once one person saw us and posted our location on social media, we've had crowds of people popping up out of nowhere to gush over Jason.

I'm having Lotte World flashbacks and sweat is pouring down my legs, but the cameras are rolling and I have no choice but to keep a smile plastered on my face. The director leads us around the middle of Times Square, positioning us on the bottom row of the red TKTS bleachers, gesturing at me to recite my line about how this is my favorite spot in the whole city and it was where I would come and imagine my future as a famous K-pop star. (For the record: it is not and no native New Yorker who values their mental health would ever willingly come to Times Square.)

We walk past a halal cart, and the smell of grilling meats practically makes me swoon. I remember Umma and Appa used to buy shawarma and falafel every Friday night for dinner from the halal guy two blocks over from our old apartment. They would say he came to America to find a better life, just like they had. It was always so good too, the soft chewy pita, the grilled chicken, and the cool, tart tzatziki sauce. . . .

Suddenly, Jason's arms are around me and my cheek is pressed into his chest.

I blink. What just happened?

"Are you okay?" he asks, worry etched into his face. "You were swaying, and it looked like you were about to collapse."

"I was?" I say, my eyes squinting in the sunlight. I press my hand to my head, feeling woozy.

Jason turns angrily to the camera crew. "Stop filming! Can't you see she needs a break?"

"But, Jason, we're on a tight schedule," the director says, looking over his notes for the next scene.

"I don't care if we're on a tight schedule," Jason snaps back. "You would stop in a second if I said I needed a break."

. . . what's it really like being back in New York?"

s slowly. Now that I've eaten, the fact that Jason and
ne together for the first time since that night in the
nacha seems to be setting in for both of us.

s weird," I admit after a pause. Not sure what else to
swallow a bite of burger, my homesickness still looming
inside me.

ason nods, his eyes darting around the park, refusing to
k in my direction. "In what way?"

I sigh. It makes me think about how different things
e for me and my family since we moved to Korea. "I don't
now. In every way." Almost without thinking, I pull out
my phone and show him Appa's graduation selfie. "My dad
just graduated from law school. I'm the only one in our family who knows because he wanted to keep it a secret until he
was sure he could succeed." I look at Appa's smiling face on
the screen. "And I get that. I feel a lot of pressure too. If this
whole K-pop thing doesn't work out, all those years of training will have been for nothing, and I'm terrified of that happening."

Jason's eyes widen in slight shock as I fall silent again, but
he just nods in understanding. "Yeah. I get that pressure."

I mean to let out a small laugh, but I can hear the scornful tone in my voice. "I think your adoring fans and our lovely
director would beg to differ."

Jason runs his hand through his hair, thinking. "I know
what it must look like from the outside. But think about how

The director's head whip
you need a break? Cut! People,
some water, please?"

Jason shakes his head furiously.
what I'm talking about. The star of y
lapsed from lack of food and water an
about me."

"Because you're Jason Lee. You're DB

"You know what," Jason says, cutting
right. I am Jason Lee. And I've decided that
rest of the day off."

He grabs a pair of sweatpants, a T-shirt, and
ers off the rack holding all my preapproved outfits
and leads me away from the crew. His fans are g
with their phones, no doubt capturing the whole exch
Snapchat, but I don't care. I realize with a sudden jolt th
spent so much time in front of the cameras this past week
I barely even noticed them today.

"Come on." He grins, holding out his hand, then says th
three most beautiful words in the English language. "Let's get
lunch."

I breathe a sigh of relief as I dig into my second Shake Shack
burger, my feet tucked under my seat as we sit in our Uber by
Madison Square Park. Next to me, Jason's window is open and
he's taking pictures of tourists feeding french fries to a group
of particularly fat squirrels.

hard you're working right now—the pressure to debut. That pressure is times a million once you actually do."

My voice catches in my throat. "I've been so worried about debuting that I guess I haven't really given any thought to what would happen once I do—*if* I do."

"You will," Jason says, looking directly into my eyes. "And you'll have your whole family there to cheer you on at every concert. Leah will insist on it, I'm sure." His face breaks into a wide smile.

"You're one to talk! Your eemos could give my sister a run for her money!"

Jason smiles at me again, but it's more half-hearted this time. "Yeah. I'm sorry about that dinner, by the way—I know those three can be a little intense. Especially when there's a pretty girl involved."

I feel the spark of a familiar flutter in my chest, but I ignore it. "What was it like, being back in Toronto?" I ask.

"Weird," he says. "I love my eemos, but I rarely come home anymore. It's just . . . difficult."

I hesitate, not wanting to pry but also missing the way the two of us just fall so easily into conversation. "Because of your mom?"

Jason looks at me and gives an almost imperceptible shrug. "Yeah. But also"—he pauses—"I'm sure you noticed my dad wasn't around when we were in Canada."

I give him a quick nod.

"Growing up, it was always like me and my mom versus

my dad. It wasn't on purpose or anything. My mom and I just both loved music—and especially K-pop. She used to sing me old Chung Yuna songs when she tucked me in at night. It felt like something that was just ours." He gives me a sad smile. "My dad hated it, though. He didn't want her speaking Korean to me at home or making Korean food. He was always saying she should just assimilate to Toronto life since she immigrated as a teenager. He didn't understand why it was so important to her—to *us*—to stay connected to it."

He sighs deeply, twirling a french fry over and over between his fingers. "After she died, we both kind of fell apart. I wanted to keep her memory alive, so I'd sing the songs she taught me. But every time he heard me play any Korean music, he'd flip out. It was scary how mad he could get about a song. Just a simple Korean song."

There's a lump in my throat the size of a golf ball, and I can feel myself holding my breath as he continues.

"My eemos, they all still lived in Brantwood, where my mom grew up. I would call them crying every time Dad and I got in another fight, and it started happening so much that eventually they sued him for custody. They've always told me Dad fought hard to keep me, but I found out the truth right before I moved to Seoul. The three of them sold off some of their family's holdings and offered my dad this big cash settlement, and he took it. No questions asked. That was that. I moved to Brantwood and took my mom's last name. Things with my dad have been . . . complicated ever since. I thought

I'd try to see him on this trip, but he said he couldn't get the time off work."

My mind flashes back to the heated phone call Jason was having in the hotel lobby a few days ago. It all makes sense now.

I swallow hard, but the lump in my throat won't move. I want to reach my hand out to touch him, to tell him how sorry I am, how my heart is breaking for him, but instead I just say, "Jason, I had no idea."

"Not a lot of people do," he says lightly. "But everyone knows the next part. My eemos encouraged me to keep on playing music, especially K-pop, as a way to grieve my mom and stay connected with her. I started making YouTube covers. And then DB found me. And now," he says, opening his arms, "here I am, in Madison Square Park. Watching the world's fattest squirrels eat french fries."

I laugh, pressing my palms into my eyes. "That's quite the journey."

"It is, isn't it?" He grins, but the smile quickly disappears from his face. "I'm sorry, Rachel," Jason says suddenly.

"About what? Making me almost cry?"

He smiles a small smile and shakes his head, his face growing serious. "About the double standard. You were right. After what Kang Jina said that night, I was so convinced that you were both being too careful, too paranoid. But . . . I was wrong. I should have listened to you. I should have paid attention. But I didn't notice anything because I didn't want to. I didn't want

to see how differently people treat you and Mina and Jina."
He pauses, swallowing hard. "I was supposed to be your . . .
boyfriend." His cheeks burn as he stumbles over the word, but
he keeps going. "But I wasn't even a good friend to you. I didn't
see what's been going on right in front of me for years. And that
makes me just as bad as the execs, the fans . . . everyone. But I
want you to know that I see it and I'm here for you. No matter
what. And I'm sorry I was such a jerk about everything."

"You were," I say, smiling. "But thanks for saying that.
Friends." I stick my hand out to shake his.

"Friends," he says, grabbing my hand. He opens his mouth
like he's about to say something more, but instead, he just
closes his fingers over mine for a moment and squeezes tight.

⭐ Twenty-Two ⭐

I wake up the next morning to a loud knock on my hotel door. Did DB send me breakfast in bed or something? I swing the door open and barely have time to let out a yelp before I'm attacked by a flurry of apple flower perfume and a rainbow blur of hair clips.

"Surprise!"

"Oh my god!" I scream as Juhyun and Hyeri throw their arms around me. "What are you two doing here?"

"Our cousin's having some big engagement party in Brooklyn to show off her ring," Juhyun says, plopping down on my bed. "So we thought we'd drop in on our little international K-pop star."

"I'd say our surprise was a success," Hyeri says, grinning triumphantly. "Aww, look, you're even crying!"

I laugh, the remnants of my green tea night mask melting away as tears stream down my face. I'd been feeling so homesick for New York that I forgot how much I missed Seoul. . . .

And the twins are like a little piece of home delivered right to my door.

"You're not busy, are you?" Juhyun asks.

I glance behind me at the stack of homework on my hotel room table. The homework that was supposed to be done today, my one day off on this whole whirlwind tour. "Well . . ."

"Because we thought we could go shopping," Hyeri says.

My eyes light up. "Shopping?"

"We've got a private suite at Saks Fifth Avenue with our name on it," Juhyun says, wiggling her eyebrows.

A private suite? At Saks Fifth Avenue? "Just give me a second," I say, rushing over to my suitcase.

I disappear into the bathroom and emerge a moment later, properly dressed in a pair of white denim shorts and a silky mint-green top, my hair in a messy fishtail braid and my purse slung over my shoulder. "Lead the way."

"What do you think of this one?" Juhyun twirls around in a white silk dress with a ruffled hem and sheer crimped long sleeves.

I lean back on the velvet chaise lounge chair in our private suite, sipping a crystal glass full of sparkling water with lemon. "It's cute, but guests usually avoid wearing white to wedding-type festivities. It's kind of the bride's color."

"Please, it's only an engagement party," Juhyun says, sticking her tongue out at me. "Plus, this one's not for tonight. It's for the Molly Folly company gala. Do you know what you're going to wear yet?"

The gala. I totally forgot about that. The twins' parents throw one every summer and I always go, but with everything that's been going on lately, it's been the furthest thing from my mind. I swirl my water around, staring into the glass.

"I might not . . . have time to go this year," I say.

"Nooo, Rachel," Hyeri says. "You have to go!"

"Yeah," Juhyun chimes in. "It's, like, our best friend tradition. I give you guys a makeover, we eat a bunch of sushi while we watch my parents mingle with Seoul's most annoying rich people, and then we go home and watch *Mean Girls* in our dresses!"

I smile, guilt creeping its way into my stomach. "I know and I love it. I just don't know if I have time this summer."

"No time for free gourmet sushi and Lindsay Lohan?" Juhyun says, her mouth dropping open. "Has K-pop sucked out your soul or something? You've been working so hard it's like you've forgotten how to have fun."

Even as I laugh, I can't help but wince on the inside. Juhyun may be teasing, but she doesn't know how close to home she's hitting.

"I know what you need," Hyeri says decisively. She grabs a polka-dotted chiffon minidress from the hanger and holds it out in front of me. "You need a dress for the engagement party."

"What? I can't go to your cousin's engagement party! I don't even know her!"

"Yes, you can," Juhyun states matter-of-factly, pulling a few more dresses for me to try.

"There's no point in arguing, Rachel." Hyeri smiles. "Consider this a fun-tervention."

"Okay, okay," I say, lifting my hands in the air. "I give up."

"Good," Juhyun says, tossing a silvery strapless dress over to me. "Let's start with that one."

The last time I checked, Brooklyn Bridge Park didn't have a rosé-spouting unicorn-shaped fountain or a hot-pink inflatable ball pit filled to the brim with mini disco balls. I'm also pretty certain that Diplo wasn't livestreaming himself DJing from the second floor of a Lucite treehouse, completely covered in iridescent flakes of glitter.

My mouth drops open as I take it all in, and I turn to the twins. "How?"

"Our family rented the whole park for the evening and transformed it for the party," Juhyun says. "All this stuff is only here for one night, so we better enjoy it while we can!"

Laid out next to the grand carousel that I remember from my childhood is a gigantic table filled to the brim with macarons in the shape of wedding rings and an artisanal cotton candy bar, with toppings ranging from edible glitter to strawberry-flavored Pop Rocks. The city skyline sparkles as the backdrop to the whole thing, and every person I see seems to be glowing with what I can only describe as pure, unfiltered, radiating joy. Or maybe it's the light-up halo crowns they're all wearing. As we make our way farther into the park, I see Jason standing by the unicorn fountain,

searching the crowds of people like he's waiting for someone. My breath catches.

I wasn't expecting to see him here.

When his gaze falls on me, his whole face lights up in a
smile and I realize he's been waiting for me.

It takes me a minute to realize he's not alone. To my surprise, Minjun and Daeho are with him, helping themselves to
glasses of rosé from the fountain. Minjun sees me and beams,
raising his glass in my direction.

"About time you got here, Rachel," he says. He nudges
Jason in the side. "This guy was about to send a search party
looking for you."

"Hi, Rachel," Daeho says, sipping his rosé.

"What's going on?" I say, looking from one person to the
next and then back at the twins, who are both grinning at me
with knowing smiles.

"We'll let Jason explain," Hyeri says.

Jason smiles shyly, his gaze softening as he meets my eyes.
"I just wanted you to have some good memories of being back
home. When you look back on your first tour, I want you to
remember more than long days of filming with no food and a
thousand outfit changes. I want you to have memories that you
don't want to forget. So I asked the Cho twins for help, and
when they said they were coming for their cousin's engagement
party, well"—he shrugs like it's nothing, but the look on his face
is undeniably pleased—"the surprise just kind of fell into place.
Minjun and Daeho flew in with the twins to celebrate with us."

"Jason . . ." I think of all the things I want to say: *This is so sweet. Thank you. I can't believe you did this. This is beyond amazing.* But suddenly I feel a wave of anxiety as I take in all the people around us. The park is packed with guests. What if some of them are NEXT BOYZ fans?

Jason's smile falters as he sees my face. "What's wrong?" he asks.

"I just . . . As much as I love this . . . what if someone recognizes us?" I ask. With Jason and Minjun both here, I can only imagine the frenzy that would ensue. And I'm not sure I'm up for being harassed by their fans again today. Or explaining to DB why a picture of me and Jason at a party in Brooklyn is all over Instagram. Not when things between us finally feel good again.

"Rachel, this is Brooklyn," Juhyun says quickly, giving my arm a reassuring squeeze. "Everyone here would rather die than admit they recognize—or god forbid *like*—some shiny, perfect K-pop star. There's nothing to worry about."

I look around me and see that she's right—no one is snapping covert pictures of the celebrity DJ or sneaking curious looks at that twentysomething pop star fresh off his first world tour who's making out with his gorgeous, redheaded, Hollywood starlet fiancée in the disco ball pit. I start to relax.

"You're right," I say. I turn to Jason and smile. "And this is unbelievable. Thank you."

"All right, all right," Minjun says, jumping in. "Does this mean we can play now? Let's get rolling before this guy gets drunk on unicorn juice!"

He points his thumb at Daeho, whose face has turned bright red after one drink.

"Is it that bad?" Daeho asks, pressing one hand against his cheek.

"I think you look perfect," Hyeri says, her cheeks turning pink for a completely different reason.

Minjun shakes his head. "My man, you are literally an apple in the Big Apple."

Jason turns to me, his eyes sparkling with excitement. "What do you want to do first?" he asks, reaching toward me.

I grin at him, a familiar swoopy feeling starting to nudge its way into my stomach as I feel his hand linger on the small of my back. "What do you think?"

We both yell at the same time, "Doughnut swings!"

We run around the park, first stopping at the gigantic doughnut-shaped swings, which Minjun tries to backflip off in midair (thankfully, landing on the tropical-island-shaped bouncy house behind him) before racing over to the treehouse, Minjun throwing his arms around Hyeri's shoulders as they both belt out the lyrics to "Sucker." My hair is sticking to the back of my neck and my feet ache from dancing, but I'm high on the rush of all being together in New York at a party where no one knows who we are. Jason and I grab on to each other and scream, his arms wrapping around me, enveloping me in a warm cloud of maple and mint.

The song fades out and the DJ's voice comes booming over the speakers. "Who here is in love?" he asks. In the front of the crowd, I can see the twins' cousin and her fiancé cheering, as their friends gather around them. "That's what I like to hear! Now, this next song may be a new one for a lot of you, but it just hit number-freaking-one on the K-pop music charts and I know you're all gonna fall in love with it. Get excited!"

The crowd cheers even louder as the song begins to play. I hear Jason's voice coming out of the speakers and I gasp.

This isn't just any K-pop song.

The number one song on the K-pop music charts is *our* song!

I press my hand over my mouth, frozen.

Jason's face is in shock as he raises his arms in the air like an Olympic champion. "This is us!" he cries. "We're number one!" I can barely hear him over the guests, who all around us are cheering along to the song, dancing wildly with huge smiles on their faces. They love it.

I scream, jumping up and down. "We're number one! We're number one!"

He laughs, lifting me up and spinning me around and around.

At the feel of his hands around my waist, something inside me breaks, and all the feelings I've been keeping bottled up for so long come rushing out.

And I realize something.

The first time Jason and I kissed, I did it out of fear. Fear that this dream I've been working toward for so long wouldn't be enough or that I would fail in trying to achieve it. Fear that

I would let down my friends, Yujin, and my family. But fear can't feed your dreams.

It can only feed more fear.

What if I want to be someone who follows her heart and takes chances? Someone who can rise beyond the constant judgment and competition of this industry? Who isn't scared to seize happiness for herself, whatever that may look like? And this thing between me and Jason, whatever it is, I know it sparks a light in me. Don't I deserve to follow that light and see where it goes? To be that girl who holds hands and laughs freely with the boy who makes her heart sing?

Even if it means I might have to let go of my dreams? Or maybe just accept that I have a new one?

When he finally turns toward me, his face lit up in that familiar Jason way, it feels like a thousand tiny fireworks going off in my heart. We lean toward each other, and right before our lips touch, he pauses for a split second, everything that's happened between us lingering in the air. But I don't pull away. Instead, I throw my arms around him and kiss him. I hear our friends whistle and cheer around us, but in this moment, there's only me and Jason.

In this moment, everything is perfect.

⭐ Twenty-Three ⭐

Leah's favorite episode of *Oh My Dreams* is the one where Park Dohee and Kim Chanwoo go on their first date. He's late to meet her at the restaurant and it starts to rain. She thinks he's changed his mind and isn't coming, so she starts walking home without an umbrella—but halfway through her walk, rain stops falling on her. It's Chanwoo. He's carrying his umbrella over her head, getting soaking wet with his arms full of groceries. Turns out, he got to the restaurant early, but when he discovered they were out of her favorite dish, he ran from store to store looking for the ingredients so the chef could make it for Dohee, which is why he was late.

Whenever Leah watches it, her face lights up in happiness and she sighs. "That's what true love feels like."

I smile at the thought of my sister going giddy over her stories, but now I know I have an even better one for her: the story of me and Jason. Things are still tender and new between us, and I'm not even sure what "us" will look like once we're back home, but I'm hopeful, more hopeful than I've been in a long time.

As I open the door to our apartment, I can't wait to see my family. I know Appa will flip over his graduation gift, a leather-bound notebook with a city skyline etched on the cover. I'm even excited to see Umma and give her the snow globe in the shape of a New York City taxicab that I got for her world snow globe collection.

"I'm home!" I call, toeing off my shoes and sliding into house slippers.

"Rachel?" Umma's voice calls from inside. "We're all in the living room."

I walk into the living room, happily dragging my suitcase behind me. "Get ready, family. I've got presents—"

"Hi, Rachel," Mina says, smiling sweetly. "How was the rest of the tour?"

I freeze. Just like Umma said, they're all in the living room. Appa, Umma, Leah—and Mr. Choo and Mina. They're sitting around a wooden fold-up tea table with mugs of bori cha and a plate of neatly sliced pears with miniature fruit forks. I can tell by the untouched pears and the way the tea is still steaming that they haven't been here for very long.

Also, Leah is holding a half-eaten Melona bar in her hand, and no way Umma would have let her crack open an ice cream with guests over.

"It was great," I say slowly. It takes all my effort to keep the confusion on my face at a level of pleasant surprise instead of horrified shock to find the Choos in our apartment. "How are you doing, Mina? How's your ankle?"

"Never better!" Mina says, smiling sweetly at me. "Daddy got me the best physical therapist in Seoul, and I'm better than ever."

"Actually, Rachel, you came at the perfect moment," Mr. Choo says, smiling at his daughter and then gesturing for me to take a seat.

My eyes widen, but I quickly recover, my insides boiling over the fact that he just invited me to sit down in my own home. He's the one who looks out of place here with his overly gelled hair and his double-breasted business suit. He smiles broadly and turns toward Appa. "I was just about to offer your father a job as an in-house legal consultant with the Choo Corporation."

The room falls completely silent. My heart stops in my chest, and I turn toward Mina. She did this. I told her about Appa while we were stranded outside Brantwood. And now she's using that information to try to destroy me. But how? By . . . giving my dad a job? It doesn't make any sense.

Mr. Choo barrels on, undeterred by our lack of response.

"When I found out that you recently graduated with a law degree, I knew this would be a great opportunity for both of us. I've been looking to hire a new consultant for ages, but I've been waiting for the perfect candidate. Someone hardworking and trustworthy and who will uphold the values of our family corporation. From what I've heard of you, Mr. Kim, you would be a fantastic fit."

"I don't know what to say," Appa says, his expression a mirror of Leah's. A huge smile spreads across his face. "This is an amazing opportunity for me."

"Yes, an amazing opportunity," Umma agrees, but her eyes flash with anger. She may be fooling Mr. Choo and Mina with her pear slices and gracious-hostess demeanor, but I know her. Inside she is seething at being caught off guard with the news that Appa has been going to law school.

"Wait, so Appa is going to work for Mr. Choo as a law-yer?" Leah asks, waving her hands in excitement. Melted ice cream goes splattering all over the floor, but no one notices. "Whoa! That's huge!"

Mr. Choo laughs good-naturedly, but his eyes are cold, calculating. "It is indeed an incredible opportunity. We're all family at the Choo Corporation. Now you'll all be part of the family too. Forever linked."

Why does that sound like a threat?

I get a sudden flashback of Kang Jina's warning to watch out for Mr. Choo. My mind flits from all the SPONSORED BY C-MART FAMILY signs I've seen at DB to the Choo Corporation plane we flew to Toronto for the tour to the many times I've heard him explode in anger toward Mina.

My stomach sinks. He's a powerful man and not one to be trifled with. I don't like the sound of being linked forever with him or his corporation. I know what that really means. We're not family.

They own us.

Mr. Choo rises, extending his hand to Appa. "I'll have someone come by with paperwork soon. I'm sorry I can't stay longer to chat today, but business calls, as always."

"Of course, of course," Appa says. He and Umma both stand, shaking his hand. "Thank you so much again. I'm honored."

Leah and I both rise to bow to Mr. Choo, but my fists are clenched by my sides. He gives us a nod and heads for the door. Appa and Umma follow after him to see him out, accidentally stepping into Leah's sticky ice-cream puddle and leaving melon-green footprints all over the floor.

They don't even realize the mess they've just stepped into.

"Well, this is brilliant, isn't it?" Mina says brightly, munching on a pear slice. "We'll all be one big happy family now. And, Rachel, you know I've been *dying* to meet your little sister."

"Really? You have?" Leah says, her eyes widening. She's heard enough stories about Mina from me that she's got her guard up, but I can see that she's flattered by the idea of Mina wanting to meet her. I take a protective step toward her, glaring at Mina.

"Of course," Mina says. "I've always wished that I had a younger sister. So many of the unnis in Electric Flower treat me like a little sister, and I want to pay it forward. They give me the best advice." She drops her voice to a conspiratorial whisper. "Just between you and me, though, some of those unnis could really take their own advice. They're always telling me to take care of my health, but I happen to know that

one of the girls sews candy into the sleeves of all her stage outfits because she has such a huge sweet tooth. Now, I don't want to throw her under the bus, but Joo Semy should really be careful. I heard DB is spending a small fortune on her yearly dental bills."

Leah's eyes are practically bugging out of her head with glee. I can see her walls coming down as she leans toward Mina. "No way."

"Yes way."

I want to scream. This can't be happening.

"Anyway, I should get going too." She smiles at me. "Walk me to the elevator, Rachel?"

"My pleasure," I say through gritted teeth.

She says goodbye to Leah and my parents as we walk out to the elevator. As soon as the front door shuts behind us, her face lights up with a self-satisfied evil smirk.

"I don't know why you're doing this, Mina, but I'm going to tell my dad everything. There's no way he'll take the job after he hears what an awful person you are."

"Ah, ah, Rachel. You heard my dad—we're all one big happy family now. Proper respect must be paid. And we both know how much this job means to your father. You wouldn't want to do anything to ruin that for him, would you?"

I narrow my eyes at her, my body temperature skyrocketing. As much as I want to burst into my apartment and tell Appa everything, I know I can't. This job is everything to him.

"So how did you and Jason celebrate the big news in New York?" Mina asks, interrupting the dark spiral of thoughts crowding inside my brain.

"Celebrate?" I blink, momentarily forgetting everything about the tour. New York suddenly feels light-years away. "Oh, you mean hitting number one on the K-pop charts?"

She cocks her head to the side, raising her eyebrows as she punches the down button on the elevator. "No, that's not the news I meant."

My brow furrows, and a delighted smile spreads across her face.

"You mean you don't know?" she says, hardly able to contain her pleasure at my dumbfounded expression. "Oh, Princess Rachel, still so much to learn about the world." She takes her phone out of her pocket. She turns the screen to face me, and I realize it's Leah's favorite K-pop gossip site. Headline after headline pops up on the screen, and I squint as I take them all in.

JASON LEE GOING SOLO!

NEXT BOYZ NO MORE! LONG LIVE JASON LEE.

DB EXCITED TO EXPLORE MUSICAL FUTURE WITH NEWLY SOLO ARTIST JASON LEE.

I stand there, my head spinning as the elevator doors open. "Thanks for seeing me out, Rachel," she says as the doors slide shut, a wicked smile lighting up her face. "And hey. Welcome home."

Twenty-Four

I stare at the closed elevator doors, unable to move. Jason is going solo? Why didn't he tell me? This is huge!

I call him, wanting to be one of the first to congratulate him and ask him how it all happened, but it goes straight to voice mail. I send him a Kakao message, tapping my foot against the floor. After a minute of no reply, I can't wait any longer.

When in doubt, turn to Instagram.

I type "#JasonLee" in the search bar, and immediately, a string of photos pops up, posted by stalker fans from just five minutes ago, of him entering a familiar-looking building.

DB headquarters.

I don't even realize that I'm still wearing my sloppy airplane clothes and candy-striped house slippers as I run out of the apartment toward the nearest subway station. But my body is buzzing with excitement and there's only one thought in my brain: I need to see Jason.

As soon as I hop on the subway, my phone starts buzzing furiously in my pocket. Thinking it's Jason calling me back, I scramble to grab my phone, nearly sending it flying across the subway car. But it's not Jason.

It's Akari. Hey, can you talk?

I can almost feel my brain crunching to a stop inside my head as I stare at her text, all thoughts of Jason zooming away. Akari hasn't spoken to me since that day outside Yujin's office. My fingers hover above the keyboard on my phone. There's so much to tell her I don't even know where to start. Or how. I'm just about to start typing when suddenly a teen girl sitting across from me on the subway looks up at me, her eyes widening in recognition. She leans over to her friend and whispers, "That's her! That's the girl! It's Jason's lover!"

My breath catches in my chest. What did she say?

My blood runs ice-cold as I click out of Kakao and search "Rachel Kim." Immediately, my screen is flooded with the latest headline: JASON LEE, CAUGHT BETWEEN TWO LOVERS.

My entire body goes rigid.

What is this?

The article is full of photos of me and Jason from our self-care day in Tokyo. Walking through Harajuku; eating at the Monster Café; me rubbing Leah's back in our Mario go-kart, Then, right next to our photos, is a similar series of Jason and Mina. Eating at a candlelit restaurant with their heads bent down, laughing; going for a sunset walk at the Han River, their faces sun kissed by the golden-hour glow; sharing an ice cream with one bowl and two spoons between them.

My hands go cold and clammy. I don't understand.

As if on autopilot, I scroll through the article, skimming as fast as I can. I pick up phrases like "an impossible choice" and "torn between two girls." A wave of bile starts to churn in my stomach, inching its way up my throat. I think I might be sick.

Has Jason been dating Mina this whole time?

All around me, I hear people start to whisper, glancing down at their phones and then at me.

"Hey, isn't that Rachel Kim?"

"It is. It is. Did you read this line about her? 'Rachel Kim is especially notorious for playing mildang with Jason Lee's heart, pushing and pulling and giving mixed signals to keep him on his toes. One second she's all over him, and the next she's giving him the cold shoulder.'"

"Wow. Can you believe her? Jason deserves better."

The back of my neck prickles, and I can feel their phone cameras turning toward me. I quickly cover my face with my hands and hunch down in my seat. When the subway stops, I leap up, running past the crowds of people waiting to board and booking it all the way to headquarters. It's no better inside, though, as young trainees gathered in the lobby whisper and point as I walk past them.

"Did you see who it is?"

"I heard she's pregnant with Minjun's love child and that's why Jason left her."

"I heard she and Mina tried to strangle each other with the straps on their heels during tour."

Well, at least the DB rumor mill isn't hurting for content.

Out of habit more than anything else, I turn down the hallway toward the independent practice rooms, when I hear a familiar song.

Jason's song. The one he played for me in the music room at school.

I burst into the practice room and see Jason sitting on a chair with his guitar strapped over his shoulder. Minjun is there too, choreographing some cheesy interpretive dance moves to Jason's song. They both look up and see me at the same time, a huge smile spreading across Jason's face.

"Ah, the lovebird, responding to the song of her mate," Minjun says, pressing a hand over his heart. "Beautiful, just beautiful."

"What are you doing here?" Jason asks brightly, holding out his arms as if expecting me to greet him with a hug. "I missed you."

He *missed* me?

A million thoughts rush into my head, tangling themselves into a gigantic knot inside my heart. Everything feels like it's happening all at once, and my brain can't reconcile my Jason, sitting here with his guitar casually strung around his back, saying he missed me, with the Jason I saw in the tabloid pictures, the one who was laughing and eating ice cream with Mina. I feel nervous and hurt and like a paper pinwheel toy could do a better job of pushing air through my body than my lungs could at this moment—but most of all, I feel angry.

I open my mouth, about to let him have it, but nothing comes out. Now that we're face-to-face, there are no words. I'm totally frozen. Shock has finally gotten the best of me.

Minjun glances between us, sensing the shift in mood. "I'll give you two a minute." He walks out of the room, closing the door with a soft *click* behind him.

Jason frowns. "Rachel, is everything okay?"

It dawns on me then. He doesn't know what I know yet. He hasn't seen the article. No phones allowed during training.

Wordlessly, I hold my phone up, pictures of him and Mina splashed across the screen.

Jason takes it from my hands. As he reads, his face goes from confused to horrified, his eyes widening as understanding sinks in. He swallows hard.

"It's not what it looks like. Please, Rachel, let me explain," he says slowly, carefully.

Yes, please explain, I want to say. *Tell me something that will pull me out of the spiral I've been falling down since I got off the subway. Tell me something, anything, that will keep my heart from breaking, because right now it's barely holding together by a thread. Let this be a mistake or, better yet, a dream to wake up from and forget the next day.*

Just please tell me something that will make this go away.

But I don't say any of that. Instead I flick my eyes down toward the floor. "Go on, then." My voice comes out hoarse. "Explain."

He takes a deep breath, wiping his hands against his pants. Usually when he says something important, he looks me right in the eye, but today it's like he's trying to look anywhere but at me. "About six months ago, I showed DB my original song, the one I played for you. I wanted to go solo, and I wanted that song to be my debut song as a solo artist."

The words rush out before I can stop myself. "But what about NEXT BOYZ? And Minjun?"

Jason sighs. "Minjun understood. As for the rest of the group . . . what can I say? I told you about my mom, how much K-pop music meant to her. How much it means to me. I wanted my music to mean something again."

I nod slowly. "I understand that part. What I don't understand is what this has to do with me and Mina."

Jason swallows hard. "Well. The execs said yes. But there was a catch. They wanted to see if I could really succeed as a solo artist." His eyes flit to mine. "They wanted me to record a new single with a trainee."

"Our song," I say, understanding slowly creeping in.

"Right. It was decided that I would do a test duet with Mina, but after the video of us singing together went viral, I . . ." He pauses here, looking down at his shoes. "I thought singing with both of you would create more buzz."

My heart pinches at his words. "It was your idea?" I flash back to Mr. Han fighting for me in the boardroom, when it seemed like all hope was lost.

Jason gives a small nod, like he can't bear the thought of what he's done. "I talked to Mr. Han after we sang together."

"Right. More arm candy for the great Jason Lee."

"Rachel, no!" Jason looks at me, his brows knit together. "It wasn't like that. I loved singing with you. It was like . . ."

"We were meant to sing together?" I finish flatly.

"Yeah, exactly. Like it was meant to be."

"And the rest of it?" I ask, gesturing to my phone, which is still in Jason's hands.

"DB was demanding I do whatever I could to generate buzz for the song," he says, speaking quickly now. "You know how DB is all about publicity. They staged dates for me with both you and Mina and had the paparazzi follow us. But, Rachel, please understand." He grabs my hands, locking eyes with mine. "Everything with Mina was totally posed, just like it was supposed to be. But it was different with you. That day in Tokyo, on the plane, I meant what I said. And I've meant it ever since. I love being around you. I love y—"

"Don't!" I shout. "Don't say it. You can't say that to me right now." My mind is spinning. I don't know what to believe. What to feel. "Did Mina know?"

He hesitates. "Her dad told her the deal right away," he admits. "That day on the river she was just playing along for the cameras. We both were."

"Why didn't anyone tell me?"

Jason buries his head in his hands before looking up. "The execs—they . . . knew you had trouble in front of the camera.

They didn't want you to ruin their plans. . . ." His words fade away helplessly.

So Mina figured it out before I even had a clue. I go through every single moment of the past few months—our self-care day in Tokyo, the time he snuck into school, our dinner with his eemos in Brantwood, the engagement party in Brooklyn—feeling more and more humiliated by the second. I was so caught up in being close to Jason that I didn't even realize how big a fool I was being. How naive I was, so willing to give up my future for a boy who had only been thinking of his career this entire time. Was any of it real?

"I can't believe you. Everything you said to me that day in the park—about being here for me. Not wanting to be as bad as the execs. But you're worse than them—at least they never lie about how they are. You had me believing this was real."

"Please, Rachel, it's not like that," he says, his voice desperate now. "Since that day in Tokyo, I've been paying the paparazzi to keep the photos off the internet. I never wanted you to find out this way. I was planning on telling you everything soon, but . . ." He looks at my phone. "Clearly someone decided to leak them."

More and more articles are popping up now, the headlines all painting Jason as an innocent, lovesick K-pop star. WILL JASON LEE HEAL FROM HEARTBREAK? K-POP STAR JASON LEE, TORN FROM BOTH SIDES. KOREA'S FAVORITE STAR BOY IN THE MIDDLE OF AN EPIC LOVE TRIANGLE.

"Please don't read those," he says, but it's too late.

"'DB trainees have long had a reputation for being ruthless, doing anything to climb their way to the top, but Rachel Kim and Choo Mina take it to the next level, manipulating lovesick K-pop star Jason Lee for a chance to shine in the spotlight.'" I stop, too furious to keep going. "I can't believe this. You know, I was coming here to find you and celebrate the news of you going solo. And then this comes out at the exact moment that—"

Suddenly, I freeze, Jason's words from earlier rushing back to me. *You know how DB is all about publicity.*

And that's when I realize.

"It was DB. They leaked the photos." I stare at him, the pieces clicking together. "You thought you were holding off the paparazzi from posting, but it wasn't because of you. It was because they were waiting for a signal from DB to drop them at the perfect time."

"What are you talking about?" Jason says.

"Think about it, Jason!" I cry. "'Summer Heat' has been one big publicity stunt to create buzz for your solo act. They've set you up as a heartbroken boy caught between two girls so that when you sing your precious debut song, people will relate it to your life and eat it up. And of course they threw me and Mina into the love triangle. We're expendable trainees! If the public turns on us, it doesn't matter!"

"But that doesn't make sense," he says, frowning. "You've heard my song. The lyrics are all about being caught between identities, being caught between two worlds. It's not about a love triangle."

"Do you seriously think DB is going to let you sing about your freaking identity?" I ask, staring at him in disbelief. "'I'm back and forth, the push and pull, I'm falling fast and floating free. I'm a glass half-empty or half-full, caught in between two galaxies?'" The lyrics spill easily out of my mouth. "Wake up, Jason. Back and forth, push and pull? Two galaxies can easily be interpreted as two girls. Your sandcastle queen and ocean lover. Why do you think they set us all up like this?"

"No." He shakes his head, a nervous panic creeping into his voice. "They wouldn't do that to me. I'm telling you, they wouldn't! They called me as soon as I got into a car at the airport. They said they have big news, that I should start practicing my solo debut because . . . because . . ." His voice trails off as he loses steam. He knows I'm right. "Rachel." He looks at me with those puppy-dog eyes, and for the first time, I feel nothing. "What am I going to do?"

I have nothing left in me to give.

"I don't know," I say, my voice shaking. "But I know you won't be lying to me any longer." I turn to leave.

Jason's eyes narrow. "You're one to talk. We both know I'm not the only one who lied in this relationship," he says, his voice harsh and bitter.

"If you're talking about my dad's law school, that had nothing to do with you—"

"I'm talking about the video. At Kwangtaek." My breath

catches in my throat as he continues. "I know you and Yujin planned the whole thing so you could get attention from the execs. How is that any different from what I did? I thought when I explained this all to you, you would understand."

My stomach sinks. "You're right. And maybe I would have. But not like this."

The thread that's been holding my heart together snaps and I crumple. I reach back into my past—to all the younger versions of myself who have been keeping this dream alive for me. To my eleven-year-old self who wanted this more than anything, whose pure love for K-pop and joy for this music has been lighting my way, showing me where to go, what to do. But she's barely a whisper in my heart right now. Jason's betrayal has shattered me completely.

"Goodbye, Jason." My voice doesn't waver or catch in my throat. It's completely steady as I walk out of the practice room. Only when my back is turned do I press my hand against my mouth, tears rolling down my cheeks.

He doesn't try to stop me.

⭐ Twenty-Five ⭐

It's amazing how quickly life can fall apart and yet remain exactly the same. A few hours ago Jason Lee was my secret boyfriend, I had a number one hit on the K-pop charts, and my family was happy. Now the entire country thinks I was dating Jason (when I'm not), I still have a number one hit on the K-pop charts, and my family seems happier than ever (even though I'm pretty sure Umma isn't speaking to Appa and we now owe our livelihood to the family of my biggest enemy).

Was anything ever really what I thought it was? Or was the entire world a lie? An elaborately created fantasy that lets eleven-year-old girls believe that dreams come true, only to shatter them to pieces, all at once, after she had already dedicated her life to them.

The fan comments on the articles are rolling in now and holding nothing back.

How dare these lowlife trainees break Jason's heart!

Who do they think they are?

These bitches need to die, hurting our sweet baby Jason.

I want to rip their ugly faces off!

There's no way DB will debut me now, not with all this baggage and fan hate. And to think, they're the ones who put me in this mess. Trained me for years and then made me un-debut-able by their standards.

It's so ridiculous I almost want to laugh. Almost.

I turn my phone off. I don't want to see any more articles or read any more comments. My career may be over, but that doesn't mean I have to be reminded of it every five seconds.

I go on autopilot, wandering aimlessly around Seoul as a foggy numbness settles over my brain, until I somehow find myself outside the twins' apartment. If anyone will help distract me from today, I know they will.

I'm greeted by Hyeri, her hair in giant pink curlers on top of her head. "Rachel!" she cries. She looks surprised but pleased to see me, ushering me into the apartment. "I see you've changed your mind about the gala. Perfect timing!"

"Did I hear you say Rachel?" Juhyun's voice calls from the bathroom. She pokes her head out, her eyebrows half drawn in. "Hi. You're here! Good. Just sit down and don't think about anything. We'll help you with your hair and makeup as soon as we're done!"

The living room is in total chaos, dresses flung over the back of the brown leather couches and makeup pouches bursting open like treasure chests all over the coffee table, leaving trails of mascara and lipstick tubes spilling onto the floor. I totally forgot that the Molly Folly gala is tonight. The twins are so busy getting ready, I realize they haven't seen the articles yet. Just as well. The longer I can go without talking about it, the better.

"Sorry for the mess," Hyeri says. She leads me to the kitchen, where a row of alcohol bottles is lined up neatly on the table, all ready for the twins' predrink. She pulls out a chair for me, patting the seat before bustling back to the living room to finish getting ready. "Make yourself comfortable," she calls over her shoulder.

I do as I'm told, sliding down the chair and resting my head face-first on the lacquered table surface. I am a blob. A giant, feeling-less blob.

I don't know how long I sit like that before I notice the twins are standing in front of me. I look up at them, my hair falling in my eyes. Their perfectly drawn eyebrows are furrowed in identical expressions of concern. Juhyun's hair is in a princess bun on top of her head, and Hyeri's falls down her back in long, sweeping curls. They look party-ready, except for the fact that they're both still in their getting-ready pajamas.

"Everything okay, Rachel?" Hyeri asks.

"Yes."

"By yes, do you really mean no?"

"Yes."

Hyeri and Juhyun exchange glances.

"Do you want to talk about it?" Juhyun asks.

"No." I droop back onto the table. "I don't want to ruin your night. You have a party to go to."

They start to protest, but I wave them away. "No, no, it's fine, seriously. I just need a drink. Here."

I grab the bottle of tequila and pop it open. Still slouched over the table like a sloth refusing to let go of its tree branch, I take a big gulp straight from the bottle. Juhyun and Hyeri stare at me as I start to chug, wincing only slightly at the taste of the sour liquid.

"Okay, where's Rachel and what have you done with her?" Juhyun asks.

"If you're going to keep asking questions, at least drink with me," I say, wiping a dribble of tequila from my chin.

"All right," Hyeri says. She picks up the bottle of peach makgeolli, cracking it open. "You're obviously sad about something and there's nothing sadder than drinking alone. So we're with you. Jjan!"

Juhyun lifts a can of beer. "Jjan!"

We all cheers, and down our drinks.

An hour later, I'm buzzed.

Maybe even a little drunk. But just a really tiny little bit.

When I tell Juhyun and Hyeri that they look like they're going to a fancy pajama party, they scream and insist that I get made up too. They curl my hair and give me a fresh face of makeup with perfect cat-eye eyeliner and siren-red lipstick. Juhyun even paints my nails in the new galaxy pattern she learned how to do. At some point, one of us has the idea that we should dress up for the party even if we're not going, so we all change into fancy cocktail dresses, collapsing on the couch with a bottle of wine and a huge family pack of cuttlefish chips, our heels up on the gigantic marble and glass coffee table.

"Whose idea was this anyway?" I laugh, hiccuping over my glass of wine.

"Yours," Juhyun and Hyeri say at the same time.

We all crack up. I snuggle into the couch, resting my head against Juhyun's shoulder. I don't know if it's the alcohol or if it just hasn't hit me yet that DB is probably going to kick me out, but in this moment, all I feel is a strange sense of relief.

I feel free, normal even.

I imagine this being my everyday life, getting ready for parties with my friends, hanging out without feeling guilty for not spending every spare minute practicing, laughing as Hyeri throws chips in the air and catches them in her mouth while Juhyun tries to intercept and swat them away. It's so uncomplicated. I could get used to this kind of life.

Maybe it's what I've always needed.

Suddenly there's a knock on the door, and all three of us groan.

"Nooooo," I say, sinking deeper into the couch. "But I'm so comfy."

"Me too," Juhyun says. She pokes Hyeri with her toe. "You go get it; you're the youngest."

"You're only older by ten minutes!" Hyeri quips back.

"Fair is fair, maknae," Juhyun says as whoever's at the door knocks again.

"Fine, but I'm taking these," Hyeri says, grabbing the bag of cuttlefish chips. Hoisting it in her arms like a baby, she teeters across the room in her stiletto heels and swings the door open.

Daeho is standing on the other side, dressed to the nines in a blue velvet tux. He actually looks pretty good with his hair waxed neatly back and a bouquet of red roses in his arms. I think he even put on some BB cream. Go, Daeho.

"H-hi," he says, clearly nervous.

"Daeho." Hyeri's eyes widen. "What are you doing here?" A look of realization crosses her face and she hastily steps aside, gesturing over to where Juhyun and I are sitting on the couch. "You must be here for Juhyun."

"Juhyun?" Daeho says, a confused look flashing across his face. "Um, actually?" He takes a deep breath and thrusts the bouquet of roses into Hyeri's arms. "I'm here for you."

Hyeri's so surprised she drops the bag in her arms. Cuttlefish chips go flying everywhere, skittering across the hardwood floor. "For me?"

"There's a card inside," Daeho says, rubbing the back of his neck.

Hyeri plucks out the card and reads out loud. "'It's taken me a million years to say, but I think about you every day. My heart already belongs to you, so will you be my girlfriend?'" She looks up at Daeho, her eyes wide. "Is this for real?"

He pales. "Why? Is it too cheesy? Or creepy? Too cheesy and creepy?"

From her spot on the couch, Juhyun shouts, "Too cheesy!"

"No one asked you!" Hyeri shouts back, shaking her head vigorously. "Ignore her please."

She presses the card against her heart. "It's perfect. It's just, I always thought you had a crush on Juhyun."

"Huh?" Now it's Daeho's turn to shake his head. "No way. You're the one I like. It's always been you. I just never knew how to say it. And I thought it would be important to be nice to your sister since I know how close you are." His brow furrows. "Did I miscalculate?"

Juhyun and I are hugging on the couch, each of us watching the scene play out. I hear a sniffle, and next to me I see Juhyun's eyes filling with tears.

"No. You didn't miscalculate," Hyeri says quietly. "I really, really like you too, Daeho."

"Really?" A huge grin spreads across his face. "Because I wasn't sure how you'd feel since we've been friends for so long and I didn't want to ruin—"

Hyeri throws her arms around him and presses her lips against his. Juhyun and I cheer as Daeho wraps his arms around her and kisses her passionately back, cuttlefish chips crunching under their feet.

"You know, I never thought about it, but they're actually so cute together," Juhyun whispers to me. "I can totally see it."

"Yeah." I laugh. "I can see it too."

★ ★ ★

Morning light streams through the window. I open my eyes, feeling groggy and a bit hungover. I'm in my own bed, in my own room.

How'd I get here?

I think back to last night, rummaging through my memories. Right. After Juhyun and I insisted on giving Daeho a complete facial, he walked me home, even taking off his own shoes for me to walk in when I told him my heels were killing me.

The thought of Daeho and Hyeri brings a smile to my face, but it quickly slides off as I remember everything else that happened yesterday: Jason. The leaked photos. The comments.

The end of everything I've worked for.

I sigh and roll over in bed, my head hammering. A stack of papers sticks out of the middle drawer on my bedside table, and I pull them out. They're the college applications that Umma gave me months ago, exactly where I last put them. I haven't touched them since.

Flipping through the pages, I pause at a list of personal essay questions.

How would you describe yourself?

Where do you see yourself in ten years?

What are your greatest passions?

My mind is a blank. How can I answer any of these when my life with DB is over? Without K-pop, do I know who I am or what I want? Do I even have any other passions? It feels like my future has been swallowed whole by a giant question mark, when for so long, I knew exactly what I wanted it to look like.

Maybe it's time I tried to imagine something new.

I get out of bed and take a seat at my desk, tying my hair back into a loose bun. I am slowly working through the applications when there's a knock on my door and Umma pokes her head in.

"Hey," she says softly. "What are you doing?"

I gesture to the applications on the table without looking up. "Preparing for college."

My voice cracks on the last word, and the reality of what is happening finally sets in. It's like Umma's question punctured straight through the numbness I've been wearing like armor, finally allowing the pain to flood in.

And it hurts.

"It's over," I say as Umma makes her way into my room, sitting on my bed next to me. "The whole K-pop thing is done. Nothing has turned out the way I thought it would. I thought I knew exactly what I was getting myself into when I first started, but I didn't know anything. I was wrong. About everything."

"You were eleven," Umma says gently.

"I had no idea what sacrifices would go into this life," I say, wiping my eyes. "It's too much. I don't have what it takes. Maybe I never did."

I feel tears building behind my eyes, threatening to spill out. Umma sits on my bed, looking at me long and hard. As sad as she looks to see me in pain, I think that a part of her must be relieved about this. With K-pop behind me, I can focus on school and college, just like she's always wanted me to.

I expect her to start helping me with my application questions, but instead she gets up and leaves my room. I hear her in her bedroom, rummaging through her dresser, and when she returns, she's holding an old photo album. "Umma," I ask, "what is this?"

"Just take a look."

I take it from her and gingerly start to rifle through the pages—it's picture after picture of my mom spanning over what must be fifteen years—from playing volleyball as a young girl to pictures of her standing on podiums receiving medals and trophies. Something heavy clunks in the back of the album, so I flip to it and a gold medal is taped to the back cover. It reads *1st place in Women's Volleyball, South Korea National College Championship, 1989.*

I'm speechless. "Umma, I . . ."

"I should have told you about my past a long time ago, Rachel. About how volleyball was more than just a high school hobby for me. Halmoni didn't approve, of course. She wanted me to get an education, get a real job—but I didn't listen. I wanted to go to the Olympics." She lets out a deep sigh. "But it didn't happen for me. I was good, but I wasn't good enough. Unfortunately, it took me too long to realize it and I suffered—"

"Umma, you don't have to worry about me anymore. I'm . . . not good enough either. I'm done with K-pop."

Umma cups my face in her hands. "My daughter, you misunderstand me." She smiles. "Why do you think we came to Korea?"

I shrug my shoulders. "I dunno. Halmoni died. I guess I never really wanted to question what changed your mind."

"You're right. Halmoni died and I came to Korea for the funeral. I hadn't seen my mother in years, and although I wanted to cry for her, to be sad for her, instead I was angry. I was so angry that she hadn't supported my dream and hadn't pushed me to follow my passion. I didn't want that for you and me, so I made a choice to move our family here so you could follow yours." There are tears in her eyes now as she looks at me. "I guess the apple doesn't fall far from the tree because I haven't done a very good job of supporting you. It's just such a competitive world," she says. "And what mother wants their child to suffer? I knew you would struggle on this path, and I wanted to protect you. Like my mom tried to protect me."

She pulls out her phone and plays a video, holding it out for me to see. It's my performance with Jason and Mina at Seoul Olympic Stadium. A shaky fancam version that's mostly zoomed in on me, capturing my every step and note and facial expression. I look up at Umma, who has a wistful smile on her face.

"Leah sent this to me," she says. "I was never good enough to make it. But *you* are. You have what it takes, Rachel. You always did."

She holds her hand out to me, and I grab it, inexplicably thinking of Jason's dad as I do.

Umma and I may argue, but I could never imagine her walking away from me for any reason. No matter what, I've always been able to feel secure in her love and in the knowledge that all she wants is for me to be safe and happy, even if it gets lost in translation sometimes. It's so easy to forget how lucky I am to have a mom like her.

"I'm proud of you," she says. "And Umma is sorry. Sorry that it took me so long."

Tears finally start to roll down my cheeks. I feel like all I've been doing is crying lately, but these are the good kind of tears, the kind that make you feel like you're a little more whole than you were before.

"Thank you, Umma." I squeeze her hand tight. "Does this mean you're not worried for me anymore?"

"I'm terrified." She laughs. "I don't know if that will ever go away. It's part of being your umma. But you deserve to take your chance, Rachel. You've earned it. Don't let anyone take that from you."

I nod and pull her in for a hug.

Before I can pull away, the door slams open. "Are you two done crying yet? I've been waiting and waiting to come in!" Leah shouts as she scrambles onto my bed and squishes herself in between me and Umma.

I laugh and wipe away more tears. "Yes, we're done, I promise." I grab Leah into a bear hug and smile at Umma over the top of her head. I feel a lightness in my heart that I haven't felt in a long time, but it's not quite complete yet. There's one more person who I need to check in with. I put my hands on Leah's shoulders and turn toward her. "Do you hate me? Do you hate this? You never asked to come here, and now here you are and . . ."

Leah scoffs easily and swats my hand away. "Unni. I'm fine."

"Seriously, Leah. I know life here hasn't been . . . the easiest," I say, thinking back to Leah's middle-school mean girls.

I can feel my eyes filling with tears again, but Leah gives me a small shove. "No more crying! You promised!"

I choke back a sob and laugh. "I'm not crying!"

"You know, Rachel, for a big sister, you sure are clueless sometimes," Leah says with a smirk. "You think I care about what those girls at school do? You're my sister. Your dreams are my dreams. And that's more important that anything." She tilts her head toward Umma and flashes her a quick, devilish grin. "Plus, DB auditions are coming up soon . . . and now that I'm thirteen, I think it's about time that I start K-pop training. That way Rachel won't have to be the only K-pop star in the family!"

My mouth drops open, and out of the corner of my eye, I see Umma's face go a little pale. Umma's phone rings, and she reaches for it, not taking her eyes off Leah, who seems to have gone into her usual, oblivious, K-pop gossip spiral as she scrolls through her Instagram feed. Umma pokes me in the side. "It's Yujin. She says she's been trying to reach you."

I realize I haven't checked my phone since I turned it off yesterday. As soon as I turn it on, several missed calls from Yujin and a string of urgent Kakao messages pops up on the screen.

Come to DB headquarters ASAP! I need to see you!

⭐ Twenty-Six ⭐

Yujin is waiting for me in the lobby when I arrive at DB head-quarters. As soon as she sees me, she rushes over and pulls me into a tight hug.

"Rachel! I heard about everything that happened."

"Everything?" My heart nearly jumps into my throat. Does everything include my relationship with Jason? Oh god, I hope not.

She steps back, anger flaring in her eyes. "I heard that Jason is going solo and how DB used you and Mina to promote him." Sharp as ever, she raises her eyebrows and gives me a searching look. "Why? Is there something else I should know?"

I shake my head, inwardly breathing a sigh of relief. "Nope, not at all."

She gives me a suspicious look, but her face softens anyway. "Listen, Rachel, I honestly had no idea DB was plotting any of this. If I knew, I would have done everything I could to stop them." Her lips press into a hard line like she's trying to keep herself together. "I'm so sorry I couldn't do more to protect you."

My heart twists at the thought that Yujin might feel responsible for any of this. I never once thought that she might be involved, and if there's anyone who should be apologizing, it definitely isn't her. "Please don't be sorry," I say. "You've done nothing but support me since day one. And all things considered, I'm doing okay."

It's only half a lie.

"Really?" Yujin gives me another searching look. "Are you sure there isn't something else you want to tell me?"

She knows me too well. For a second I think how nice it would be to tell her everything about me and Jason. It would feel so good to get everything off my chest.

No more secrets. No more lies. But then I imagine the disappointed look on her face and put on my best smile.

"Really. Don't worry."

She sighs. "No use telling me that. There's always something to worry about."

Across the hall, two second-year trainees come out of the cafeteria, chattering a mile a minute.

"Did you hear about Akari?"

"Yes, I can't believe it! Of all the girls at DB, I never thought . . ."

I strain to hear the rest of what they're saying, but their voices fade as they continue down the hall.

I look over at Yujin. "Did you hear that? What's going on with Akari?"

"You mean you haven't heard?" Yujin says, her eyebrows shooting up in surprise. When I stare at her blankly, she bites her lip, an apologetic look on her face, as if she's sorry for the news she's about to give me. "Akari's been traded to another K-pop label. She's no longer with DB."

My stomach sinks. "What?"

No. That can't be true. If it were true, I would have known about it. Wouldn't I?

Even as I think it, I know I'm wrong. I've been so absent in Akari's life lately that how *could* I know about it? My mouth goes dry as I remember that she messaged me yesterday, right as everything was blowing up. I just totally blew her off.

Again.

I grab my phone and text her now, but the message comes straight back as undelivered. I call her and even try to FaceTime her, but everything bounces back, telling me that her phone's been disconnected.

She's gone.

"Come on," Yujin says gently, taking my elbow and guiding me down the hallway. "It's newbie day today. I know you may not be up for it, but it'll be a good distraction. Let's go."

I follow her woodenly to the auditorium, my mind a blank. Yujin nudges me toward the stage, where all the other trainees are standing to receive bows from the newbies. Everyone, that is, except Akari. My stomach drops even lower.

She should be here. I can't believe she's really gone.

Onstage, Eunji gives me a scathing once-over. "Look who

decided to show up." She blows a watermelon-scented bubble with her gum, letting it pop over her lips.

"We thought you'd probably died of embarrassment by now," Lizzie says, narrowing her eyes at me as I move toward the head of the line.

"Come on, Princess." Mina smiles at me with all her teeth, blocking my way. If she's reeling from the recent article scandal, she doesn't show it. She looks as poised as ever. "You'd think you'd know your place by now."

Mina's final comment makes me snap back into focus. She's right.

I do know my place.

I step into the front of the line, right next to Mina, exactly where I belong on the trainee hierarchy.

"I believe this is my rightful spot," I say.

The entire stage falls silent as Mina and I glare at each other, the friction between us practically ricocheting off the walls. It feels like everyone is holding their breath, waiting to see what will happen next. But as soon as the newbies come out and begin their bows, Mr. Noh following right behind them, Mina looks away.

Everybody exhales.

I straighten my back, determination coursing through my veins. I'm not going to let anybody step on me today.

Not when I've worked so hard to be here.

Not when I've earned this.

Not even the DB execs can take this away from me, I

think, as a group of them stop right in front of me, broad but unforgiving smiles on their faces.

"Rachel," Ms. Shim says.

I bow. "Ms. Shim," I respond before turning to Mr. Noh.

"How are you?" Mr. Noh says, a slight note of hesitation in his voice. I can see my pale, tired face in the reflection of his glasses.

"Yes," Mr. Lim chimes in, barely able to hide his disdain, "we weren't, uh, sure we would see you here today."

I look up at them, my jaw set. There's an angry glint in Mr. Lim's eyes, and Mr. Noh keeps fidgeting with his satin pocket square—and suddenly I realize they know I know everything and they're trying to see how I'll play my cards. Well. When it comes to playing games, I've learned from the best.

After all, I have been trained by DB.

"I wouldn't miss this for the world. And I don't plan on going anywhere anytime soon." I beam, the picture of a perfect trainee, and lock my gaze on Mr. Noh. "Remember, we're family. And family is forever."

Mr. Lim's face grows icy, but Mr. Noh throws a small, resigned smile in my direction. "I wouldn't expect anything less from you."

There's a calculating look in his eyes that I'm not sure what to make of, but he's already moving down the line, away from me. I don't relax until we all file off the stage and into the auditorium seats for announcements. I take a seat in the back by myself and finally let my body sag. I close my eyes, leaning back against the velvet covering. At least the worst of it is over.

I feel the chair next to me sink as someone takes a seat. My eyes fly open.

It's Jason.

For a moment we just stare at each other. I don't know what to say, and from the way he's jittering, his leg bouncing up and down against his seat, I can tell he doesn't either. He looks tired and defeated in a way, like a shadow of his former self, the self that overflowed with confidence and knew without a doubt that the whole world was his best friend.

"Rachel . . . ," he starts, but his voice trails off. It looks like he's about to reach over and grab my hand, but he stops himself midway and grabs the armrest instead. "Congratulations," he finally says, smiling tightly at me. Then he pushes himself out of his seat and walks away, disappearing down the aisle.

I stare after him, dumbfounded. Congratulations?

Congratulations for what?

Mr. Noh takes the stage for announcements. I'm so busy trying to process what just happened with Jason that I almost miss what he's saying.

It turns out, there's still room for one more surprise.

"We are so thrilled," he says, his voice booming over the auditorium, "to be debuting DB's new girl group, Girls Forever! Please join me as I welcome the nine ladies who will be the new faces and voices of what I'm confident will be Korea's biggest stars!"

The room is like a live wire, trainees and trainers frantically trying to guess who will be announced, craning their heads to see who is in the room. I sit up straighter in my chair, shock zipping through me like a lightning bolt.

I had no idea DB was announcing a new debut group today. And judging by the stunned look on everyone's faces, no one else knew either.

"I'll ask the girls to come up to the stage," Mr. Noh says. "First we have Shin Eunji, who brings a firecracker energy to everything she does. Ryu Sumin, the picture of grace and elegance. Yoon Youngeun, a master harmonizer. Lee Jiyoon, a creative artist. Shim Ari, power vocals to challenge any ballad singer. Im Lizzie, dancer extraordinaire. Choi Sunhee, the most skilled rapper in our trainee class."

He takes a significant pause, looking around the auditorium. The air is so thick with anticipation I can almost feel it pressing down on my chest. Mina is leaning forward in her seat, her nails digging into the armrests. He hasn't called either of our names yet.

Is this the moment he's going to drop us from DB? Will he announce it in front of everyone after naming all the new members of Girls Forever? What a cruel way to let us go, and yet how on brand for DB. I steel myself for whatever he's about to say next.

"And lastly, I'd like to announce our final two members with particular pride." He spreads his arms open wide, the picture of a proud father. "These two young ladies have already brought an incredible amount of success to DB. They epitomize everything that we are as a family, and I know they will continue to be model examples of what it means to be perfect DB stars going forward." His smile turns almost sharklike, a subtle threat laced in his words. "I am pleased to announce Rachel Kim as lead vocalist and Choo Mina as lead dancer of Girls Forever!"

I am pleased to announce Rachel Kim as lead vocalist. The words play over and over in my head as my legs go totally numb. I don't know how I do it, but I somehow manage to walk down the aisle and up to the stage, my knees wobbling like Jell-O, barely registering the cheers that echo across the auditorium.

This morning I thought my career was over.

Now I'm about to debut.

Mr. Noh shakes my hand with a toothy grin.

"Congratulations," he says. And then, as if reading my thoughts, he adds, "Your dreams are becoming reality."

I don't realize I'm crying until I feel the wetness on my cheeks and quickly wipe the tears away with the back of my hand. This is happening. This is real. It's finally happening.

Almost reflexively I scan the crowd for Yujin. She's clapping and crying too. I want to run and hug her, but I know now is not the time. Instead, I spot Jason standing in the far corner of the auditorium. I realize with a jolt that Mr. Choo is standing next to him. He leans down and whispers something in Jason's ear and Jason nods resolutely. As the announcements wrap up, Mr. Noh walks down from the stage to join them. Jason shakes both men's hands, a grim but determined look on his face.

A nervous flutter erupts in the pit of my stomach. This

must be what Jason was congratulating me on earlier. He knew I was going to debut today. That I wasn't being kicked out of DB. How did he know?

And what did he do to get me here?

"Congratulations, Rachel."

I turn to see Mina standing before me, Lizzie and Eunji on either side of her.

"Lead vocalist," Lizzie says, her voice dripping with fake enthusiasm. "That's an impressive title."

"It'll be so great being in a group all together," Eunji adds. "Imagine how much fun we'll have."

"Girls, give me a minute alone with Rachel," Mina says. "I want to give her a personal congratulations."

Ever obedient, Lizzie and Eunji flounce off the stage. Mina turns to me, all smiles, but I can see a familiar evil glimmer in her eye.

"That little stunt at the bowing ceremony was cute, Rachel," she says, her voice dropping into a low whisper. "But don't think it changes anything about where your real place is. Now that we're debuting together, Yujin-unni won't be around to protect you anymore. You really think you'll be able to survive for very long without her?"

"I think I can hold my own, Mina," I say, crossing my arms. "After all, I am the lead singer."

She smiles on, unfazed. "I wouldn't let that title get to your head if I were you. You shouldn't get too comfortable. You never know when you might . . . lose your step."

She pulls out her phone and presses play on a video, holding it up for me to see. It's another shaky fancam video from Seoul Olympic Stadium, but this time it's of Electric Flower singing "Starlight River." I frown, shooting her a wary look. Why is she showing this to me?

And then I see it. The starry night cover is lifted, and as soon as the lights turn on, there, in the corner of the screen, is a glimpse of me and Jason kissing backstage. It's only half a second, but it's unmistakably us.

"Where did you get this?" My voice is shaking so hard I can't even pretend to hold back my alarm.

"Leah," she says smoothly. "That day I came over. Before you got there, she was showing me some videos from the concert and I happened to notice something very interesting about this one. I asked her to send it to me. You know I'm a big Electric Flower fan."

I swallow hard, my jaw clenched. If this video were to ever get out, I would be ruined, just like Kang Jina. Jason was confident that the K-pop industry was changing, but if the past two days have taught me anything, it's that it isn't changing quickly enough to make a difference for me. "You wouldn't," I say, even though I know of course she would. She wouldn't hesitate.

And that means she owns me.

She smiles, tucking the phone back into the pocket of her skirt. "Congratulations again, Rachel. This next year is going to be *so* much fun."

✦ Twenty-Seven ✦

"Girls, you're about to go onstage for your *debut performance*! How has the past month been, preparing for this moment?"

I sit with my eight fellow Girls Forever members, all of us in coordinating electric-blue outfits layered with patterns of neon flowers. My halter dress fits snugly on my body, hot-pink with petals climbing up the sides. On my feet are thigh-high white knee socks and spotless white high-top sneakers. I brush my perfectly curled hair over my shoulder and smile at the interviewer, batting my lashes.

Head up, legs crossed. Tummy tucked, shoulders back. The camera zooms in on my face, airing live to millions of people all over Korea.

"It's been a challenge, but we've been working really hard and we're as ready as we'll ever be," I say easily. I gesture to the other girls. "It's been such an inspiration working alongside such talented members. I've learned so much from all of them."

Like how to watch my back at every hour of the day. From

bubble gum in my hairbrush that Eunji swore wasn't hers to my shoes mysteriously disappearing every time we had a wardrobe fitting, my life of debut prep has been a constant rerun of training, sleepless nights, and dodging vicious prank after vicious prank from the girls the whole world believes are my best friends.

I smile at the camera.

If only they could see what our lives are really like.

All the girls "aww" back at my sweet comment, Sumin and Lizzie even leaning in on either side of me for a group hug. I squeeze back tightly like I'm in the middle of a full-on lovefest. Their long nails scratch against my arms as the interviewer beams on, all bright eyes and gleaming teeth.

"It sounds like you all work really well together," he says.

"Absolutely," Mina says, her voice a pitch-perfect tone of mastered enthusiasm. "I couldn't think of anyone better to be on this journey with." She casts a fond look over all of us, her gaze resting on mine. She smiles. "We have a beautiful road ahead of us."

I stand backstage before our performance, taking deep breaths. This past month has flown by in a whirlwind, and now it's finally time for us to debut. Here we come, world.

It's time to finally show you what we've got.

A burst of giggles catches my attention, and I turn to see Mina showing a video to the other girls on her phone. They're all leaning in, laughing and pushing one another for a better view.

"Holy shit, this is gold."

"I can't believe she caught this on video!"

My stomach clenches. Is that what I think it is?

I run over and grab the phone from Mina's hands. It's an Instagram video of a girl playing a piano duet with her dog. Chopsticks. My face warms all over.

"What the hell, Rachel?" Eunji says. "What's your problem?"

"Don't mind her, girls," Mina says breezily, sipping a glass of water. "Princess Rachel's not a fan of viral videos that she's not the star of."

My fist tightens around her phone. Mina may be holding her video blackmail over me, but that doesn't mean I have to take it lying down. I slam her phone right into the glass of water, everyone shrieking and jumping away as water droplets fly everywhere.

Mina's mouth falls open in shock.

"Woops, sorry, Mina," I say sweetly. "My hand slipped. But you know what, maybe it's for the best. You know the rules about social media. Wouldn't want you to get in trouble."

I turn away. Then I pause and look back over my shoulder, glancing pointedly at Mina's wrist and her ruby-colored watch. Mr. Han's watch—his one-of-a-kind heirloom from his grandfather. I recognized it in Toronto but didn't say anything. I don't even know for sure why she has it.

But I can guess.

"By the way, do you know what time it is?" I ask innocently.

Her eyes widen. Flustered, she looks down at the watch, covering it with her hand. "It's, um, almost one."

"Thanks," I say. "Almost time for the performance, girls."

The girls look back and forth between us, trying to figure out what's being left unsaid. Eunji and Lizzie glance at each other, then walk over to me. "We're ready!" Out of the corner of my eye, I see Mina's face fall. But I'm already walking away.

I have a song to perform.

We go through a final round of makeup touchups and assemble on the stage, waiting for the curtain to go up. I take my place in center position, four girls in a horizontal line on either side of me. Cameras are pointed at us from all directions, and I can hear the cheering crowd beyond the curtain.

They're excited to see us. I lift my chin. Good.

We're about to give them the performance of their lives.

If someone had told me when I was eleven years old about everything I'd have to sacrifice to get to this point, everything that would be stolen from me, I would have said they were writing a K-drama. The path to get here has turned out to be harder than anything I could've ever imagined, but here I am.

Despite it all, I made it to my debut moment.

I think of the haenyo: *When we feel like we cannot do this any longer, we remember that we already have, and we will again.*

I think of Leah: *Your dreams are my dreams.*

I think of Umma: *You deserve to take your chance. You've earned it.*

Just as the curtain goes up, I make a decision. Staring

straight into the center camera, I take a big step forward, leaving the other girls in a line behind me and stepping into the spotlight by myself.

This is my time to shine.

And I won't let anyone stop me.

herself together. "I'm so sorry I couldn't do more to protect you."

My heart twists at the thought that Yujin might feel responsible for any of this. I never once thought that she might be involved, and if there's anyone who should be apologizing, it definitely isn't her. "Please don't be sorry," I say. "You've done nothing but support me since day one. And all things considered, I'm doing okay."

It's only half a lie.

"Really?" Yujin gives me another searching look. "Are you sure there isn't something else you want to tell me?"

She knows me too well. For a second I think how nice it would be to tell her everything about me and Jason. It would feel so good to get everything off my chest.

No more secrets. No more lies. But then I imagine the disappointed look on her face and put on my best smile.

"Really. Don't worry."

She sighs. "No use telling me that. There's always something to worry about."

Across the hall, two second-year trainees come out of the cafeteria, chattering a mile a minute.

"Did you hear about Akari?"

"Yes, I can't believe it! Of all the girls at DB, I never thought . . ."

I strain to hear the rest of what they're saying, but their voices fade as they continue down the hall.

I look over at Yujin. "Did you hear that? What's going on with Akari?"

"You mean you haven't heard?" Yujin says, her eyebrows shooting up in surprise. When I stare at her blankly, she bites her lip, an apologetic look on her face, as if she's sorry for the news she's about to give me. "Akari's been traded to another K-pop label. She's no longer with DB."

My stomach sinks. "What?"

No. That can't be true. If it were true, I would have known about it. Wouldn't I?

Even as I think it, I know I'm wrong. I've been so absent in Akari's life lately that how *could* I know about it? My mouth goes dry as I remember that she messaged me yesterday, right as everything was blowing up. I just totally blew her off.

Again.

I grab my phone and text her now, but the message comes straight back as undelivered. I call her and even try to FaceTime her, but everything bounces back, telling me that her phone's been disconnected.

She's gone.

"Come on," Yujin says gently, taking my elbow and guiding me down the hallway. "It's newbie day today. I know you may not be up for it, but it'll be a good distraction. Let's go."

I follow her woodenly to the auditorium, my mind a blank. Yujin nudges me toward the stage, where all the other trainees are standing to receive bows from the newbies. Everyone, that is, except Akari. My stomach drops even lower.

She should be here. I can't believe she's really gone.

Onstage, Eunji gives me a scathing once-over. "Look who

ACKNOWLEDGMENTS

I have so many people to thank for helping make this dream of mine a reality! I must start with my Golden Stars, for your epic and endless support and enthusiasm. It has kept me encouraged and inspired through it all!

I also want to thank the entire team at Simon & Schuster, the US home for the book—most of all, my shining star editor, Jennifer Ung. Jen, you've truly helped make this book sparkle (inside and out)! Thanks are also due to the inimitable Mara Anastas; the powerhouse marketing and publicity teams including Caitlin Sweeny, Alissa Nigro, Savannah Breckenridge, Anna Jarzab, Emily Ritter, Nicole Russo, and Cassie Malmo; and last but certainly not least, enormous thanks to Sarah Creech, the superb designer who came up with the amazing star-filled cover and got all those sparkling rays of light just right.

I'm eternally grateful for my incredible representatives at United Talent Agency—Max Michael, Albert Lee, and Meredith Miller—for helping get this book into so many countries across the world, many of which I've spent time in and can't wait to connect with readers there. Equal thanks to the talented Stephen Barbara of Inkwell Management for believing in this project from the beginning, finding *Shine* its first home, and championing it always. I couldn't have done it all without the fabulous women of Glasstown Entertainment. Thanks are due to Lexa Hillyer, who has listened to many tea-spilling stories (over actual tea!), as well as the inimitable Rebecca Kuss, who made sure every single detail was ab-so-lute-ly perfect. Thank you to Laura Parker and Lynley Bird of Glasstown, and to Matt Kaplan, Max Siemers, and everyone else at Ace Entertainment, for your hard work in turning this baby into a story that will hopefully one day soon hit the screens! Thank you, too, to Sarah Suk—you are a true star, and your work has made the book sing.

I owe such a huge debt of gratitude to my whole family, too—for supporting me unconditionally. To my parents, you were always there for me and let me be who I wanted to be. And most especially Krystal, the best sister one could ever, ever wish for. I love you with all my heart.

Lastly, I want to thank Tyler. You've been with me through so much of my journey, and I couldn't have done this without you. Your fervor and passion to help is above and beyond—I can't wait to see what the next adventure brings.